ACROSS SEWARD PARK

ACROSS SEWARD PARK

A NOVEL

GAIL LEHRMAN

PENNY TUNES PUBLISHING

Across Seward Park

By Gail Lehrman

Published by Penny Tunes Publishing

Copyright © 2023 by Gail Lehrman

All rights reserved.

Edited by Kerry Cathers

Cover Art by ebooklaunch.com

This book is a work of fiction, and all names, characters, places, and incidents are fictional or used fictitiously. Any resemblance to actual people, places, or events is coincidental.

ISBN-13: 979-8-218-21087-8 (paperback)

ISBN-13: 979-8-218-21086-1 (ebook)

First edition

1912-1916

IRV

ONE

Manhattan, Lower East Side

Artie's over on the bed. I'm hanging out the window scouring Rivington Street, eyes peeled for something I'm praying I won't see. Down below Mr. Klein, the fruit seller, paces behind his pushcart, batting his shoulders against the cold. I feel like I've been watching him my whole life, but, in my fright, the cobblestones go fuzzy with memory.

I was five the first time.

IT WAS AUGUST AND OUR TENEMENT WAS AN OVEN. PAPA BOASTED he'd bargained getting us street windows instead of an airshaft, but in the scalding summer heat, the sunlight shot in hot as flame. Trapped in the sweatbox, I pressed my cheek to a bare spot in the linoleum where pops of air sometimes darted between the bare floorboards.

My sister Miriam wasn't allowed to lie idle like me. Her ten-year-old fingers were nimbler than mine. Before he left, Papa had pointed to the almost empty cupboard. "You don't work, you don't got nothing to eat." So, stripped to her chemise, Miriam sat next to Mama, stitching red and white bits of fabric into appliqué flowers. Papa had put a basket in front of them, commanding, "*Onegfilt bey haynt bay nakht.*" Filled by tonight. He'd taken a contract. They didn't dare disobey.

I spread myself across the floor, flipping from front to back, back to front, waiting the hours for my big brother, Arthur, to come home. He'd whispered in my ear that he had a secret penny. He said that later, when the iceman came, he'd buy a bag of ice to hold against my neck. "It's so cold, you'll shiver like in Russian winter."

Artie was born in Russia. So was Miriam, but she doesn't remember. So Artie took it upon himself to tell about the muddy, ugly *shtetl*, rampaging Cossacks, and winters that froze your nose off. He was fifteen and an apprentice bookbinder. Sometimes he brought home cast-off pages from work and read tales of Moshkeleh, the Horse Thief, and Tsireleh, the tavern keeper's run-a-way daughter, or The Dybbuk, Stealer of Souls. The pages held only half a story, so Artie would make up the rest, one leg on a chair, waving his arm, his voice booming like the great Thomashefsky.

I was curled in a half-doze, when Miriam wiped an arm across her eyes, bleating, "I can't see," and the needle slipped from her clammy fingers. Mama took a damp cloth to Miriam's face, tied her braids higher off her neck, and set her back at the table. I was awake enough to hear Miriam mutter, "I wish Papa would go back to Russia," before she picked up her needle.

I got up to check the basket. If it was close to full, that meant the day was almost over. Artie would soon be here and so would the iceman. I was struck by a new and terrible thought. What if the iceman got to our block before Artie? Mama and Miriam didn't know about the secret penny. The guy would roll past our door and I'd never get my ice as cold as Russian snow.

I crept to the window and listened for the thud of the iceman's wheelbarrow. Propped against the wall, I listened with all my might, but I couldn't hear him coming, so I climbed up to look. Five stories down, the apple man stood with his pushcart in the blazing sun. He doffed his bowler and wiped a rag over his sweaty head. I decided he must be waiting for the iceman, too. When he turned and looked up the street, my heart jumped. I crawled out another inch, but I still couldn't see if it was the iceman. I crawled out an inch more. And more again, tipping up my tush and pushing my face around the window frame.

The front door scraped against the linoleum.

"God in Heaven, Irving." Artie practically ripped my pants down yanking me off the ledge.

Miriam vaulted from her chair. Mama screamed, "*Oy gevalt.*"

Artie tapped my head. "Hey, Irving, don't do that again." He stood and lifted me toward my mother. "See, it's all right, Mama. He's okay." He said again so she would understand. "*S'iz gut, Mama. Er iz okay.*"

"*Neyn. Neyn.*" Mama clutched me in so tight I could barely breathe. "*Meyn tatelleh.*"

Artie patted her on the back, repeating, "*S'iz gut, Mama. S'iz gut.*"

"No, it's not." Miriam's hands were clenched into fists and tears cut the grime on her cheeks. "It's lousy Papa's fault for keeping us in all day." She said it in English so Mama wouldn't understand. Mama never let us speak against Papa because, even if he was away, he might magically hear and make us suffer.

Artie walked over and hefted the basket, feeling the weight of the day's labors. "Yeah, he's a real *schmuck.*"

That's when it happened.

His warm eyes went blank. His jaw clamped shut and his mouth twisted into a knot. In the space of a heartbeat, his torso jerked, and everything that was Artie disappeared. As if possessed by the Dybbuk himself, his arms heaved in a wild swing, scattering the flowers across the floor.

Mama shrieked, "*Deyn fater vet aundtz teytn.*" Your father will kill us. Dropping to all fours, she groveled to gather up the flowers while Miriam slammed into Artie's chest shouting, "What did you do?"

Artie blinked. He swallowed. He shook himself. Wiping a dab of spittle off his chin, he stared at the catastrophe.

———————

IT ALL WASHES OVER ME, VIVID AS A PHOTOGRAPH, WHEN MIRIAM grabs the back of my shirt shouting, "Come off Irving, you'll kill yourself."

"Cut it out," I kick her away.

I don't need to be dragged off a ledge anymore. I'm twelve and I know what's dangerous. It's not the window. It's what's outside. With a jingle of traces and pounding of hooves, the black wagon rounds Clinton, grazing the pushcarts and sending shoppers scrambling as it thumps against the curb. Two uniformed burlies jump down and yank a stretcher from the side. I run to shake Arthur's chest. His jerking's over, but he's frozen, eyes rolled to the ceiling.

"They're coming. Get up, Artie. You gotta get up."

Mama throws her shawl over her eyes, wailing my father's name. "Yitzhak, Yitzhak, *vas hastu?*"

What has Papa done? I think in my fury. *What has he done?* He's been threatening it for weeks, growling that he doesn't feed those who cannot work. Yesterday, Artie got fired.

Papa snarled, "Enough. Charity is for the rich," and he slammed out.

The two hulks hammer the stairs, sending Mama cowering into the corner. Miriam runs to the hall while I spread-eagle the door to keep them out.

A rough hand pushes me aside and a voice snarls, "Shit. He's out cold. We'll have to strap him in." Grunting, the men roll Arthur onto the stretcher, ignoring Mama's howling sobs. I crouch down, blocking the door a second time, but Miriam drags me away.

"Cut it out." She shakes me. "They showed me where Papa signed the papers."

I kick at the heavy banister.

"Get out if you can't watch." She pushes me toward the stairs. "Go ahead. Get."

I bolt, hitting the street at a run, pounding east toward the river, but it's not far enough to blot out what's happening. I run harder. Under the Williamsburg Bridge, past Grand, past Pitt. My lungs burn and my chest heaves, but there's no stopping. At last, my legs flounder. It's cold. It's dark, and I'm hungry. So, I limp back home.

Miriam's sitting on the stoop with our satchels packed. She's waiting for me, even in the dark, even in the chill.

I sink to the frigid step. "Where's Papa?"

"Who cares? We're getting out of here, you and me."

"What about Arthur?"

"Papa crowed he'll never be bothered with him again." She glances up at the building. "I hate that bastard. I hate his guts."

"Mama?"

Her face goes hard. "A rabbit too scared to run."

I nod. My head drops to my sister's shoulder. "Swear to God, I'm gonna find Artie. Swear to God, I'm gonna bring him home."

"Fine." She's on her feet, picking up her bag and handing me mine. "You take care of Arthur. I'll take care of us."

Two

Miriam is ferocious. "Try to quit school, I'll cut off your *schmeckle*."

The only place rattier than home is where my sister moves us when we leave—two filthy rooms up five flights on Norfolk Street. Tilting floors, peeling wallpaper, a couple of rusty beds, and a window over the alley. We have to rent the beds to boarders and share a mattress on the floor.

"Once I'm a bookkeeper, it'll be better," Miriam insists. A shop girl during the day, she studies from the library every night. "Bookkeepers know about money. I'm smart. Watch, it won't take long."

"At least let me work after class," I grouse. "Something in the trade."

I don't have to name it. A single industry dominates these swarming streets—the ready-to-wear clothing business. Like Jonah's whale, it swallows any and all who come within range of its gaping maw.

I start part time as a bundle boy, carrying piecework to the poor *shlubs* sitting night and day in their homes sewing cut parts into apparel. One pile on my back, a second on my head, up through dust and rat shit to where people are stuffed, five, ten, fifteen to a room.

Ludlow Street, Delancey Street, Stanton or Essex, anywhere and everywhere, they irrigate the district with their sweat.

True to her word, Miriam rises to office work. We kick out the boarders and sleep in our beds. I keep my nose to the grindstone. By 1916, when I graduate high school, the best jobs have moved to the "inside shops," the factories and lofts where crafty owners can better control their workforce. We bribe a foreman for me to go in as an apprentice at Niedermeyer's Garment Cutting, a small specialty shop on Broome Street, called cushy because Niedermeyer plays ball with the union, meaning decent money and regular hours. All day, up and down, hauling thirty-pound bolts of cotton, it doesn't feel so cushy to me.

We unroll them, twenty-five feet down, twenty-five feet back, until we have a foot deep river of fabric. Thick cables dangle from the ceiling, giving power to electric knives that can glide the length of the long table. I stand in a corner as the air goes thick with dust and the ocean of fabric becomes a string of islands floating on a dark-wood sea. The triumphant cutters step back, clear the pieces to the sorting table, and begin again with different forms for a different size. By the end of each day my arms are rubber, my legs are lead, and my chest is filled with cotton powder. But there is one giant gift. I learn from a master.

Leo Hirsch is an artist of the cloth. He guides his blade along the table, back and forth, up and down, every gesture a dance, his body a miracle of grace. Not an inch of fabric is wasted, not a thread is lost. The foremen need him so bad they put up with his jabber about the International and the Triumph of the Proletariat. Leo is a Marxist.

"It's not right," he sings under the hum of his knife. "It's not right." Work for a pittance, die as a pauper. "It's not right." Ninety hours a week, never a day of rest. "It's not right." Rats in the workroom, sewage in the hall. Like God pointing a finger, "It's not right." I ask him how a man can stay so mad all the time. He bangs his fist on the counter. "Right is Right."

I'm curious to know how a Jew comes by white-blond hair and sky-blue eyes. Leo is blithe. "Somewhere, there must have been a Cossack. Probably a rape."

When he hears I've never tasted beer he pulls me into Cepulski's. "Today you become a man."

It smells of sauerkraut and sausage and sawdust. Guys in derby hats yakkity-yak, their feet propped on the railing. The waiter drops us a tub, spilling white suds onto the table.

"Drink." Leo guzzles, wiping away the foam with the back of his arm.

I swallow, burping out rye, caramel, and gas.

"Good start." He drains his glass and pours another. "Did you read it?"

From my back pocket comes the pamphlet.

"Society is splitting into two great hostile camps—Bourgeoisie and Proletariat..." My second swallow goes down easier. "I don't get it."

"*Schmendrick*." He slaps the back of my head. "Look." Up comes his beer mug. "What turned a handful of sand into this beautiful object of utility?" Up comes his fist. "Human labor. All value commences from human labor. We workers create the wealth but the capitalist reaps the benefits. Why? Because he owns the means of production."

"Niedermeyer bought that shop with his own money."

"A slave's answer. Any accumulation of capital always begins with the exploitation of someone else's labor. Listen, Irving, there's a whole world to make. When we stop fighting over the pitiful droppings left us by the bourgeoisie and come together as brothers, we will let loose beauty like the world has never known." He downs his glass. "Come to our study group. You'll learn something." I get an elbow in the ribs. "And bring your pretty sister."

Everyone knows Miriam is a looker. My friends joke I should walk in front of her with a baseball bat, but Miriam doesn't need any help from me.

"Forget it, Leo. My sister has her own plans for owning the means of production."

"*Schmendrick.*" He throws two bits onto the table. "A good revolutionary knows that all things come to he who waits."

THE MEETING IS IN A BASEMENT ON LUDLOW. WOODEN CHAIRS, A couple of ceiling bulbs, and a coal stove, about thirty men and women. I take a back seat afraid I'll be asked things I don't know. The dust-covered workman to my right sits with folded arms, but the woman in front is a jumping jack, craning to catch every random utterance so I have to keep ducking around her to watch as the panel at the front is introduced. Tall, broad Leo, Bessie Gerstein with the shoulders of a wrestler and fingers thick as cigars, and scrawny Mendel Stern in a collarless shirt and brown vest, who immediately upon sitting plunks down three glasses and a bottle of schnapps. Leo waves it off but Bessie takes a quick snort before banging her gavel to begin. One after the other, they berate the horrors of the sweatshops and the evil of the contract system whereby the manufacturer pays the contractor a set price per bundle and the contractor extracts his profit from the workers in blood.

Leo flings a copy of this morning's *New York World* on the table.

"Today Bloomingdales is selling middy blouses at ninety-eight cents. These prices are only possible because the bosses exploit us as slaves."

Bessie's face is a mask of disgust. "Those bastards stop at nothing, adding work hours, dropping the bundle price at will, and tossing you to the gutter if you object. They skulk the docks for fresh victims right off the boat, greenhorns too scared to breathe, much less comprehend their exploitation."

"Vile, immoral, and illegitimate." Mendel shakes his head. "The Protocols should be eliminating such abuses."

Leo snorts his contempt. "The manufacturers will comply with the Protocols when dogs shit gold bricks. We all smell the stink...how the manufacturer curtseys and says, 'Sure, I'll agree to play by the rules.'

Instead of manufacturing his own garment, he buys the cloth and contracts the cutting out to a Cutter. When you go to the cutter about working conditions, he says, 'I'm not a manufacturer, there's no protocol for me.' The manufacturer, who now calls himself a Jobber, contracts the sewing out to a subcontractor. The subcontractor says, 'I'm not a manufacturer, there's no protocol for me.' Next comes the Presser, who says the same thing. 'I'm not a manufacturer, there's no protocol for me.' Add to that the inside shops where owners simply do as they please. Your damn Protocols are a capitalist ploy to lull us into submission. Only after the triumph of the worker's International—"

"Marxists." Mendel interrupts, looking to Heaven for agreement. "Tell me, where is your sacred International today, with workers killing each other all over France and Germany?"

Leo leans across the table. "Don't start with me, Mendel. You know I stand opposed to the European debacle. The French and German workers have been duped by false notions of patriotism. Class warfare is the only real battle."

"So, making life better for the poor *schnooks* in sweatshops isn't enough?"

"Exactly how much are the Protocols helping the poor *schnooks* who made those middy blouses?"

"For God's sake, what are these *fakakta* Protocols?" I carp, then slap a hand over my mouth, but the jumping jack woman swings around. Only it's not a woman. It's a young girl with fervent grey eyes that pin me to my seat.

"The Protocols of Peace. The Strike of Nineteen Ten made the uptown big shots nervous. They wrote rules about wages and working conditions, making it look like we could expect justice. The manufacturers signed the rules and cheerfully ignore them without consequence." She looks me up and down. "Are you a greenhorn, you don't know this?"

The heat rises from my neck to my hairline. "No, just...doing other things."

She sniffs, leaving me the back of her tawny head.

Down front, the rancor is cooling. Mendel concedes that the Protocols have failed to deliver as promised. "Clearly the only permanent solution is a powerful union."

Leo sits back, satisfied. "Mendel, we finally agree. Workers must take charge and rule their own destiny."

A murmur of concurrence circles the room. My little instructress can no longer contain herself. She jumps up, waving her arm for attention.

"I'm Nettie Bloom. I work at Margolis Shirtwaist Company, one of the foulest shops in the district. Mendel can vouch for me."

"Which I most proudly do." Mendel waves a salute.

"A few of us favor unionizing, but we're not enough yet, and the interested ones have no experience."

"It's a dangerous undertaking." Leo rubs his chin, eyes narrowed. "I know of Margolis. Word is he's an authentic barbarian. If he catches on, you'll be out on the street with teeth missing. The only way is having good organizers on the floor, talking in whispers."

"Where do we find these masterminds?"

Nettie Bloom's question hangs in the air as the three panelists look at each other. Mendel Stern slaps the table.

"Presuming Margolis is hiring cutters, I will come lead the effort."

Bessie stares in surprise. "You'd quit a good union job to go work for a *mamzer* bastard?"

"Sure, why not?" He throws back a shot. "What better have I got to do with my time?"

Leo is not about to cede the night to Mendel. "You can't do it alone." He stands. "Count me in."

Seeing Leo on his feet, I panic. Leo is my education, my future. What is Niedermeyer's without Leo? My arm goes up before I can think.

"If I can still apprentice, I'll go too."

They all turn to Leo, questioning. He nods and it's done.

THREE

Miriam slams her book shut, sending the papers flying. I bend to pick them up and she hits my shoulder so hard it draws a welt.

"I thought I raised you smarter than this."

"It's just until it's organized."

"Which will probably be never." She makes as if to hit me again but whacks the table instead. "What about my school? What about her?"

She points to the corner, where our mother sits in her rocker. She came six months ago, after our dog of a father kicked the bucket. She doesn't talk anymore. All we hear is the creak of her chair and the click of her fingernails drumming on the tabletop. A ghost haunting our kitchen.

Miriam's voice drops. "That's not gonna be me."

This shuts me up, but I volunteered. Only a *schlemiel* goes back on his word. And Niedermeyer's without Leo...

"Miri, Leo Hirsch is going. He's my apprenticeship."

"Leo Hirsch." She's on her feet. "Get your coat."

Leo lives two blocks over on Clinton. When he opens the door he is in shirtsleeves, his brown suspenders hanging at his waist.

"Bastard," Miriam hisses from the hall. "He's a baby, and you trick him with your stupid theories so you can show what a *macher* you are. What about his family? What are we supposed to do with this idiot plan?"

Leo is big and blond. Miriam is small with hair dark as onyx. They face each other in the doorway, her eyes hurling fire.

He steps aside for her. "You are mostly wrong, but a little right."

The ceiling bulb shoots sparks off Miriam's black hair. Leo offers a cigarette, which she disdains. He lights up, slowly shaking out the match.

"You're wrong about me showing off. A true revolutionary is not concerned with personal glory." He sighs. "But you're right in that I didn't think about his family. That was an ideological error."

Head down, Leo circles the room, palms out like they're weighing something. Finally, he looks up.

"Until we have successfully unionized the shop, I will make up the difference in Irving's salary so his family doesn't suffer. About the working conditions and extra hours, I can do nothing. That must be his contribution to the struggle."

Miriam is a balloon with a pinprick, all the air fizzling out at once. "What...why would you do that?"

"We stand by our beliefs or we are nothing. Marx says, 'From each according to his ability.'"

"You are a madman." She turns to me. "He's a madman." My eyes do the pleading. "But...if the money stays the same...and Irving continues to learn the trade..."

I grab her hand. "Thank you, Miri."

Leo grunts as if hit with a new thought. "I will come by every week, personally, to hand you the money."

Miriam slowly nods, her eyes locked on his. "Yes. That is acceptable."

FOUR

"It's your funeral," Niedermeyer said when I quit. Now it's six in the morning, the city is an iceberg, and I'm standing with Leo, Mendel, and a hundred other phantoms, waiting for Margolis to open his doors. Nettie Bloom huddles in a crowd of women, blowing warm breath into her cold hands. She is tiny, a little porcelain doll. I shoulder my way over.

"Ready to do battle?" My words come out in a cold puff.

"Have you ever done sweat work?"

"Come on, what could be so bad? I am a soldier of the revolution."

"Quiet, fool," she hisses and kicks my shin. I step back just as fat Margolis pushes through wearing a fancy wool coat with a Persian lamb collar. His scrawny contractor, Schneiderman, skuttles behind, a scavenger fish following a shark. We've been warned to watch out for Schneiderman. Keys jangle, the door opens, and the women shove. I'm heaved against the wall, watching the row of hooks inside the door disappear under their coats.

Upstairs, the loft is endless, whitewashed brick smeared with grease and dust. Rows of black sewing machines run down the center, thread from the skeins circling like spider webs. The right wall is a fleet of ironing tables for the pressers. The back is for the cutters. On every surface there is cloth, Everests of cloth on the sorting tables, puddles of cloth on the floor, neat little armies of cloth by the pressers.

I watch Nettie take a seat at the far end. Schneiderman circles her, eyes gleaming. He knocks his clipboard against the table to get her attention then leans across her, pointing at something, dipping his face into her breasts. She whips herself erect. He walks away with a smirk.

One by one the women pick up a bundle, find a place and turn on their machine. Soon the whole room is clattering. Tic-a-tic-a-hum. Tic-a-tic-a-tic-a-hum. The sound rattles the light fixtures and jumps off the walls. Tic-a-tic-a-hum. Tic-a-tic-a-tic-a-hum. Paid by the piece, speed is money. This bundle is supper. Tic-a-tic-a-hum. That bundle is the rent.

Leo ties on an apron and checks the knives as the other cutters stroll in. Some, like Leo, wear grey work shirts with sleeves rolled up their arms, but others are in collars and ties, demonstrating to any and all that they are the cream of the cream, the highest-ranking workers in the shop.

Margolis manufactures lady's shirtwaists. A sample of today's garment hangs against the wall as the cutters huddle, dissecting the pattern. I look from their template to the blouse but cannot imagine how those odd little pieces will come together into a garment. Not a problem for the master cutters. When Schneiderman sidles over, they close ranks so he has to stand on tiptoe to peek over their shoulders. Schneiderman is Margolis' rat. He lives to report a mistake. The women can't object, but the cutters are less afraid. His eyes darken at their contempt. When he sees me staring, he barks "Are you loafing?" and I run.

In the middle of the room, the women never stop. Some baste white ribbon for collars and cuffs. Some stitch ties, some sew sleeves, others assemble. Right sleeve. Tic-a-hum. Cuff. Tic-a-hum. Left sleeve. Tic-a-hum. Cuff. Twist the fabric this way, then the other, with the speed of a flying bird, their fingers are a blur. Finish a bundle. Pick up the next. Tic-a-tic-a-tic-a-hum. And everywhere there is Schneiderman, counting, weighing, sneering. In Italian, *"Più veloce."* In Yiddish, *"Fastn."* In English, "Faster."

As cold as it was in the morning, the heat from the pressing tables makes this a steam room. The women get up only to relieve themselves, even then, Schneiderman glowers. Around noon I see Nettie pull salami and bread onto her lap, wiping a greasy hand against her skirt so as not to soil the fabric. The sun rises, fills the room with light, and falls away. By five o'clock, it's dark, but the sewing never stops. Tic-a-hum. Six o'clock. Tic-a-tic-a-hum. Seven.

Margolis reappears a little before eight, frowning at this, barking at that. He moves to the front and pulls the chain on the big brass bell that hangs by the door. Like a locomotive pulling into a station, the clacking gets slower...slower...and slower. Until it is still. The scratch of the chairs and shuffling of feet as the women stand. After all day with the clatter, the silence hurts.

Schneiderman guards the exit. Every bag and pocket must be checked against thievery. God forbid Margolis should lose one piece of ribbon. My feet are so heavy I can hardly move but my mouth is sour with rage.

They've been here all my life, limping to work early and staggering back in the dark, carrying bundles to do more at home. All my life. Until Leo, I never really saw.

FIVE

Tonya Wojcik looks maybe ten years old. If it were washed, I think her hair would be blond. She sits with nine others next to a bin that holds the assembled sections. Using scissors too big for their hands, they trim the threads left by the operators when they cut the garments from the machines. Schneiderman's wife Gussie, a forewoman, circles them, cawing orders like a sharp-nosed crow. Every few minutes Tonya's green eyes shoot to the bench where her mother Klara sews trim. If Schneiderman goes to harass the mother, Tonya darts over. Her mother speaks only Polish, so Tonya must translate the insults that Schneiderman rains upon them.

"Don't the Protocols have rules about children?" I mutter as I push a broom past Tonya's table.

"Grow up, kid." Manny Zukerman turns around. He was a couple of years ahead of me in high school and is almost done with his apprenticeship. He elbows me and whispers, "Notice the size of the bin? Big enough so when the inspector comes, they dump the girls under the fabric. And, trust me, Margolis shells out to know when the inspector will come."

"Are you being paid to prattle?" Schneiderman yells from across the room. I give my broom a thwack to push up a cloud of fabric dust for him to see. "Loafer," he yells again. "Go get the delivery."

I have to wait for Margolis to lumber over with his key. The door stays locked so no one will leave early. I know, we all know, the world knows, that a fire killed one hundred forty-seven Triangle Shirtwaist women this way. It doesn't seem to trouble Margolis. I maneuver past mounds of fabric, empty barrels, oily rags, and coils of old wire. More echoes of murder. In the street I throw two bolts over my shoulder and lurch back upstairs. Brutes. I see it all now. They are brutes. Bertha Mandelbaum coughs up blood from the dust. She is docked for soiling the garment. Loretta Benvenutto runs her finger under the needle. She sews without stopping. Gussie Schneiderman follows them to the stink hole of a toilet, counting the seconds it takes them to shit. Brutes.

On Friday, Margolis closes before sundown for the Sabbath.

"Such a good Jew," Mendel Stern sneers as we walk down to the street. "I wonder what he says to God on Yom Kippur."

The more I know Mendel, the better I like him. His stubble comes in white and his thin hairs make grey lines across his scalp, but he's still full of vinegar, in the needle trades since a child and a committed orga-nizer. By the end of the first week, he knows the name of every worker in the shop. No matter how hard he and Leo argue, he always ends with a joke and a slap on the back.

"You should've been here for The Uprising of Twenty Thousand. Can you imagine, Irving? Strikers like an ocean filling the streets. Pickets marched from Grand to Canal, from the river to the park. We ruled the district until they called in the gangsters. Then it was war, terrible and vile. Mind you, we didn't win all we wanted, but at least they don't have to bring their own sewing machines and pay the owner for needles and thread. For that they can thank us."

I know from that first meeting that Mendel is no fan of Leo's Marxism.

"I don't trust it. It asks for a perfection that is not human." He glances at Leo and Nettie walking ahead of us. "Leo imagines a world where every evil will be washed away in the great awakening of the worker's paradise, but these are childish fantasies. Give us a workday that doesn't last forever, a clean place to shit, and twenty dollars at the end of the week. That will be miracle enough."

A beer wagon passes us. The big horse clip-clops around the corner, leaving his droppings behind.

"How about Nettie?" I ask.

He bumps my shoulder. "A pretty girl, no?" I feel the heat rise in my face and blush harder when he laughs. "Nettie is the third of six. Her mother, may she rest in peace, went from tuberculosis. The two older girls were out as soon as they found husbands. Nettie supports, working since thirteen. She understands if nothing changes, this will be her life forever."

"Is she a Marxist, too?"

"Maybe, maybe not. She is a heart in search of direction."

The sun has dropped behind the buildings and the streets are blue with shadow. Lights from Shabbos candles shimmer up and down the block. Passing a corner shul, we hear the wail of the Friday prayers. I shake Mendel's hand, wave to the others, and turn up Norfolk, my fists deep in my pockets. Four and a quarter dollars for the week. It's shameful. In the apartment, Miriam is at the stove. When I place the money on the table, she doesn't bother to look. She turns off the flame and calls for Mama to light the candles, one of the few things to rouse her from her perpetual trance.

We're finishing the last of our soup when the knock comes. Miriam waves for me to sit but stops at the dark window to check her hair before opening to the door. Leo has put on a fresh shirt and a brown jacket. His hair is parted in the middle and smeared with pomade, like some suitor in a Mary Pickford movie. He holds out a roll of cash.

"I have come to honor my commitment."

Miriam thumbs the wad, counting, as Leo leans in the doorframe. She slips the money into a drawer. "Thank you. This will do."

That's when he pulls his other hand from behind his back,

thrusting out a bunch of white daisies. I cannot imagine where he found a florist open on Friday night.

"Would you consider accompanying me to the Rialto to see Charlie Chaplin?"

Miriam doesn't blink or look surprised. She holds the bouquet to her nose before handing it off to me.

"Let me get my hat," she says, and they are gone.

By the end of three weeks Leo is with us for dinner every night. Miriam, who finishes her workday like a normal human being, has food waiting for us when we get home. Leo rips off a chunk of challah and talks between chews.

"Irving, tomorrow you help Nettie distribute handbills. Find a spot where Margolis and Schneiderman won't see you. And, for God's sake, when you come inside, keep your mouth shut. One whiff you're talking union and you'll be lucky to have teeth."

I look up from my soup bowl. "But Nettie whispers union all the time."

He tosses a piece of bread at me. "Nettie knows what she's doing."

"So do I." I toss it back. "I'm not a baby, you know."

"Yes, you are," Leo and Miriam say together.

Leo keeps on. "We need to get the shop signed up soon. Things are on the move. The union is starting negotiations with the Manufacturers Alliance. We'll make demands. The manufacturers will refuse. The union will strike."

Miriam pours the last bit of soup into her bowl. "How can you be so sure the owners will refuse?"

"This is capitalism. They always refuse."

"Then why make trouble?" She sets down the pot and comes to the table. "Everyone knows these strikes never work. At the beginning it's all brother and comrade, but soon it's only what about me? It's human nature. People want for themselves."

"Like me," I raise my hand. "I want more soup." They both scoff. "No, I mean it. I want more soup and there isn't any. When I'm hungry I care about my own stomach, not anyone else's."

Leo grabs Miriam's bowl and pushes it toward me. "And if I say the only way to fill your stomach is to take the soup from your sister—would you do it? Because that is capitalism."

Miriam grabs back her food. "Let me state clearly, no one takes away what I have."

With both hands, Leo lifts his own bowl as if making an offering. "But, unlike the capitalist, you give as well as you get. Look what you have provided." He reaches across the table to cover her hand in his huge paw. "But I must admit, there are things I too want that I don't yet have."

Miriam blushes. She does that a lot these days, my stern, serious sister. I am not the only one seeing the world with new eyes.

Six

In the hour before work, Nettie stations us on Allen Street, knowing that Margolis and Schneiderman will walk up Grand. We thrust a handbill at each person who passes, "Attention! Garment Workers! Improve Your Conditions!" in English, Yiddish, Italian. Some sneer. Some ignore. But most grab as they go.

Tonya Wojcik approaches, holding her mother's hand.

I hold up the paper. "Can you read?"

She nods and snatches it into her pocket. It's a good thing, because a cop strolls onto the block, twirling his billy club. Nettie pulls me into a doorway, "Come on, you idiot." I shove the papers under my coat and we dash up to the loft.

I'M AT CEPULSKI'S WITH LEO, MENDEL, AND IGNAZIO CAPAMAGGIO, an old comrade of Mendel's who also works at our shop. Ignazio's an anarchist. He's drinking grappa and holding forth on the fundamental error of Marxist ideology.

"*Basta* on your communist state. The State is just another tool for domination. Human beings can unite in cooperative brotherhoods without supporting corrupt political institutions."

Our glasses jiggle as Leo's stein hits the table. "Such thinking is naïve. The central state is a necessary step in the..."

Socialism, anarchism, Marxism—around my third beer they all start to sound the same. No matter which kind of -ism, the job still stinks. My attention wanders as Nettie Bloom walks by, surrounded by four of Margolis' operators. I jump to the window and wave. Her eyes brush my way, but she acknowledges me not at all. I plunk back to my chair as Capamaggio removes himself to the privy.

"Irving?" Mendel notices my pout.

"It's driving me crazy. She's all *schmoozy* with the girls, but with me, it's only Yes. No. Maybe. She's like the pirate chest in *Treasure Island*. There's gold inside, but I don't have the key."

Leo tips up his chair, sipping his beer. "Well, you can always share your political views."

Mendel looks disgusted. "With advice like that, the boy'll die a bachelor." He ignores Leo's scowl. "Listen, Irving, you gotta relax. Act like a person. If she gets to know you, you'll get to know her. Trust me." He tosses back a vodka. "I've been married twice."

Next morning, while we are waiting for the doors to open, Mendel gives me an "accidental" shove so I bump into her. I manage to squeak would she want to come out with me? I endure a full minute of a stare before she nods.

ON SATURDAY NIGHT, I STAND IN THE MIDDLE OF THE KITCHEN while Leo instructs me how to drop my arm just right so it's easy to take a girl's hand. Miriam looks me in the eye, says, "Act right," then slips some coins into my pocket.

All the way down Suffolk Street I keep checking myself in the store windows. It's my life's curse that I'm short. The *shmeggeges* in school used to call me Chicken Little and ask if my pecker was tiny, too. Some joke. On her stoop, I practice pushing my shoulders back and sticking my chin up. Maybe my cap adds an inch or two. I try it this way, that way, and give up. She's so small herself, maybe she won't notice.

I climb to the apartment, take a deep breath and rap my knuckles on her door. A kid yells, "By me, by me," and, lined up at the threshold, two girls and a boy. The boy gives me the onceover. "You takin' my sister?" The girls titter. Behind them, in the corner, in a black yarmulke, the fringes of his tzitzit hanging out under his shirt, sits their father, a Yiddish newspaper in his lap. I make a polite nod, but he doesn't acknowledge. Nettie comes from the back in a creamy shirtwaist, smoothing her black skirt. Air whistles through my teeth before I can help it. Her eyes get cool and I cover my mouth.

"*Jakie, bay 9:00 ir gat tsu shlofn*," she says to the kid. Pointing a finger to the older girl, "Remember, Sadie, nine o'clock."

"For sure." Sadie nods solemnly.

"Yeah, sure for sure." Nettie glances back at her father, but he is engrossed. She sighs, grabs her cloak off a hook and we head downstairs.

It's a frosty night. The puddles are cracked glass and ice collects on the tarpaulins covering the pushcarts, but Shabbos is over and people are out for fun. Kitchen vents pump steam and warm air hits us with each opening of a restaurant door. Elbows bump, shoulders rub. The sidewalks are so full the crowd makes heat like a blanket. We get trapped in a throng surrounding a hurdy-gurdy at the corner of Essex and Delancey.

"There is a moving picture at the Sunshine," I say when we break free. "From a Dickens book."

"Who's Dickens?"

"You know. Charles Dickens."

When she drops her eyes, I want to bite my tongue off. She's never heard of Charles Dickens. Such a thing never occurred to me—all that zeal and fervor, but Nettie left school at thirteen. No literature. No science. No geometry. No nothing. She's looking down at her feet. I bet she's thinking I'm a snooty show-off. I'm about to grab her hand and apologize, but she grabs mine first.

"Would you tell me one of his books? I love hearing stories."

We pass under a streetlamp. It's like someone turned on a light inside her.

"Sure, sure, I can do that. Just let me think...how about *Oliver Twist*? He was a poor kid, like us." Miriam's coins jangle in my pocket. "We could sit at Katz's. Would you maybe like a hot dog?"

I get my first giant Nettie smile.

It's work to remember the whole story. Some things she asks to go over twice.

When I tell about the workhouse she's spellbound.

"Was Charles Dickens a Marxist?" she asks as we walk out.

Clouds ring the moon and an icy drizzle is falling. We try to walk under the awnings. Nettie's shoulder brushes my coat.

"How about you tell me a story," I say, moving a step closer. My arm has a mind of its own and creeps across her back. "Tell how you started with this union business."

"Really?"

I nod so hard my cap almost falls off. She looks around like she's searching for words. "Well...you know about the big shirtwaist strike?"

"Of course." I send Mendel a silent blessing.

"Mama was going out every day, carrying a sign, 'Picket! Ladies Tailor Strike!' I kept pleading with her to take me along. I wouldn't stop begging. Finally, one day, she wrapped me in a sash that said, 'Abolish Slavery!' There was snow on the street. I remember how warm my fingers were, holding her hand. There were so many women, I couldn't see where the line started or ended. Someone started singing." Nettie's voice is thin. "*As we go marching, marching in the beauty of the day.* I felt like a big hero, just being with them, you know?"

I wrack my brain to see if I'd ever felt like that but find nothing.

"When we got to Lafayette, the street was filled with blue coats and the paddy wagons were waiting. The coppers used their night-sticks to make a circle and pulled people into the wagons, it didn't matter who. 'You're one of them alley cats working the Bowery' or 'Hey, floozie, I seen you at Randy Rick's.' It was their excuse, see? It's not against the law to picket, but they're allowed to arrest prostitutes. One of the cops grabbed Mama. She swung me behind her and the other women kept pushing me back 'til I was buried by their black skirts. Mama yelled 'I ain't no whore.' Then she was gone. They kept her in the workhouse for two weeks. When she came out, she was coughing up blood."

"You joined the union when you were nine?"

"Don't be a dope. But I was thirteen when Mama died, still eighty hours a week, still paid by the piece. I knew that it would always be like this—we get tiny dribs and drabs but never all the way. I knew we had to fix it."

We've gotten to the Sunshine. The sign reads, "New release, *Great Expectations*."

I reach to help Nettie across the street. She grips my hand. "It shouldn't be *Oliver Twist* forever," she says. "It's got to be better."

SEVEN

I f you ask me, the Seward Park Library is as grand as any synagogue and I cannot believe my ears when Nettie says she's never been.

"Papa commands no. He says women can't read Torah, so why bother?"

I hatch a plot. We wait 'til Saturday. Once this monster of a father has disappeared into his shul, I proudly escort Nettie through the door. High arched windows, paneled walls, rows of cherrywood shelving with books beyond measure—all commissioned by the great Mr. Andrew Carnegie himself. Like all temples, it has a priestess—the spectacled librarian who stands at the door, ensuring all hands are clean enough to touch the sacred texts.

Inside, I become a tour guide. Would Nettie like to study the latest fashions? Here are the magazines. Not of interest? How about science? I walk backwards to watch her face and assess what appeals. Does she read Yiddish? The collection is upstairs. No? Perhaps more stories? A-ha, there's the smile.

I lead her to American Fiction. On this account, I must apologize —these volumes are often used, so the bindings have become threadbare and the pages ragged. She runs her hand across the covers. Washington Irving. Harriet Beecher Stowe. Henry James. She kneels.

"*The House of Seven Gables*—what's a gable?"

God curses me. She's picked a book I haven't read. Reluctantly, I'm forced to acknowledge my ignorance. She pulls it from the shelf.

"So, if I read, maybe I can tell it to you for a change."

I make a face. This is not going as planned. "Wait...follow me."

A wide set of stairs leads to the roof. The sign says, "Closed." Nettie holds back.

"It's okay, I promise."

She glances around for the librarian but lets me lead. Outside, the sun has heated the black tar surface and the brick ramparts keep the wind at bay.

I open my arms wide. "Marvelous, no? In summer, they put a garden up here."

Nettie looks over a parapet, knitting her brow.

"An awning...do they have a big awning?" Her hands wave above her head. "And yellow lights?" She waits for my nod. "Irving, I was here with my mother. There was a table." She runs to the middle. "Right here. Mama had some pieces from the shop. It was hot so she came to work outside. We had books with pictures." Her eyes fill with tears. "Mama wanted me to read."

She is so beautiful. I move toward her, but get shy, and I only take her hand.

"I told you this was a palace of marvels."

She leans against the wall. Wisps of hair escape their pins and catch in the sunlight. She's small, like Miriam, but so different. Her waist is narrow, her breasts tight. Miriam is the trunk of a tree. Nettie is a blade of grass. When our arms touch, electricity flows to my groin. For shame I flash on the French postcards the boys sell on the street.

"How did you ever find this place, Irving? Was it Miriam?"

Jolt. My daydream disappears like smoke. Such a natural question. Anyone would ask that question, no big deal, but I am speechless. I twist away so she won't see my confusion. Our family's unspoken pact. From that day to this, I haven't said a word. Tell Nettie the truth, it is a betrayal. But lying to her is also a betrayal. I study the snowy rooftops as if they have an answer, and there is Arthur, floating in the air, tall and skinny with his scrawny beard and his worn black coat, his hand on my shoulder as he walks me through the door. "Come, *bubeleh*, we've been given a gift of great value."

"No, not Miriam. My brother, Arthur."

She catches my tone. Her voice drops. "Is he dead?"

Good question. What is dead?

"He's...away...He has fits."

"Fits?"

"On the floor, jerking, twitching...fits."

"You mean your brother has the epilepsy?"

I go red. Papa whacked me when I used that word.

"My father always complained how, in the *shtetl*, they banished those who ate but didn't work. One day Artie had a terrible attack, the worst. Papa shook him, *Get up, you bum*, but nothing, so Papa went for his belt. Miriam...Miriam held him back. He almost hit her. Instead, he kicked the bed and barked Artie had to go."

A gust of wind blows some old newspaper against my leg and I flick it away, looking north, over the traffic, to the spot where the ambulance had parked.

"Where is he now?"

I shake my head. "Miri said we couldn't live there anymore, see? So, she and I left. After that Papa wouldn't give us the time of day and Mama would never say a word against him."

We go to the empty park next to the library, shoving a pile of snow off a bench in order to huddle. I lean forward, rubbing my hands together, figuring how to tell about my brother.

"There was the time...Papa came in ready to bash something, anything. I was playing on the floor. One swipe and I hung in the air, screaming. But the whack never came. Instead, 'Grr, grr, grr.' Arthur had the Hoffman's mongrel, Goliath, lunging on its leash. When Papa dropped me, his snarl was darker than the dog's." I lower my head into my hands. "That was my big brother Arthur. Until the fits."

She slaps her knee. "You gotta find him."

"How am I supposed to do that?"

Nettie bats my shoulder. "You're the smart one. Figure it out." Her voice is firm. "Wherever he is, Irving, you got a right to know."

EIGHT

I bolt awake, sucking in the dark. It takes a minute to settle...the apartment, my bed, Miriam snoring quietly across the room. Since telling Nettie, the nightmare is back. Used to be, when it came, Artie would wake me whispering, "I'm here *tateleh*," and bring warm milk.

I swing out of bed and pad to the kitchen, my toes curling against the icy floor. It would be nice if once in a while they left the heat on at night. There's a shuffling by the window—my mother. Even with a cot for her in the back, she sits up half the night, rocking. Creak, creak, creak, her face goes from white to black to white in the moonlight. I can't remember the last time we were alone in the dark. When I was a baby, maybe.

"Mama?" Filmy eyes swivel in my direction. "Mama, do you know where Arthur is?"

"*Vas?*"

"*Tsi ir visn vu Arthur iz?*"

The creaking stops. "*Ver iz Arthur?*" Who is Arthur?

HANDS SHOVED IN MY POCKETS, I KICK A TIN CAN FROM LEFT FOOT to right foot to left foot. "Mama's *meshugeneh*. Miriam's a blank. Nobody knows anything."

Nettie shoots out her boot and knocks the rusty thing under the hooves of a draught horse, who immediately stomps it to bits.

"Enough *kvetching*. You got feet. You got a mouth. How many hospitals can there be?"

"Sure. Fine. I'll go up and down Manhattan, every day, in all those wonderful hours when I'm not toiling like a dog for Morris Margolis." I look longingly at the dead can.

Nettie sniffs. "All right, so that's not so easy. But for sure somewhere there's a way."

I shrug and keep walking. Nettie catches up and prods me with her shoulder. I don't stop. She does it again, a little harder, but I'm not in the mood for ha ha ha. A third bump, hard enough I collide with an old woman who curses, "*Nudnick*" and returns me a *potch* on the arm. This is too much. I shoulder Nettie back. For ten steps it's a war to see who can shove the hardest, but it's not a fair fight—she's so tiny. I straighten up so fast she stumbles and I have to catch her from tripping. My arms around her waist, I hold her to me. She rests her head against my chest for one breath, then we start walking.

"You know, Irving, after Mama died, my papa disappeared into his synagogue and my sisters left. Mendel was our neighbor. He saw I was all the time crying. One day he said, 'Maybe if you understood what really happened, you wouldn't be so sad.' He started taking me to his meetings, The Workman's Circle, The Labor Temple, places like that. He was right. The more I understood, the less sad I got because, what happened to my Mama, it happens to a lot of us. If I fix it for everyone else, I'm fixing it for her, too. Could you maybe see your Arthur that way?"

We've gotten to Grand and Allen. Margolis is pushing open his doors and the workers are piling in. As we cross the street, a blast of steam from a manhole cover shrouds us in white mist.

"I don't know...Maybe."

NINE

Tonya's mother Klara is pregnant and even I can see it's not good. Her face is grey and her hands are slow. She is all the time bent over a slop bucket she keeps at her feet. Day after day she stays late, struggling to complete her bundles, but the seams get twisted or the ribbing torn. Nettie and the other girls sneak this piece or that to finish for her, but Margolis is relentless, docking her for every spoiled ribbon or misused thread. At the end of seventy hours, she takes home *bubkes*.

"How is this allowed?" I fume. We're all leaving for the night with Klara still stitching and Tonya asleep at her feet.

Leo's voice is heavy with frustration. "For God's sake, how many times do I need to tell you? This is capitalism."

"Stop pestering the boy." Mendel is sharper than usual. He was often at Klara's machine today, his face grave. "We all agree this is a crime and, God willing, we will put an end to it, but, enough about revolution." His breath is ragged. "When I was seven my parents were murdered in a pogrom. My uncle carried me to America on his back. Ask a hundred people on this block and you'll hear the same story—pogroms, murders, rapes. Life here ain't perfect, but no one here is burning my house or slaughtering my family. America is better than where I'm from."

Leo looks back at the lights still on in Margolis' loft. "Not better enough, Mendel. Not better enough. I believe it's time."

THE ROOM IS A MAP OF WARRING EUROPE. YIDDISH, ITALIAN, Polish—each sits with his own. On top of that are the different trades. The cutters associate only with each other. The pressers cluster behind them. The sewers, trimmers, sorters, and finishers—all women—are in the back. Antoni, the Wojcik's youngest, plays on the floor with Elena Carpaccio's son. Sophie Bowser peruses a pamphlet with Seraphina Redondo. Nettie, who never ceases to amaze, has a heated conversation in Italian with Rosa Delacosta. After the meeting I ask her where on God's earth she learned Italian. She is casual. "Neighbors."

I am assigned to the door.

"It is urgent to admit only workers from our shop," Leo says. "Let me know instantly if anyone else tries to enter."

I'm honored by the unexpected responsibility.

"You'll be a good decoy," he teases as he flicks some dust off my jacket. "Nobody takes you too seriously."

I give him a dirty look but go to my post. At 7:15 sharp, Mendel bangs a gavel. People settle into their seats and Leo stands.

"Brothers, sisters, comrades." His booming voice needs no megaphone. "I am a cutter, I am a worker, and, like the rest of you, I am a slave."

Esther Mandelbaum translates to Yiddish, Seraphina to Italian, little Tonya does Polish.

"If Morris Margolis berates me, I must bow my head. If he lowers my wage, I must accept. If he works me 'til I drop, I must comply. Speed-ups. Docked wages. Noxious conditions. Complain, and Margolis fires me. Without his job, I starve."

Around the room there are nods and titters of agreement.

"But, I ask you, can Margolis make a single blouse alone? Can he cut and sew and press and package? We are the makers. We are the builders. We are the creators. We deserve the fruits of our labor."

Those who understand English immediately stomp their approval. The others lean in for translation and add their voices. Rosa Delacosta shouts, "*Va bene!*"

"But, Leo, you might say to me, Margolis owns the machines, the police, and the politicians. How am I to oppose such domination? To which I say, alone you are a tiny pebble tossed by the surf. But, stand shoulder to shoulder with your comrades, and you become a mighty sea wall. The union is that wall."

Climbing onto a bench, Tonya prances in circles to capture the passion of Leo's words. One of the Italians twirls a red handkerchief over his head. The toddlers on the floor stop playing to gawk at the adults.

Leo waits for calm. "It is time to stop being cowards and demand our rights. I motion we join with the union."

"Second the motion," someone yells from among the pressers and everyone cheers.

"Does anyone else get to talk?" a deep voice calls over the chanting. The English-speakers look around to find the source. Others pull at the sleeves of the translators. Confused, Tonya steps down from the bench. Pincas Gutzman, a big man with a face like an ox, stands up from among the cutters.

"You union people spin a pretty tale, but you leave a few things out. I used to work for Stern and Company Remember them? A small outfit on 12th Street? Long hours for bad pay, like always. The union said they could improve our lot. Twenty-five dollars it cost me to join. Twenty-five dollars that could've fed my family and paid my rent. When Stern wouldn't negotiate, they called a strike. Stern was just getting started. The strike drove him out of business. My family almost starved that winter. I say to hell with your union."

Manny Zuckerman growls, "Coward." Abe Feingold, another cutter, answers, "At last a little truth."

The translators inform their constituencies. A dark murmur circles the room. Leo is about to respond when tiny Angela Costorini raises her hand. Her small voice barely carries and people shush each other to hear.

"My papa was a cloak maker. He got pneumonia two years ago. Because he was in the union, he had sick days and didn't lose his job."

Her face gets red and she plops back down. Nettie gives her a hug.

The debate rages. Angry words. Reasonable words. Everyone has to be heard. After all the arguments have been exhausted and our brains are filled to overflowing, Mendel takes the floor.

"Friends, I think we can all admit that there is no such thing as a perfect world. Likewise, there is no such thing as a perfect union. Any association will be as good or as bad as we make it. But I put to you, whatever we do in this life, we are better off doing it together."

We vote on secret slips of paper. A committee, one representative from each trade, tallies. At the end, Nettie picks up Tonya Wojcik and twirls her around. Despite the cutters' peevish grumbling, the die is cast.

TEN

We're at union headquarters on 16th Street. After the successful vote, Leo and Mendel decided the smart thing is to consult the officials for our next steps. Nettie comes to represent the women and I come to be near Nettie. It's a good thing, too, because Leo's contact, Myron Dickstein, a spindly, sharp-faced redhead, will only confer with the men, saying secrecy is paramount in these things and women talk too much.

Nettie prepares to let the bastard have it, but Mendel yanks her aside. "So, he's a *schmuck*. What's more important, putting in your two cents or our shop getting the help we need?"

Though steam comes out hear ears, Nettie agrees to wait outside. "But you'll give me the real dope right after." She pokes his chest with her finger. "Or else."

Mendel puts up his hands like a scared child and agrees. He and Leo disappear into the office.

We kill time circling the lobby. Corkboards on the walls display a gallery of broadsides. Most are bright red with black lettering, though some are white with red lettering.

GENERAL STRIKE!

CLOAK AND SUIT MAKERS—
GENERAL STRIKE CALL:
Wednesday Morning, January 17, promptly at 7:30 AM a general strike
in the...

STRIKE!
Sisters And Brothers And Workers Of The Ladies Garment Shops

MEMBERS AND NON-MEMBERS ALIKE
A STRIKE is declared in your shops.
STOP WORK NOW and come to the
K. of C. Hall, Cor. Water and North Sts...

The final sign advertises the goals of the current negotiations:

The workers of the ladies' shirtwaist industry assert and avow the
following conditions as our natural right:

A Forty-four-hour workweek
   Paid overtime
   Scheduled daily lunch times
   7 annual holidays
   Sick leave
   Union inspections for proper sanitary conditions
   Union inspections for appropriate safety precautions

Forty-four hours...I'd actually have time to begin the Artie search.
I start a mental list of the hospitals when Nettie yells from the other
side of the room, waving frantically. "Irving, come, you gotta see this.
Look, look." She stuffs a thick pamphlet into my hands.

THE GARMENT WORKERS UNION CREATES
AN EDUCATION DEPARTMENT

Industrial unions exist to assist in the all-important task of making a better world for all to live in. Economic strength is much more effective if directed by intelligent, well-informed, clear-thinking citizens. The purpose of the Education Section is to provide the Labor Movement with such men and women.

Nettie's shaking finger runs down the page.

Professors from the City College of New York. Classes will be offered on Saturday afternoon and Sunday morning in English, Yiddish or Italian. Programs in Literature...History...Psychology...Economics...

"God, Irving, see, Social and Industrial History of Europe and America, Applied Psychology and Logic, Tendencies in Modern Literature. And, oh, oh, see this one." She's making little jumps. "A Woman's Place in the Labor Movement." She waves the pamphlet. *"This* is what we are fighting for. *This* is what our lives are supposed to be."

Watching Nettie's gorgeous eyes dance, becoming an intelligent, well-informed, clear-thinking worker is the last thing on my mind. I lean in for a kiss, but before I can achieve my heart's desire, Leo and Mendel emerge and Nettie dashes toward them.

"Well?"

Leo is jubilant. "Dickstein says the negotiations are nearing an end. There's a rally next week to announce the results. Organizing rogue shops like ours is one of their priorities." He makes a fist. "We came just in time."

ELEVEN

A beefy guy with a big white mustache leans down, shaking hands from the podium before picking up his megaphone.

"Welcome, fellow workers. Your attendance today demonstrates to all the world the strength and solidarity of our membership."

Leo leans across Nettie to explain. "He's Edelman, Chairman of the Joint Committee. A smart operator but I believe he lacks revolutionary spirit. The Marxist caucus voted against him."

She and I sit on a long wooden bench shmooshed between Leo and Mendel. Every few seconds someone else squeezes us more with, "Maybe there's a little room?" So many cram the hall, a rumor starts flying that the coppers, who infest like cockroaches, will call it a riot and shut us down, but the gallery keeps filling. I twist and turn, marveling at my first rally, the union in all its glory.

People from our shop are scattered around the hall. Sophie, Esther, Angelina, and Seraphina sit a row ahead, gaping and awed. Even Gutzman attends, wary and watchful against the back wall, his arms crossed over his chest. Nettie is spinning in happy circles, waving this way and that.

She hugs my arm. "We did it Irving, you, me, Mendel, and Leo, just like we planned."

There's a wave from the podium. Conversations end, people shush each other, and Edelman commences his speech.

"Welcome fellow workers. We, the members of the Joint Committee, have called you together to report on the state of our negotiations with the Manufacturer's Alliance. No labor organization on earth is more committed to bringing you the justice you deserve."

A roar of approval bounces off the ceiling and the walls. He waits for the clamor to ease and raises the megaphone again.

"I can say, with extreme pride, that your leaders have done everything humanly possible to put forth your just demands. We argued eloquently and have done all that persons with feelings of pride and self-respect could do to convince the manufacturers of the righteous necessity of our cause. But, I also must say, that from the very first, the manufacturers balked, and all our meetings ended without results."

Imagine a ceiling filled with buckets of ice water when someone pulls a rope. The room goes from rowdy to silent in the space of a breath.

"I know there are those among you who see no alternative but to strike. But your elected officers believe that the cost of such an action, both to you, the workers, and to the industry as a whole, is too high."

A wave of discontent floods over the assembly. People jump to their feet, pumping fists, and yelling. Edelman bangs his gavel, commanding order. In the angry silence, one official after another takes the podium. The treasurer tells of the limited funds in our war chest. The vice-president points to the severity of the winter and the difficulty of mounting picket lines in the cold. A fiery, black-haired Italian brings up the war in Europe and our patriotic duty to stay prepared in case America is called to fight.

Shouts of "Coward", "Weakling", and "Fink" follow the speakers off the podium. Leo pushes Nettie and me out of his way in his rush to organize the Marxists in mounting an official denunciation. We are trapped in the aisle as a quarrel breaks out. Insults are thrown, then fists.

I'm working to shield Nettie from those flailing arms when we see Rosa Delacosta waving frantically from the back door. I force open a path and Nettie runs. Rosa grabs her by the shoulders and shouts into her ear. Nettie jumps like she's been bit. Rosa nods, lays her head on Nettie's chest. Nettie breaks out of Rosa's arms, her eyes burning. She turns, heaving aside men and women alike, forcing her way to the front, where she leaps onto the podium, practically launching the speaker over the edge. The sight of tiny Nettie pushing aside a big *macher* grabs everyone's attention, and the noise cools enough for her to be heard.

"Do you know Klara Wojcik?"

Nettie's voice, usually so soft, booms to the back wall. She points to some random guy sitting in the front row.

"Do you know Klara Wojcik?"

The *schlemiel* holds up his hands and shakes his head as if he's been accused of a crime.

"Of course, you don't know Klara Wojcik. How could you? She sews seventy, eighty, ninety hours a week, though pregnant and sick. Sometimes she works all night. Ever hear of such a thing?"

The room has gone silent. Everyone, men, women, officials, watching coppers, everyone, waits on Nettie.

"Well, I am sorry to tell you that you will never know Klara Wojcik. Her daughter found her on the shop floor, dead, along with the unborn child!"

A communal moan spirals the room.

"How long will you allow this to go on?" Nettie is a warrior woman. Her voice is the voice of the prophets. She turns to face the union officials behind her. "How long will you allow it?" Back to the rank and file, she raises her fist. "I say strike. Strike now."

The crowd roars. In the blink of an eye, the whole room is a whirlpool of bodies, circling, eddying, shouting.

"Strike now. Strike now. Strike now." The chant bounces off the walls and ceiling. "Strike now. Strike now. Strike now."

Nettie stands, a statue, tears streaming down her face.

And that is how it begins.

TWELVE

"And what about the rent?"

Miriam is at the counter, cutting vegetables. Thwack, the celery stalks are hacked into tiny bits. Thwack, there go the parsnips.

"You're still working." I twist my hat in my hands, blushing with mortification as I utter the words.

"Thank you so much for the privilege of supporting us, yet again." She wrenches the greens off the carrot heads.

I bite my lip and search for what will make her not so mad.

"Leo says it probably won't be a long strike because it's the busy season and the owners will go broke if they don't deliver. Not to mention the money they will make if we enter the European war. With any luck, those *mamzers* will surrender in a week."

"With any luck..." A scraper flays skin from the first carrot. Slam, it goes to the cutting board. Whack. "Always the same thing. A dreamer with no sense." The carrot slides into the pot.

"Miri, think about Klara Wojcik. Think about her kids."

She grips the sides of the sink, her head lowered. Finally, "Okay, I'll admit, that bastard Margolis should be hung by his *baitsim*—a pregnant woman with children." She wipes her hands on a rag and reaches into the cabinet to pull down the tea tin that hides a roll of bills. She strips off five and offers them to me.

"For the Wojciks. But, never forget, Irving, family always comes first. Even Klara Wojcik would say that. When it's really either-or, you have to take care of your own."

I take her rough hand into both of mine. "I know, Miri. I will."

We are standing like that as Leo stomps in, a bundle over his shoulder and a wicker suitcase in his hand.

"I got home and I said to myself, Hirsch, why are you paying rent to your capitalist landlord when you promised a monthly sum to your comrades?" He slings his bundle onto a chair and his suitcase thuds to the floor. "Your Mama can share Miriam's bed and I'll take her cot in the back. The place will be a little crowded maybe." He plunks his tush down on one chair and his feet up on another. "But think of all the advantages."

I am awed. Leo's mind is like one of Margolis' sewing machines. It never stops working. But Miriam is no pushover. She folds her arms across her chest.

"Listen to Mr. Can't-Get-Over-Himself. First you get us mixed up in this union *mishigas*, now, you're the hand of God, saving us from Pharaoh's chariots. Tell me, for your next trick, do you plan to part the Red Sea?"

Leo's feet bang to the floor. "No. I am a man who knows where his responsibility lies. I made a promise. I will honor it, no matter what. Besides," his eyes don't leave her face, "at a time like this, a man needs a family."

Someday, please God, Nettie will look at me the way Miriam looks at Leo.

She squeezes out one last objection. "What will the neighbors say?"

Leo wraps her in his huge arms and winks at me over her shoulder. "They'll say Miriam Friedman is one smart cookie. She always makes the rent."

THIRTEEN

The strike is set for nine a.m. At six o'clock we assemble like always, but today there is no morning chatter. We shuffle our feet and talk in whispers. *He has to know. Maybe he'll lock us out. Maybe he'll bring in thugs.* Everyone watches Nettie, Leo, and Mendel who stand at the front like the pointy tip of an arrow.

"He'll be here," Mendel assures. "He doesn't believe we have the *chutzpah* to walk out on him."

As if Mendel were the prophet Elijah, Margolis pushes through, his frog face frozen with disdain. He pulls out his keys, bangs open the doors and marches up the stairs. We follow him in and go to our stations. The sewing machines start clacking, the ironing tables hiss steam, and the cutter's blades eat fabric. No one has uttered a word.

At 8:55, all eyes turn to the clock over the door, seeing the second hand navigate its little circle. The pressers keep their hands suspended. The cutters hold up their knives. I wait in the entranceway, a bolt of cotton hanging on my shoulder.

Is it possible we'll really do this? The newest trimmer is only thirteen and has never disobeyed her papa, who decried the loss of her salary. The hand finisher in the corner has a sick husband. The seam-checker at the end of the bench is only two months off the boat and speaks not one word of English. The lead presser has four hungry kids.

The minute hand moves another tick, and, again, the second hand begins its rotation. 8:59. The machines keep clattering, but no one in the room breathes. The hour hits nine. A hundred and fifty hands reach for their switches and the room falls dead.

Margolis, his white shirt rolled to his elbows and a tape measure around his neck, steps out of his office. Leo removes his apron and lays it across the table. Nettie rises from her seat. I drop my bolt. We look around, waiting. Pincas Gutzman nods and off comes his apron. It is the final sign. Like a trained army, the sewers, trimmers, finishers, pressers, and cutters fall into line and march out the door, leaving Morris Margolis alone in his factory, staring at their departing backs.

When Nettie, Leo, Mendel, and Rosa Delacosta walk into the space we've rented in the musty basement of Kaufman's Candy Store, everyone shouts *mazel tov*. Leo holds his hands over his head like a champion prizefighter, but Nettie ducks, red as a beet and comes right over to where I'm standing. There's a minute of me hemming and hawing, tongue-tied because Nettie is a Somebody and I'm just me. But when she puts her hand on my arm, it's still Nettie, small and warm, sending shivers down my spine.

"Can you believe it?" she says. "Just like we said we'd do."

All I want is to snatch her up, but the whole world is watching. Someone shoves me so hard I fall into her.

"Celebrate, *Schmendrick.*" Leo passes without losing a step.

My arms are wrapped around her waist. Her face is glowing like a Shabbos candle. She is irresistible. I close my eyes and take my first kiss. Her lips warm to mine until she pulls away, blushing.

Down front, Leo bangs on a table.

"Okay, comrades, let's get organized. Today, instead of garments, we manufacture a strike."

I JOIN A CREW CUTTING FABRIC INTO SLOGAN-SASHES. MENDEL supervises a gang of men sawing wood for picket-signs. Rosa yells instructions to a line of sewing machine operators turned sign-painters. Elena Carpaccio is trying to copy out a slogan. She curses when the watery paint drips down the side of her board. Sophie Bowser, an expert hand-stitcher, clucks disapproval. Her lettering is perfect. Voices shout over the sawing and banging. Faces shine. People make jokes. Is this not what work should always be like?

Leo sits at the desk, scribbling a handbill, "Why We Struggle." Esther Mandelbaum pecks it out on an ancient typewriter sent from union headquarters.

"We need this translated and printed. Rosa, could you maybe do the Italian? Irving," Leo shoves the paper in my face, "do the Yiddish and bring it to the *Forward* to publish."

I point up to the narrow window. "Don't you see what's doing out there?"

It was only flurrying when we left Margolis' shop, but the drifts have risen to our knees. Mounds of horseshit melt steamy puddles into the roadway and the motorcars are sliding in the mush. Our sour basement stinks extra from the damp.

Leo is not perturbed. "You're a Jew. Did you think God would make it easy?"

Muttering curses under my breath, I slowly tug on my coat, moving like a snail to stay inside as long as I can.

"Well?" Leo's eyes travel from me to the door. What can I do? I wrap a scarf around my neck and throw myself into the storm.

The wind whips the snow into needles. My toes freeze and my eyes crust with ice. I have to turn around every few feet to catch a full breath, berating Leo with each new shiver. Look at the fool's errand he sends me on. Obviously, everything will be shuttered in this misery, but when I get to the *Forward* building, lights glow onto the white sidewalk and the place is buzzing. I stick out my tongue to the plaster faces of Marx and Engels etched over the entrance, and push my way in.

I realize I was given no instructions. Is this to be an article, an announcement, a what? There's no money to pay for an ad. At the editorial desk, an ancient clerk in beard and yarmulke takes my hand-bill and waves for me to wait. Dripping snowmelt, I inhabit a dark wooden bench, twiddling my thumbs, until I pick up a wrinkled copy of yesterday's *Forward*—proudly the largest Yiddish newspaper in America. Artie used to bring it home every day, but I've barely read it since he went. I take off my wet gloves and start thumbing the pages.

Dispatch reports describe the nightmare of the European battle-field. A boxed editorial rebukes President Wilson as a pro-war hypocrite. The women in Brooklyn riot over food prices. Finally, relief from the wretchedness, there's everyone's favorite advice column, *A Bintel Brief*.

This used to be Mama's delight. She didn't read, but she adored hearing other people's troubles. Artie would orate from the kitchen table, waving his arms to convey all appropriate emotions. Mama stopped her chopping or scrubbing or baking to berate a wandering husband (*Er zol geyn shpringen in di ozere*—He should go jump in the lake), criticize a daughter's disobedience (*As meydl is kukn far konflict*—That girl is looking for trouble) or drop a tear at a poignant death (*Oy gevalt, di nebekh muter, di nebehk froy*—Oh, the poor mother, the poor child). We'd hear Papa's boots clomping up the stairs. Artie would close the paper, I'd bury myself in my schoolbooks, and Mama would bend back to work.

There's a good assortment today.

"Worthy Editor, I am a Socialist and Freethinker. My sister demands I say Kaddish on the anniversary of our mother's death. Will I be too much a hypocrite if I go to shul not believing?" (Editor: There's nothing hypocritical about honoring your mother's memory.)

"Mr. Editor, My husband threatens to desert me because of my night school classes." (Editor: Tell your husband he's in America.)

"Dear Editor, I am in agony. My husband was quarantined at Ellis Island because of a cough. When we went to get him, he'd already left. My cousin had to take us in. He has written this for me. How can I get my husband back?" (Editor: The National Desertion Bureau, 356 Second Avenue, locates missing men. We refer you to them for help.)

I feel the blood rush to my face. I read the letter again, dizzy with surprise. It's still there, in black and white. I look around. Someone else should see this...Miriam...no, Nettie. I should be telling Nettie...Look...Look what they say...Right here...Look...They locate missing men.

When I run through the *Forward's* door, the stinging snowflakes are mere pillow feathers on my cheek. In black and white, I can see it, like a motion picture. Me, Mama, and Miriam, sitting around our table. The door flings open. Artie, in rags, totters across the room, arms outstretched. The film's dialogue card shows "*Mamashe*! I'm home!" My sister falls back, flabbergasted. From her rocker, Mama's dreamy eyes go wide with shock, then recognition. Her hands cover her heart while tears stream down her wrinkled face. She reaches for Artie, fingers beckoning. We read her words, "Arthur, my beautiful boy!" Sobbing, he falls into her arms. A single violin sings in the background. "It was Irving. Irving saved me." I hear the music while I run. I hear it all the way back to the basement. It plays a sweet song as I push open the door, where the racket hits me like a punch in the face.

Women are yelling. Men are cursing. Angelina and Sophie are gawking at the white footprints tracked across the floor. Clumsy Elena Carpaccio has kicked over a whole can of paint.

"*Idiota*, out of my way." Pulling a big pail of hot water, Rosa elbows me in the gut.

From the top step, I cup my hands and shout, "Nettie, Nettie," but, hard as I try, I can't get her attention. She is surrounded by a gaggle of women, her head twisting from one direction to another as if it could spin a full circle.

Sophie Bowser shoves a mop at my face. "Help already."

Who cares about the *fakakta* strike? God has given me a miracle. But my words sink under the din like rocks in the ocean. In this whole, howling mess, no one cares about Irving Friedman's earth-shattering discovery. There's nothing to do but throw off my coat and take the mop.

We slave until ten o'clock, me tracking Nettie's every move, waiting for an opportunity. The whole night, she never stops. By the time we're ready to lock up, she's so worn-out she can barely slip into her coat.

The snow has stopped. Our footsteps crunch on the icy concrete. She takes my arm and her head falls against my shoulder as her eyes droop. Three times I open my mouth to speak, but my tongue won't move. This is impossible. I can't spill my heart like this. There's no room in her for me tonight. When we reach her street, she gives a dim smile. "Sleep good. We got lots to do tomorrow." She squeezes my hand and peels away.

The night is colder than ever. I curl tight into my coat, waiting on Leo and Mendel, who are also moving slow. When they catch up, Mendel stops to ask Leo for a cigarette. He cups his fist to light the match and the flame glows red against the dark. I've never seen Mendel smoke before.

"Margolis could have coppers there tomorrow, or scabs, or even gangsters."

Leo's hands are buried in his pockets and he, too, is shivering. "We know this. We all know this. We're prepared."

Mendel takes a deep drag. "They're *pitseles*, babies. They have no idea what can happen."

Leo's foot plays with a snowdrift. "Have some faith, Mendel. This is a revolutionary act."

Mendel flings the butt into the street. "Enough with your exalted theories Hirsch. Remember the people here."

"Without ideas those people have nothing to sustain them—"

I lurch away. Who cares? The same debate, endlessly and forever— who cares? This fresh tactic, that radical formulation—enough already —who cares?

Five in the morning, I'm sipping tea with only the dark sky for company. Miriam is asleep and Leo is already out the door. All night it whirled through my head. I'm seventeen. No one needs to hold my hand. I could go to the Bureau by myself, tell them about Artie, maybe get them started. Okay, I know, it's the strike. But there'll be a hundred people on the picket line. What's one more or less?

Leo bangs in, red-cheeked and grinning. When he sees me, he holds up a *Forward* he got off the earliest newsboy.

"I told you the snow wouldn't kill you. Look." His article made the front page. He rolls up the paper and bats me over the head. "Get dressed, we got plenty to do."

Miriam stumbles to the stove, hair down, eyes half-shut, still mussy from sleep. She was in bed when we got home. I couldn't tell her my news.

"Do the heroes want some food before they go save the world?"

As Leo bends to nuzzle her neck, I almost choke on my drink. Leo doesn't know about Artie. I divine it with utter certainty. I told Nettie, but Miriam never told Leo. It's the family secret. We talk about it to no one. I watch my sister moving around the stove. Whatever happens, I can't act without telling Miriam first.

Leo bats me again. "Come on, *Schmendrick*, move. We got work to do."

It's easier to obey than to explain.

FOURTEEN

DON'T block entrances. Walk up and down the block.
DON'T shout or use abusive language.
DON'T touch the sleeve or coat of a person you are speaking
to. It could be called a technical assault.
DON'T threaten anyone.

Mendel points to the sign he taped to the wall. "Remember."
"Enough," Gutzman booms from the back. "We know you organizers love the sound of your own voices, but, for God's sake, get out of the way."

Sashes are pinned onto woolen winter coats. Gloved hands hold signs. "Abolish Slavery." "Garment Workers Strike." "We Fight Until We Win." Everyone carries fliers for explaining to the public. With a nod from Mendel, Leo throws open the door and we surge out. We arrive before sunrise and we take possession of the sidewalk but carefully, carefully not blocking the door—that's against the law.

"Keep walking," Mendel calls. "And nothing nasty."

His timing is perfect because here comes Margolis. Behind him, the *fakakta* Schniedermans are herding a crew of scraggly women. "Scabs," someone hisses and a heave of resentment flows from the line.

Schneiderman's sneering eyes are shifty with malice. Look, they are saying, look what I brought.

Leo holds out his arms. "Move. Come on, everyone. Get going."

Like the treadle belt of a sewing machine, we snake in thin circles on the sidewalk, all the time staring at twelve grimy women, barely dressed against the cold whose eyes dart from Schneiderman to Margolis to us. One guy shouts, "Dirty Scabs." Mendel tries to shush him but someone else picks it up. "Dirty Scabs." We're all chanting in time with our steps, "Dir-ty Scabs. Dir-ty Scabs. Dir-ty Scabs."

Margolis bares his teeth. "*Kush mayn tuchas*," he growls and shoves his key into the lock, but it sticks, frozen with encrusted ice.

I'm marching with Nettie and Rosa. When we reach the door, Nettie suddenly hops out of the line. Leo grabs for her, but she shakes him off to run at the huddled scab women.

"This is a bad thing. You shouldn't do this. *Farshteyn? Das iz a shlekht zakh*."

A tall, skinny girl, shivering from fright or cold or both (she is wearing only a thin cotton coat), raises her hands in utter confusion. "*Vayl vos?*"

Nettie indicates the picket line. "*Dos iz a strayk…a strike*."

Schneiderman rushes at Nettie just as Margolis swings back the door and yells "*Kumen in*." Schneiderman snarls but swerves to drive the scabs up the cold, dark stairs, slamming the door behind them. Nettie stares at the pocked black iron.

"*Schmuck*, he took them right off the boat."

But Leo is gleeful. "How many blouses do you think they'll finish today—that handful of greenhorns? Don't you get it? He's running like a chicken without a head." Filled with new gusto, Leo turns back to the picketers.

"Keep it moving. Keep it moving, everyone. We're doing good."

At first we kid, make jokes, encourage, but soon it's just step, step, step on the frozen street. Around and around while my feet become bricks and my hands red turnips. Once in a while a bite, some tea, a piss. To keep myself warm, I invent ten different ways Arthur will look when I find him. Older, not so old, happy, miserable, healthy, sick. He recognizes me and falls into my arms. He doesn't until I say, "It's Irving. I'm a man now," and he almost faints.

It's after dark when the black door bangs open and Margolis sneers past, pushing out the scabs. Everyone collapses, claps each other on the back, pledges they'll be here tomorrow. I hug the paper in my pocket, not making any promises until I speak with my sister.

Fifteen

"You know who makes your Desertion Bureau?"—waving the *Forward* under my nose—"Fancy-shmancy uptown Jews, that's who. Heaven forbid the *goyim* should think all Jews are trashy kikes who leave families to starve, so those big shots pay for an office to chase down bastard husbands. That way they can say, see, we're *allrightnik* Americans."

She opens to the back page, which I never read. Photographs of men, like on a police roster—Eliezer Cohen, father of four…Immanuel Rosenzweig, husband of Sadie…Meir Moskowitz, left a wife and new baby…A headline in big Yiddish letters, "The Gallery of Vanished Husbands."

I twitch. Clearly she's missing the point. "They find missing men." I stab the words. "It says so."

"Irving, Irving." She takes my face between her hands. "Such a smart head and no sense. If you're not a miserable, deserted wife, that place got nothing for you."

A fury so big I can't swallow boils to my chest until the room gets fuzzy and the lamp hurls sparks. When the words come, I don't recognize my voice.

"Miriam the boss—Always in charge. Always pushing me around, like nothing I say is any good. God forbid baby Irving should have a mind of his own. Don't you think I see? I got eyes, Miriam. All these months, you never said one word to Leo." I point a finger into her face, shaking the air with my words. "Stop lying. You hate Arthur. You're glad he's not here. You hope Arthur's dead."

Red blotches crawl up Miriam's face. Her hand goes up to strike and I shut my eyes for the sting, but nothing. The bedroom door slams so hard the walls rattle.

I wrap my hands under my arms to stop the shaking. So she hates me. So she kicks me out. Who cares? I'm done licking Miriam's boots. It's there in black and white. 356 Second Avenue. Right there. I use an arm to brush away the tears. I'm still bent over against the counter, when the bedroom door creaks open. Quietly, she pulls two chairs out from the table.

"Sit, Irving." I waver—Miriam is tricky—but she pats the chair. "Come sit."

We're face to face, eyes locked. "Do not go searching for Arthur."

"For god's sake, Miri, why?"

"All your life, you live by what you wish, not by what is. This time you must believe me. Artie's not right in the head. They got him away someplace all these years. Maybe if they learn he's still got family, they'll say enough is enough. He's yours, you take him. We already got one ghost in this house. You want another? Three of us working to make the rent, one bedroom, Leo in the closet. You gonna feed him, dress him, be his minder? You'd rather do that than make nice with your little girlfriend?" She sees my expression. "See... You can't have both. You gotta choose. One way or the other. Either or."

Only Miriam can turn white into black and black into white, like chasing the truth through a maze. I struggle to hold the one thing I can still see.

"If you think you're so right, why didn't you tell Leo?"

A quick sniff. She brushes some crumbs off the table. "What's done is done. You make a new life, you don't drag the old one along."

"But it's not done. If we desert Artie, we're just like the *mamzer* husbands in the paper."

"For me, Arthur is all the way done." She sighs. "But, you're right. It's time Leo should know." She puts both hands in her lap, sitting up tall. "We're getting married." Her head is high. Her brown eyes are steady. "We have to."

The floor drops out. I grab the table to hold myself steady. I know I'm supposed to make words, but my mind is a white blank. I never considered...it never occurred to me...Leo over every night...moving in...I never thought...I could punch myself for being such a little *pisher*.

She almost giggles. "You can close your mouth, Irving. It's not a tragedy. Leo and me, we're okay. He's already thinking names."

"But the union...the strike?"

"One way or the other, the strike'll be done. And the union... Things change when you have a mouth to feed." She stands, smoothing down her skirt. "You go looking for Arthur, you get no help from me." Her hands rest on her belly. "I got my own either or."

———

EITHER OR. EVEN IN SLEEP, MIRIAM'S WORDS ARE A SONG I CAN'T escape. Either Nettie or Artie. Either a baby or a brother. Either a union or a wife. Nah, Leo has no either ors. After his golden revolution, no one will have to choose because everyone will have everything. Look at him—the strike...my sister. His sacred Marx would surely approve. To each according to his needs, right, Leo?

I flip onto my back to stare at the ceiling. He came to me before bed. "I promise, Irving. You have no worries about Miriam." So earnest. So respectful. No more *Schmendrick*. It's Irving all the way. I'm supposed to be his friend. He couldn't ask before taking my sister? I snort loud enough to make Mama stir in the other bed. Tonight, she shares my room. Leo and Miriam stopped pretending and moved to the cot in the back. I don't want to imagine what the two of them have to do to sleep on that tiny thing.

I pull up the covers but the chill seeping through the window wraps me in a blanket of ice. When was the last time I was warm? Ten thousand years ago, in that basement, kissing Nettie. My feet hit the floor. I pull on my pants, coat, cap and tiptoe out, carrying my creaky shoes to lace in the stairway.

The night is a frigid blue. Up and down the road empty wagon poles freeze against the cobblestones—even the draught horses are home in their warm barns. I could be alone in the world except that in the alley I make out the purple skin and icy hands of paupers in boxes and barrels, asleep under old straw. Who knows? Artie could be one of these foul wretches. My stomach twists and I bolt, dashing past Norfolk, Essex, Ludlow, stopping to rest only when I reach the market at Orchard and Delancey. The stalls are closed, awnings dented with ice. I lean against an iron lamppost, breathing hard, remembering.

I was eight. Shabbos was coming so Mama sent us to the swarming sidewalks to buy a chicken from the slightly honest butcher on Orchard Street. I scuttled and ducked between the legs of the hagglers. Miriam said, "Cut it out, you're too big for tricks," but I didn't listen and soon I lost her. When I reached an opening in the crowd, surprise of surprises, there was Arthur on his way home from work, smiling when he saw me. I was about to wave when I found a clean new marble hiding in the dirt. "Artie, see." But Artie wasn't looking at me anymore. His neck was thrown back and his eyes scanned the sky. I twisted to look up, too, but couldn't see anything. When I glanced back, Artie was down, rolling in the mud like a crumpled doll. His head thudded against the stones while his torso jerked up and down, his fingers like chicken claws and his wrists curled into knots. A woman yelled, "*Oy mayn Gott*," and jumped like from a gunshot. It was a fit. He was having a fit right where anyone could see. I screamed, "Miriam," craning to find her, but everyone was too big.

I dropped the marble and ran, but it was too late. Artie's eyes were hideous white balls. He was snorting, "Chnurgh, chnurgh, Chnurgh," like a snuffling pig as a dark stain spread across his groin and spittle foamed from his mouth. I threw myself across his chest, trying to cover him up. If Papa found out, he'd whip Artie to shreds. Like riding a donkey, I was thrust up and back, up and back, so hard my palms slipped off his face. He gave one vast final heave, tossing me into the muck. Then he was still.

I pushed myself erect. Trousers, skirts, and shoes swirled in a black whirlpool. All the faces were dark with revulsion. "Devil", "Animal", "Dybbuk." An old woman pointed her thumb and pinky at Artie, mouthing a curse. A second spit between her v-shaped fingers to ward one off. Red with shame, all I could think was, "Don't tell Papa, don't tell Papa." One by one, they turned their backs.

That's when I heard it.

"Artie Friedman, hoo hoo hoo. Oinks like a pig and stinks like one, too."

Izzy Schwartz from two doors down. His pinkies were in his ears and his thumbs pulled his nose into a snout. He stuck his tongue out and, as I found a rock to heave at him, he ran down the street, singing at the top of his lungs.

The streetlamp pops off. The sky is brightening over the Williamsburg Bridge. I step away from the post, pulling my coat and straightening my shirt. Silhouettes from the early-bird peddlers float on the walkway. I'll leave the place to them. I know where I need to go, but I have to make one stop first.

———

THE BASEMENT SMELLS FROM FRESH BREAD AND COFFEE THAT ROSA and Esther lay out for those strikers who can't afford breakfast. Sophie is separating a big stack of handbills into smaller piles for distribution, and, in the back, Nettie is nailing more picket signs. From her giant yawn, I bet she's been up all night, too.

"Nettie, I gotta talk."

She reaches for my hand only to dump me a fistful of nails. "Work while you talk."

I juggle the tacks from one palm to the other while I tell her the whole *megilleh* from finding the *Forward* to Miriam's objections to now. Nettie never stops whacking. I drop the nails and grab her wrist. "Enough a second."

She sighs and wipes an arm across her forehead.

"I need for you to tell me—I have to try to find him no matter what, right? It's a sin to say, 'Tough luck, Artie, bye-bye' when I have a way."

Nettie folds her arms over her chest, thinking. "You want my opinion? You're absolutely right. Miriam's talking *drek*."

I slap the top of the worktable. "Thank you."

"But, I gotta ask...*now* Irving? Do you have to go Artie hunting *today?*"

My eyes go wide and she holds up her hand. "I know Arthur is important, but," she waves her arm to the room, "we're at war. You can't just desert. A week, six weeks, he wouldn't know the difference. You and me, we're comrades. We got a battle to win right here."

I open my mouth to register my objections as a ruckus erupts at the food table. Two street kids are pounding each other over a piece of bread. Nettie awards me the hammer and runs to play Solomon, dividing the food between them. Sophie pulls her over for advice on I-don't-know-what, and she's gone.

All my logical arguments still unsaid, I hammer signs onto handles. Whack. First, she says do. Whack. Now, she says don't. First, it's "You have to Irving." Whack. Now, it's "No, this is more important." Whack, whack. Everyone's for themselves first, even Nettie. Not like Miriam but just like Miriam. I drop the hammer and kick the signs away. I lean against the wall, chewing my grievances.

The room crowds up. A bigger horde collects outside. Leo prances in waving a stack of newspapers, "Look what the world is saying." A fracas of arms and hands competes for the pages. Mendel moves to stand at the top step. He sees me stewing and waves me to come, but I'm not in the mood for kindly Mendel right now. He makes a mock frown, shrugs, and calls out, "Ladies and gentlemen, it's time."

The door is flung open. A cold draft blows in. Nettie, Leo, and

Mendel step to the lead. The strikers follow, locking arms to form phalanxes as they leave. Rosa starts singing, "*As we go marching, marching...*" Voices echo from building to building. I follow as far as the doorway. So many strikers, so many hands, what's one more or less? Does one more person matter? No one would miss me.

I watch them round the corner, then turn and walk to 356 Second Avenue.

SIXTEEN

My foot taps the floor so hard the whole bench shakes. Just like Miriam predicted, I am a rooster among the chickens —me and five women filling out our *Form of Application*. The women scritch, scritch, scritch, while I am stymied by "Husband's Name (and Alias)" "Name and ages of children." The lady sitting at my shoulder wears a threadbare grey coat and smells faintly of garlic. She watches my leg do its dance.

"I bet you search your papa." She makes a huge sigh. "Ach, it's always so hard on the *kinder*."

She retrieves an orange from her worn carpetbag and, saving the rind in a graying hanky, offers a section. I shake my head, "No thank you," so she extends the fruit across to a girl in a fine white shirtwaist with a little black bowtie, sitting so stiff her back could be glued to a piece of wood.

The girl's eyebrows go up, but after a second, she peels off a slice. "*Adank*."

The older lady nods. "Better we should suffer together than alone, no?"

The younger woman's lips curl a dainty grimace. "Best is that we shouldn't suffer at all."

The old lady kisses her fingers and raises them to heaven. She takes another bite of orange. "My *alter kocker* could drop dead tomorrow and I wouldn't care except he took the money, may he forever crap blood and pus. You?"

The girl's cheeks bloom, but her voice is harsh. "As soon as I said a child was coming." Suddenly she doesn't look so young. "I want, if they find the *mamzer*, they'll make him give me my divorce or else go to jail. Enough with that *schmegegge* making the rules."

The secretary calls, "Kominski" and the older lady pulls together her carpetbag, coat, and hand muff, but pauses to shake the other's hand. "*Zol zein mit mazel*." Go with good luck. She strides into the office.

Enough *schmegegges* making rules. My eyes scurry back to my paper. I scratch out "Husband's" next to "Name" and write, "Brother's." At "Cause of Desertion" I scribble, "A callous and brutal father." Then, "My brother, Arthur Friedman, suffers from the curse of epilepsy. Five years ago, when he was helpless, my father removed him from our house by force. This heartless man has passed away. We believe Arthur is locked in a hospital or asylum, but we don't know where. My poor, ailing mother suffers greatly from the loss of her beloved son."

The secretary looks annoyed at my scratch-outs, but I don't care. I sit down, curl in close, and ready my spirit. That's what our crazy gymnasium teacher, Mr. Abrahams, taught us. Bums from Norfolk Street don't run foot races, but Abrahams decreed that if snooty uptown schools could make a team, so could he. We were skinny, tenement kids, shivering in ratty school uniforms. Doesn't matter, Abrahams insisted. Just ready your spirit. Down on one knee, toe to the block, hands to the ground. Close your eyes. Ready your spirit. Our *farshlugginer* team won every match. So, I shut my eyes and ready myself. The next thing I hear is, "Friedman" and the secretary is holding open the door.

The plaque on the desk says Monroe Goldstein. His black hair is slicked to leather and his white collar is so stiff it makes my neck raw to see. In gold-rimmed glasses, he holds my application an arm's length from his nose, waving me to a chair at the side of his desk. Since when is a Jew named Monroe? He drops my papers and laces his fingers.

"A very sad situation, but we can't help you."

I show him my golden *Forward*. "It says you find missing men."

A glance, a prim frown. "A poor choice of words. We locate missing *husbands*." I open my mouth, but he holds his hand for me to shush. "Mr. Friedman, you're clearly a fine young man, and I admire your devotion to your family. I wish to God all men were as upright as yourself, but I deal with rascals who think coming to America gives them the right to violate the laws of man and God. You saw the women out in my office. We are their only hope of penalizing those miserable scoundrels who confirm the Gentiles' worst misconception of the Jewish people." He offers me back my paper. "There's only so much I can do. I have to stay true to our mission."

He makes as if to stand, but I hold my ground. Would Leo crawl away like a beaten dog? Would Nettie? I scour the room, the desk piled with applications, the walls papered with men's photographs. So many women, so many stories. This guy spends his life listening to their sorrows. Somewhere, he has to have a heart. I pretend I can hear it beating under his fancy wool suit, and the words pour out.

"Excuse me, sir, but what happened to my brother is as much a stain on the good name of our people as your *fakakta* husbands. Who allows a sick man to be robbed of his family and leaves him to rot in some God-forsaken hole? This you hold up to the Gentiles as an example of our upstanding moral responsibility?"

Something stirs behind his eyes.

"You talk about God's law. Where was God's law when my father beat my brother blue and tossed him away like garbage? Where was God's law when my mother's soul was ripped from her body and my sister's heart turned to stone? Desertion? I can tell you about desertion." I point out his window. "I work ninety, a hundred hours a week in a sweatshop, a slave and a pauper. Right this second my friends are down on the street, striking against the monster who abuses us, but I deserted them. Me, Irving Friedman, turned traitor so I could come here today and beg." My voice cracks. "How can I save my brother if you won't help me?"

Monroe Goldstein doesn't blink. In my whole life, I've never spoken like this to another human being. The seconds tick away, both of us so still we can see the air move. Slowly he takes a handkerchief from his pocket and starts to clean his glasses. He clears his throat. Back go the glasses.

"You should think about changing jobs, Mr. Friedman." He picks up a pen and reaches for my application. "You make a great salesman."

THE STREETCAR SWAYS AND I AM CONTENT TO ROLL WITH EACH bump and swerve because, look, I am a *macher*. I opened my mouth and out came gold. So, what if Goldstein cautioned, "We never make guarantees." I know they'll find him. This is America. The streets are paved with jewels.

When I swing off the trolley the sidewalk is blocked by a row of stinky pickle barrels that a sourpuss grocer guards from his doorway. I bounce past him, holding my nose and he throws me a sneer. The clock on the corner says eleven-thirty. See—only a couple hours, easy as pie. Nettie probably didn't know I wasn't there. I'll tell her I, too, did a great thing, a radical thing. In this revolution, everyone gets saved.

I hum a tune Mendel taught us over beer at Cepulski's.

It's a strike, yes a strike,
A big cloak maker's strike.
The Manufacturer's Association
Had to go on vacation,
Because of the cloak maker's strike.

I stop dead, slapping my forehead. Nettie is going to meet Arthur. Never have I anticipated such a miracle, but it will happen. I try a wave of my hand like in the motion pictures. "Nettie, I'd like you to meet my brother Arthur. Arthur, this is my sweetheart, Nettie Bloom."

Bent forward in my elegant bow, I suddenly hear them—the whinnies and the heavy clop of hooves against cobblestone. I look around, not telling from where, until I cross to Grand and turn a circle, thinking I must've walked the wrong way.

Not a striker is to be seen. Instead, in the dark shadow of the elevated, a sea of navy-blue coppers is hooting and cheering, slapping their clubs against their black leather gloves, while a dozen paddy wagons roll over the remnants of tattered banners and shredded cardboard pickets.

My heart becomes a thrumming drum. Where's our strike? Scouring up and down the street for my people, there is only a torn coat sleeve, a woman's hat, pools of red melting into the snow. I stumble forward. An audience of *kibitzers* is gawking from the sidewalk. Mamas cover the eyes of their little ones, with cries of "*Oy, gevalt*" and "*Gott in Himmel.*" An aproned workman bangs his fist against his leg, his face black with anger, "Butchers."

I tremble, hearing Mendel's voice from a hundred years ago, "It was war, terrible and vile."

The strutting coppers clap each other on the back and croon loud congratulations. Their whoops ricochet off the iron railroad beams and echo down the shadowy street. Pushing aside the onlookers, I search frantically to see someone, anyone, I know.

There, under the train tracks, a bear in a brown coat, Pincas Gutzman struggles to stand. I yell his name, but the rat-a-tat of an overhead train drowns me out, so I dash into the street, who cares about the coppers. His great weight almost buckles me as I help him stand. A trickle of blood runs from his ear and his cheek is scrapped raw.

"Pincas, what happened?"

He sucks in air and leans against a girder. "Margolis." He releases a deep breath and sucks again. "Margolis brought the coppers. Said he needed protection for his bastard scabs." He leans over, his hands on his knees. I'm afraid he's going to pass out, but he rights himself. "Something happened...I didn't see...they started with their sticks..."

My chest is pounding. "Nettie Bloom...did you see Nettie Bloom?"

He shakes to clear his head. "Some fought...some ran...I fell..."

The gangs of blue gorillas swirl around, assembling for the march back to their precinct. One bulky goon with the yellow eyes and bulbous nose of a boozer catches sight of Pincas' face.

"Sheeny scum." He aims his stick and lumbers toward us.

The hairs on my neck bristle. Like the flipping cards of a nick-elodeon, I can see the club swoosh, my bloody head in the snow, and the breath leaving my body. With strength I never knew I had, I hoist Pincas up. Before that hulking lump of flesh can get close I have us around the corner. Pincas gives me a shove. "Go...get going...I'm okay...go."

I swivel to run, but my shoe hits ice. Down on one knee, my wrist on fire, I jump. I'm jabbing through the crowds on Orchard, darting past the dutiful at the synagogue on Ludlow and spinning by the sweatshops on Essex. My feet have wings. They don't touch the ground.

Half a block away, the basement door's been flung open. Groans reach out to the sidewalk. At the top of the entryway, my stomach rises to my mouth. In coats, hats, and gloves, the people litter the floor —bent over, on their backs, curled into balls. On the top stair, Esther Mandelbaum retches into a bucket. When I step down, she tries to grab my hand but has to turn away with another heave. I swallow my own bile. I'm ready to bellow Nettie's name when I catch sight of Leo lying stretched across his desk. Leo. Vaulting the stairs, I grab him up then spring back. His teeth are red with blood and a jagged gash cuts across his mouth.

"Leo..."

Glazed eyes squint. He licks his lips, mouths "water." The samovar is still on the food table from this morning. I frantically empty it into a teacup. Leo winces when it touches his lips. I want to wait until he's breathing easier, but I can't contain myself.

"Do you know...Leo...where's Nettie?"

A hoarse rasp. "In the paddy wagon...Didn't you see?"

Blood pounds in my ears. The workhouse...her mother coughing blood...I wheel for the door as I comprehend that Leo doesn't know I wasn't there. His grasping fingers crush my sleeve, holding me back.

"Wait...you gotta let the lawyers."

Behind us, sighs and moans as people gather themselves together, testing to move a leg, an arm, gradually rising off the floor. Word has spread. The mamas, papas, wives, and husbands are rushing in. I tug my arm, ready to punch him to get free, but Sophie Bowser stumbles over, shoulders curled.

"A runner came." She drops her head onto Leo's chest. "Mendel is dead."

Seventeen

I'm at my kitchen window, staring into the black pit of the night.

"Swine. Bootlicking capitalist lackies." Leo holds a rag full of snow against his face while Miriam caresses the smashed knuckles of his hand. His words are slurred by the bottle of vodka at his elbow.

"The Mick captain said they were there to protect the legitimate employees of the establishment. 'Not to quibble,' Mendel says, 'but we're the legitimate employees of the establishment.' A good answer, no? A Mendel answer." He stops for a swig and his eyes go glassy. "So, we let the scabs pass, only a little name-calling. But then, at the back, comes Gussie Schneiderman." Leo's jaw works. Another swig.

"Then what?" As long as he's talking, I can picture Mendel's face.

"That *chaleria* ghoul was pushing the little ones who do the trimming, hocking them to move, move, move. Worst of all, she's hauling Tonya Wojcik. When Tonya sees us she starts twisting away, yelling, 'I didn't want to. Papa made me.' She cries it over and over. 'Papa made me. Papa made me.' Gussie is tugging and tugging, but Tonya won't budge, so the witch throws an arm back and, across the face, bam." He slaps the table hard enough the floor shakes. "You could hear it a block away. Mendel...Mendel couldn't abide. He ran to take the child up. That's all the excuse those Mick bastards needed."

This time he doesn't bother with the glass. He grabs the neck of the bottle and guzzles. Miriam reaches to stop him—we've never seen Leo drink like this—but he bats her away. After everything today, it doesn't take long. His eyes droop and his head sags to his chest, but Miriam keeps holding his hand. Miriam, who never loved the strike in the first place. After he snorts a raspy snore, she props him up with her shoulder. Patting my arm, she mutters "Thanks to Gott at least *you* ducked the clubs." She shambles him to their closet cot.

I contemplate Leo's vodka bottle, but it's drained. Why correct her? Everyone will know it soon enough. Once again, I have failed to be where I was most needed. I raise the empty tumbler to my eye. The chipped crystal splinters the light into a hundred yellow beams.

You gotta admit, God has some sense of humor. It's just like Nettie said. I proudly picked this day, this exact day, this one and only day, to seek a brother who's missing years. Let me proclaim my brilliance as an orator. Let me demonstrate it when we bury Mendel. Irving Friedman, the great orator, wishes to eulogize his fallen comrade. I hear Leo's body thump into the bed. His shoes thud to the floor and Miriam coos as she tries to remove his pants.

Yit-ga-dal v'yit-ka-dash sh'mei ra-ba...Let the glory of God be extolled...We say Kaddish when family dies and Mendel was certainly family. On my feet, reciting the ancient prayer. *Yit-ga-dal v'yit-ka-dash sh'mei ra-ba*...

The big joke is, I was also right. My presence would have changed nothing. Little Irving Friedman could not have kept Nettie Bloom from the paddy wagon. Little Irving Friedman could not have halted the club that murdered Mendel Stern. I suck my fist and fall into a chair. I'm supposed to be a man, but my shoulders shake and the sobs will not be contained.

A feathery hand flutters my head. I look up. Mama, in a white nightgown, her milky eyes combing my face. Does she know who I am? Her quivering voice drones a tune from another world.

Ey leh leh,
Ta-tel-eh.
A lullaby so remote it is fog in the wind.
Ey leh leh leh,
Ta-tel-eh.

Did she ever sing it to me or was it only for Arthur? I can't recall. Her parchment-dry fingers brush my hair and she hugs my head to her chest. I inhale her age, stale and pungent. I don't care if she knows which son I am. I wrap arms around her and weep.

I must have fallen asleep because I am alone at first light. Leo hobbles into the kitchen. His purple bruises have turned black and his lips are swollen shut, but his red eyes are savage with purpose. He spits, "Office. Now," and pulls on his suspenders.

Cold sunbeams fire the narrow alleys between the buildings. There is only the rhythm of our footsteps and the soft slush of our breath puffing mist into the icy air. We don't talk. Leo's mouth is too broken and my head is filled with dark imaginings, wondering if it's time to tell of my desertion. Before I can form the words, we turn onto Essex and stop dead in our tracks.

The street is packed—men, women, young, old, grey-haired grand-fathers, burdened mamas, and rosy-faced working girls. They surround the open door of our basement office, murmuring quietly. When they spot Leo, all talking stops. As if by universal accord, a path opens. Hands brush his shoulders as he passes. "*May Gott treyst ir tsvishn di murners fun irushlim.*" May God comfort you among the mourners of Jerusalem. "*Mendel vet zeyn revengd.*" Mendel will be revenged. "*That Margolis, trinkn zoln im piavkes.*" That Margolis, leeches should drink him dry. Leo nods and bows at each passing caress, his face heavy with emotion, but I have not earned these benedictions, so I skulk quickly to the office.

Gone is the gossip. Gone is the laughter. The women stalk the room with iron determination, their reddened eyes focused only on the work. I go alone to the back table to affix safety pins to sashes. While my hands dance between the pin box and the fabric, I bite my tongue and remind myself I'm a nothing, a no one, and not a single person in this room cares where I was yesterday.

A tumult of cheers comes from the door as last night's prisoners return home. Nettie is in the lead, covered in grime but chin held high. My whole body yearns toward her, but I duck back as she receives Leo's hug, Sophie's kisses, a chorus of *mazel tovs*. The assembly demands a full report. With rising outrage, they hear that the cops forced the women to stand for hours, that they were spat upon by whores and loonies, that they were caged with vermin, that the judge reproached, "You earn your bread by the sweat of your brow." A furious cry goes up, "Justice. Avenge Mendel Stern."

People rush to my table. I frantically dole out sashes until a set of strong fingers clutch my hand and won't let go. Nettie. Her face is stiff and her eyes hold me tighter than her grip. I step from behind the table—let them get their own sashes—and follow her to our quiet corner. Her arms go around me, her knees buckle and the dampness of her tears waters my shirt.

"Mendel," she whispers.

What can I do? I wrap her in my arms and stroke her hair. I know what I'm supposed to tell her. I start to say it, but she melts into me, overcome. With all this grief, isn't it selfish to burden her with a story about my bad judgment right this second? She's been through so much. I tighten my grip and hold my tongue. Silence is an act of mercy. Tomorrow. I will tell her tomorrow.

It's such a pretty idea.

EIGHTEEN

As fate would have it one of the onlookers watching the assault that day happened to be a reporter for the *New York World*. Knowing a good story when he saw one, this would-be Pulitzer followed the paddy wagons to the courthouse. The next morning the whole of New York woke up to front-page headlines about the tragic striking garment workers and the tiny, courageous tenement girl who stood up to the big bad judge.

By the time Nettie was released from jail she was no longer just a shirtwaist worker. No. Nettie was a *Universal Symbol of Labor's Oppression*. So said the wealthy matrons of the progressive Women's Trade Union League who all read the *New York World*. Up went their hue and cry—we must act to aid these poor, exploited working girls in their time of need.

The Strike Committee immediately sends Nettie to a WTUL session. As a man, of course, I can't attend. I only get to hear it from Nettie later, *kibitzing* at the fringes as a circle of women drink in the juicy details.

Apparently, Nettie laid bare the abominable conditions under which working women live and the injustice of the system under which they labor. "A system that produces the garments you ladies are wearing, in this very room." While Nettie orated, Sophie, Esther, and Rosa passed the hat. They hold up a wad of bills, chortling how they got more money that one afternoon than our local dues could produce in a month.

Nettie is radiant. "They want all women should vote. And all the children should be at school instead of work." Her voice drops to almost a whisper. "One says, after the strike, I could maybe get a scholarship."

The room is alight with Nettie's dreams. This is not the place to tell her about mine. She doesn't notice when I leave to walk home alone.

Mendel's funeral. I solemnly don a yarmulke and prayer shawl to sing Kaddish with the other men in the wood paneled sanctuary of the Eldridge Street Synagogue. The women look down from the gallery, their sighs and sniffles filling the silences between the rabbi's prayers. Only Leo boycotts—religion being the opiate of the masses—but he meets us at the cemetery, somber and subdued. Enough stay to drop a handful of earth on the coffin, they do half the gravedigger's job.

At the union hall, over the pastrami, pickles, beer, and schnapps the mourners sing a chorus of praises. "A genuine *mensch*." "Every cause should have such a champion." "Filthy Cossacks."

Rosa dabs a wrinkled hankie to her eyes. "If I knew which *bastardi poliziotto*..." She bends her arm into a *basta*.

"I was too busy ducking to see." Zuckerman makes a demonstration.

Abe Feingold blinks a blackened eye. "I should only have ducked so good."

Nettie was silent at the cemetery, her face pale. I reached for her hand as we left, but she gave only a quick squeeze and walked away, eyes glued to the ground. She looks at me now.

"Irving, I never saw you. How did you dodge the coppers?"

My stomach drops. I frantically scan the room for a quiet corner where we can talk, but before I can figure it out, Leo pulls her into a different conversation.

The cloud from a putrid cigar curls around my face. I back away to wander the room alone. Over at the bar some comedian has used a whiskey bottle to prop up a photograph of Mendel, his cap cocked to one side, his hand flicking in a salute. I run my hand over the frame. Mendel had wisdom for everything. He would have had something smart to tell me in this situation. He ought to be at Cepulski's, feet up, chair tipped back, contemplating the best solution to my problem. I pour myself a glass.

"*L'chaim*, Mendel."

I grimace as it scalds its way down, but I pour a second anyway. Not as bad. After the third, the babble recedes and the edges around the crowd blur. Stumbling against a table leg, I turn a circle to search out Nettie. She's across the room, surrounded by the powerful of the Joint Committee, her eyes darting from one guy to the next as they compete for her attention. Is that not a wonder? Is that not an amazement? In the middle of all this misery, Nettie has become a celebrity.

I pour another drink and lift my glass. Here's to you. By the grace of God and Mendel's demise we have a queen. Down the hatch it goes. Blessed art Thou, oh Lord, King of the Universe, who creates the fruit of the vine.

"Irving?"

The floor tilts. There is another presence in my vicinity. The presence seems to have a shoulder, so I reach for it.

"Mendel said people are more important than philosophy." I pound my fist on the presence's shoulder. "I struggled to ease my brother's suffering. Is that not a moral act, too?" I fumble to set the glass back on the table but it hits the floor. I lurch to my knees to retrieve it.

A hand grabs my arm. "Let's go, *Schmendrick*. Enough mourning for today."

Leo. The presence is Leo.

Nodding requires great concentration. My head drops forward, but lifting it up again is hard work.

"You're so right." I let my weight fall against him. "Enough mourning for today."

NINETEEN

Mama snores in the other bed. My head pounds in what must be God's continuing punishment. I stumble into the kitchen to wash away the rot in my mouth. I'd expect to be alone at this late hour, but the front door swings open—Miriam returning from the hall toilet. She pauses in the shadow of the hall lamp.

"I don't sleep so good these days. Mama snorts louder than a broken motorcar, not to mention I got to pee twenty times a night." Late as it is, she drops into the chair and rocks, her hand on her belly. "This place is gonna get crowded when the baby comes." Her eyes shift in my direction. "Thank Gott you didn't go hunting Arthur."

In this blanket of darkness, it would be so easy to stay hidden, especially from Miriam. So easy.

"I did go. I was at the National Desertion Bureau the day Mendel was killed."

Miriam's face is half in moonlight, half in dark. "Leo never said."

"Leo doesn't know. No one knows."

She takes that in. "Oy, Irving. So good at making messes."

What can I say? What's true is true.

She starts back with her rocking. "You know, we were in the hold of that lousy steamship when Mama had you in her belly. I was only five, but I can smell that stink to this day. Whenever Mama started retching, Papa disappeared. It was Arthur who ran for a bucket and held her head." Miriam's face tightens. "What God did to Arthur is a crime."

"So, if I find him, it's okay?"

"No, it's not okay." She pushes out of the chair. "But ask me again if the time comes."

In the hour or two left of the night, I dream. It's hot summer. I'm at the East River with Arthur. The river looks cool and clean in the sparkling sunlight. Kids play, shoving each other around. When I look at Arthur, he's pulled off his clothes. All the other kids are shocked into silence, staring at his naked, pale member, hanging openly for all to see. He looks down at himself and grins as if to say, "What's to hide?" Waving for me to follow, he disappears into the water.

The morning is a groggy haze. It's all I can do to find my coat and shoes. Arriving late, I find the picket line in turmoil. A fleet of black vans is burping out a big crew of cutters, pressers, sewers, and finishers. These scabs are not greenhorns. Margolis has found the real thing.

"Lickspittles." "Flunkies." "Finks." Up and down the sidewalk, strikers shout their curses.

The cops build a barricade with their nightsticks and the scabs scurry, hands over their heads. Rotten tomatoes fly. Fists pump the air. One scab guy loses his bowler as Rosa stomps it. Angelina's claws pinch a woman's arm. Esther uses a hatpin. Nettie stands right by the door looking each in the eye and begging them to join us, but it's a futile effort. The *schmucks* disappear upstairs and Schneiderman slams the door.

Nettie turns to the strikers. "Sing. Sing so they know we're here." She raises her fist. "*Just fight on, just fight on. We struggle for victory…*"

We're crowded around the doorway, a mass of poking elbows and wagging arms. Suddenly a rush of bodies comes at us from down the street. I'm rammed from behind, my cheek squashed into the coarse wool jacket of the guy in front. A beefy paw jerks at my collar and I'm lifted off the ground. The heavy buttons of my coat crush in my Adam's apple. Stunned and choking, my vision goes red. It's like Papa coming again for murder but this time Artie's not here to the save me.

I snarl and twist my hands over my head, groping for my attacker's eyes. There's the satisfying gouge of skin under my clawing fingernails then something cold and hard hits the side of my head. I fall to my knees, my ears ringing, watching mute lips move in a silent movie, before the noise rushes back in. Screams. Cries. Curses. "*Stronzo* Gang-sters." "Faster, you *yutz*." "Get 'em."

I crawl to all fours and slowly pull myself up. Curled and moaning bodies litter the sidewalk. The attackers mowed through us like sickles in a wheat field then disappeared down the street. I frantically twist for my people. Nettie is untouched, standing with Leo near the loft door, screaming her outrage into the face of a copper, who folds his arms across his chest and smirks.

"Bastard." Leo jumps away to give chase. But it's too late. The attackers have already disappeared. Arms reach down to help the fallen. With groans and whimpers, we rise to assess the damage. This time no one has died, but we all understand. Margolis has brought in the goons.

The basement is dank with cold. Picketers drape over chairs, lean on tables, sag on each other's shoulders. Some women leave—"We can't keep taking chances. We have *kinder* at home"—as do some men who gripe the bruisers are too big to fight.

"*Basta* that gang," Rosa says. She presses a rag against the bloody bruise on her ribs. "Jake Rosensweig was in the lead. Also Benny Fein, that *testa di cazzo*."

Seraphina slaps Rosa's hand. "For shame, *cara*."

Sophie rubs her back. "Imagine, I got slammed by Izzy Schwartz from my own building."

Izzy Schwartz with his piggy face and nasty song. What else but end up a thug?

Pincas Gutzman, stands, his voice harsh. "I am done cowering under the boots of the Cossacks. In Russia we cried and quaked from the pogroms. This is America. A good man is dead. Hooligans knock in our heads. Margolis populates his shop with vermin scabs. I know what needs to be done." He makes a fist. "In my house, we eradicate vermin."

Nettie is on her feet. "No, Pincas. The manufacturers cry that we're a bunch of subversive fanatics. If we start acting like that, we'll lose public support."

Rosa, Sophie, and the rest nod. "She's right." "No hitting." "*Bene, cara*."

"Women," Gutzman sneers. "What do you say, Hirsch?"

Everyone turns to Leo. His eyes travel the room, touching each person in turn. "I say it's been a hard day. We're all tired. Tomorrow is Shabbos. Go home. Rest."

Gutzman slaps a hand against his leg. "God save me from women and fake revolutionaries." He picks up his coat and stomps out.

TWENTY

Saturday morning in bed, I watch the paint chips peel from the ceiling. Some genius I am, some Casanova, courting Nettie with Charles Dickens. Looks like she'd rather see me waving a red flag leading a worker's army. That would make her eyes brim with pride. That would get her chest heaving with admiration. My hand slips to my groin.

"Irving," Leo yells from the kitchen, "I got a caller coming,"

I jerk from under the blankets. "Since when do we have callers?"

"Since now."

I'm still pulling on my trousers when this caller arrives—that arrogant organizer Myron Dickstein. I offer a respectful hello, but he doesn't deign me a nod and turns his back on my ghost mother without a word. Leo's eyes order me away, so I retreat to the bedroom, but of course that's a joke. Privacy does not exist in our tiny flat.

Silently, Leo brews up tea. Can you hear someone not breathing? Because it seems to me that Leo has not taken a breath since the man entered our house. Finally, there's the whine of the kettle and the gurgle of pouring water. Dickstein tinks his spoon against the glass and blows across the rim to cool it down.

"The overall news is good. With the workers remaining committed and the season half over, many of the manufacturers are ready to capitulate."

Leo opens his mouth to cheer, but Dickstein stops him. "Unfortunately, Morris Margolis is an exception. He's gloating he's replaced all his disloyal workers and the union can go to hell." Dickstein slurps a cautious sip of tea. "If he goes through with it, your people are out."

"God help us." Leo's voice is husky. "After all this, Gutzman was right."

"Tsk, tsk, where's your revolutionary zeal?" Dickstein sounds almost cheerful. From my perch in the bedroom, I see the man prop his boot on our table and tip back his chair. "Margolis simply needs a good reason to cooperate, like, for example, the welfare of his equipment. Without machines, he can't make shirtwaists. No product, no profit. For a capitalist there is no greater tragedy."

"What are you saying?"

"Come on, Hirsh, don't play naïve." Dickstein's chair hits the ground. "The sluggers who whacked you will work for whoever pays. The owner on Monday, the union on Tuesday, who cares, as long as they get their money."

Leo's voice becomes ice. "Pay the gorillas who beat us up to attack Margolis' shop?"

"Either that or do it yourselves."

"The leadership opposes violence—"

"A bunch of bourgeois cowards with no ideology and no stomach."

Dickstein leans across the table. Gone is his nasty smile. "Use your head, man. The bosses will not hand you your rights on a silver platter. In Europe workers murder each other at the behest of the ruling class. In America, our peace-loving president quick marches us into the war. Is *that* where you want to fight? Do you want to die for *that*? If you have to pick up a weapon, at least do it to serve your class and end your oppression. Go with hammers and crowbars. Take out half the machines, then let Margolis know what he has to do to save the rest."

Leo propels out of his seat. "I don't know...I don't know...Some of the men are for it but the women object."

"Never pay attention to women. They're incapable of dialectical thought."

Stalled in the doorway, head bent in indecision, Leo glances my way almost by accident. Something cold enters my chest. Rosa's blackened ribs. My ringing ears. Mendel. I clench my fist.

Slowly, Leo nods. "The shop is empty tonight."

Dickstein rubs his hands together. "And no coppers if you're lucky."

"Since when have we been lucky?" Leo goes back to the table. "Come in, Irving," he calls. "You're part of this, too, now."

Over the next hour, they formulate a plan. I am to hide under the elevated on Grand as a lookout. Leo and Dickstein will assemble five or ten guys for a destruction committee. I'll be there to stop the action if the coppers are around. Otherwise, we get in and do damage. The three of us rise. We share a round of solemn handshakes and the two recruiters leave.

Outside, ropes of wet laundry sway over the alleyway. I used to hide from roughnecks in that alley. Izzy Schwartz, Blackie Birnbaum, Benny Fein. They lurked in the doorways, prowled the carts while I cowered under wet clothes. What kind of man am I? My eyes scour the room, past empty Mama, to Miriam's iron fry pan hanging by the stove. I seize the handle and step clear of the furniture. "For Mendel," I shout and swing. Heavier than a baseball bat, it scorches the air. Another swing. "For Klara Wojcik." The blood rushes in my ears. "For Arthur," I cry and swivel in a final sweep. I grab my jacket and rush out the door.

Shabbos. The streets are teaming. I have to shoulder through noisy hawkers, mamas with screaming babies and gaggles of street kids. When I reach Rivington and Grand, the rattle of an overhead train briefly drowns out everything else. I keep to the shadows of the black girders, not knowing if I'll encounter a lone patrolman or a battalion of Cossacks. But when I arrive at Allen Street, I stop short.

The loft door is wide open. A parade of sewing machines, cutters' knives, cotton bales, and thread barrels stomp down the steps. Like an ant army, the porters follow one after the other into the flotilla of trucks parked at the curb. None other than Morris Schneiderman is supervising the demolition. When he sees me frozen in the street, his face twists into his rat grin. He points at the waiting wagons.

"We closed the shop," he cackles. "Go ahead, go make your union now."

I'm waiting there when the committee arrives, Leo and Dickstein with Gutzman, Capamaggio, Manny, and Abe, all with hammers and crowbars bulging under their coats. The news I have for them is not what they expected.

TWENTY-ONE

Leo stands facing the assembled employees of the Margolis Shirtwaist Company, his hand resting on Mendel's empty chair. He raises a gavel but doesn't bother to bang. The room is already quiet as death. Leo's voice is deep and slow.

"You all heard. Margolis is gone. Yesterday Irving here found men emptying out the shop. We've confirmed it. He moved lock, stock, and barrel out to Jersey City. He's beyond the reach of our activity."

In the front row, Nettie holds Rosa's hand. Rosa has Sophie's, who grabs Esther, who throws her face into Seraphina's shoulder. Men mumble curses. Women do the same, even as they dab their eyes.

Tonya Wojcik looks from face to face. "What's Jersey City?"

"Tell her," Pincas Gutzman calls out. "Go on, Hirsch, tell her."

Leo's face is gray granite. "We have no more jobs, Tonya. The job moved away."

The child drops her head to her knees. "Papa's gonna kill me."

Sophie wraps her up, but Tonya's sniffles fill the silence.

Leo takes a step forward. "You all should know—many bosses are capitulating. Up and down the district, the job will be safer, better hours, more security. This strike will be a victory for the workers."

"If they have a job." It's Gutzman, of course.

Leo doesn't flinch. "Yes. If they have a job."

The meeting is done, but no one wants to leave. People gather into small groups, figuring, commiserating. How do you find a new job mid-season? Maybe the capitulating shops will need extra help to make up for lost time. But with the higher pay, maybe the owners won't be able to hire. They will if they take less profit. What owner's gonna take less profit? *Mamzers* like that have dollars for blood and wallets for hearts. Maybe it would have been better to leave well enough alone. And live like slaves? Better a slave than a corpse. Stinking capitalists.

I wander from this group to that, uncertain where to help. I give Rosa a hug, shake hands with Abe and Manny, wish Ignazio luck. The whole time my eyes keep shooting back to a single soul who sits, talking with her friends. The sunlight starts to fade from the windows. It's getting late. Slowly, one by one, the newly unemployed wander out into the blue dusk.

The last of us fold the chairs, straighten the benches, sweep. Esther covers the old typewriter that will go back to union headquarters. Nettie and Rosa stack picket signs against the wall. Then, there's nothing left to do. We snuff the lights and climb out into a dark, cold drizzle. Nettie, Rosa, Sophie, and Esther give a last hug then turn away home. Shoulders curled, hands in my pockets, my eyes ask. Nettie smiles. Side by side, we head north, stopping at the corner to let the traffic pass.

"You'll get another apprenticeship?" she asks.

I shrug. "Miriam says maybe she can get me in at Hoffman's Department Store. Someone once said he thought I'd make a good salesman."

The rain is pelting. We wait under the big transit kiosk in the middle of Delancey. A trolley rattles through and we squeeze to let the passengers go by. Pressed against her, my eyes lock onto the fine soft hairs on her neck. The crowd eases. We step apart.

"And you? Another shop? More unionizing?"

She looks past my shoulder to where the motorcars rumble out over the East River and the lights of the Williamsburg Bridge sparkle in the rain.

"A WTUL lady is sponsoring me to go to school. I'm moving to Boston."

I stare at the distant windows of Brooklyn until breath comes back to my lungs. "Your dream come true."

The downpour eases. I offer Nettie my arm and tuck her hand tight against me as we cross the rest of the way. When we get to Rivington, she lets go. Her chin is high, her face smooth. Her grey eyes glow in the lamplight.

She rests a hand on my chest. "*Zol zayn mit mazl*, Irving. Go with good luck. May your dreams come true, too."

Holding her hand one last time, "*Zol zayn mit mazl*."

I watch her disappear into the dark street.

1917
IRV

TWENTY-TWO

The Jersey ferry thuds its flat prow into the berth. Green water twists into whirlpools. The floor stops vibrating and the motor drops to a dull hum. A deckhand swings open the gate, shooing off a parade of clomping horse-wagons, snorting motorcars, and soot belching vans before waving us pedestrians down the ramp. It took only twenty minutes for me to cross the wide Hudson River and leave Manhattan Island for the first time in my life.

Monroe Goldstein's letter arrived three weeks after the end of our strike, two weeks after Miriam and Leo recited their vows at the Eldritch Street Synagogue, and one week after I give up on finding another apprenticeship.

It was the simplest of investigations, he wrote, right there in the records of Bellevue Hospital. Arthur Herschel Friedman was admitted November 4, 1912, in a "morbid epileptic paroxysm." The instigating relative, the father, declared the patient to be a man of low moral character, "a vicious, degenerate pervert prone to violent outbursts. He refuses to work. He abuses his mother and is a threat to his brother and sister, a constant danger to the family. He brings us only shame." An order of commitment was signed on the basis of the father's testimony. Arthur Friedman was transferred to the state's newly opened facility in Rockland County. "Any further inquiry should be directed to the authorities where your brother is being housed."

So began my monumental correspondence with Superintendent Dr. Charles S. Little of Letchworth Village Asylum for the Feeble Minded and Epileptic. Back and forth the letters flew, explanations, rebuttals, entreaties, and legalities until I am at last granted a visit to their hallowed institution in Thiells, New York.

The conductor nips our heels, yapping that the Rockland County rail service has a schedule to maintain and the train is waiting. Before I can blink, I'm installed in the scratchy seat of a coach car, staring through a grimy window as the conductor pushes the last straggler aboard, bangs the doors, and waves to the engineer. The train-whistle answers with a deep bellow and we bounce into motion. In my pocket I carry a sheaf of letters, in my satchel the gift of Miriam's best fruit-cake, in my heart...uncertainty.

Dr. Little's final message arrived with my permission slip.

If you hold some fantasy of reclaiming your brother to normal life, let me state in the most adamant terms, that the vast majority of epileptics are incurable, becoming demented, feeble-minded, imbecile, idiotic, or insane.

"This *schmuck* sounds just like the bastard judges during our strike," Leo's voice was harsh. "More concerned with your capitulation than your success. Do what you set out to do, Irving. Go see for yourself."

Thiells, New York, is a red brick stationhouse and a road. The other passengers putt-putt off in waiting motorcars. I'm alone excepting the two workmen shoveling coal into a rusty van at the platform's edge. When I ask, "Letchworth?" one of them waves, "Two miles," without looking up.

Grey road, telegraph poles, grass, and weeds. It's noon, so peaceful you can hear the air hum. The sun paints black lines from the telegraph wire onto the roadbed. Out in the field, some insect drums a tick-tick-tick. My boots crunch the gravel. In my whole life I've never walked in such emptiness.

Three-quarters of an hour later, jacket over my shoulder, shirt-sleeves rolled up, I stop to wipe the sweat off my face. The coal truck rattles past me, kicking up a smoky cloud. When the dust clears I see where it is headed—a black iron arch with the words "Letchworth Asylum." I start to run.

The grey stone building at the top of the lane says "Administration." Its hallway smells of bleach and lye soap. Bright as it is outside, the window blinds slant the light to dim as the receptionist examines my documents. Turns out I'm not to see the exalted Superintendent Charles S. Little, but some lackey assistant, Dr. Bertram Barnsby.

Hidden behind thick glasses and a bushy goatee, he taps his pen as he reads from a thick file.

"Trust me, Mr. Friedman, your brother is best served at Letchworth. Although our primary mission is the maintenance of feeble-minded children, we also retain facilities for permanently impaired adults." My knee starts twitching in time with his pen, so I put a hand on it to hold it still. The pen stops. "On that score, the record is unequivocal. Your brother is an incorrigible epileptic. Such degenerate conditions necessitate an environment of rigorous discipline, orderly routine, and productive work."

My fists are balled in my lap. "Arthur was a bookbinder...if we would take him..."

"You would have to petition the state Supreme Court to overturn his commitment. Frankly, I doubt they would allow it."

"But I can see him. Your boss said I'm allowed." I reach to my pocket to produce my documents, but he waves them away.

"Certainly, certainly. That's not at issue."

"So..." I'm half out of my chair.

"A question, first." I drop back. He clears his throat. "The etiology of epilepsy is obscure, but we know there is a strong hereditary component. Whenever possible we try to obtain a complete family history. Now that you're here..."

I twist my cap as if it were this bastard's neck.

"Ah, I see you're on pins and needles. Why don't we send a case-worker to interview your family at home?" His lips turn up in a weasel smile. "That way you can go right to your visit."

"Yes, sure, fine, anything."

"Good." He makes a note in the file. "Most of our inmates are working the fields in this lovely spring weather, but Arthur's been assigned a dormitory job. An orderly will walk you over." He offers me his fish handshake. "We'll be in touch about the other matter."

A brawny guy with a red face and bad teeth cools his heels on the front porch. When I come out, he flicks off his cigarette and cocks his head for me to follow. I trail him over grassy hills and around budding trees. This could be a stroll in the countryside, if it weren't for the hulking stone buildings, one after the other after the other.

"They sort 'em into clans." He's a Mick, sounding right off the boat. "One for the Idiots, another for the Morons. Your fella's in Epileptics. That's what the docs call 'em. I call 'em Mexican Jumping Beans." I'm thinking to bash in his head with a rock when he stops at the top of a rise. "There's your guy."

Sitting at the bottom of the hill. I make out a silhouette against the bright sun. The Mick makes as if to walk down with me.

"You can go," I tell him.

"I'm supposed to stay and—"

I shove my face an inch from his nose. "You can go."

"What the hell," he gripes, and away he stomps.

I order my heart to stop thumping. I breathe. Go too fast, maybe I'm scary, so I make myself walk slow.

Arthur is on a bench next to a basket of pea pods. He scoops, slits with his thumb. The round green pebbles plink to the metal bowl in his lap. Scoop, slit, drop. Scoop, slit, drop. Regular as a machine.

"Artie?"

The peas stop pinging. His head comes up. Narrow face, sharp nose, cleft chin, a moon-shaped scar next to his left eye, and white welt on his neck. Sunken cheeks, deep lines etching the mouth. Pale and rail thin. But my brother, still my brother. His brows fold in concentration. I step closer.

"They told you I was coming, yes?"

Carefully, carefully, carefully like he's handling precious gems, he places the pot on the bench. His knees unfold and he's on his feet. Eyes wide in wonder, he throws open his arms.

We are enfolded. Crushing the rough cotton of his shirt, I bury my face into the soft folds of his neck. My cap falls to the ground as his fingers caress my hair. He smells of salt and sweat and—how can it be? —of Mama. We hold each other where we stand, rocking back and forth, five minutes, ten minutes. Our throats are too full to make words, so we share our tears.

After an eternity of embracing, we push apart. He runs his hand over my cheek. "Irving. Little Irving."

It is the gentle voice from my dreams. Arthur's brown eyes are holes too deep to fill. With all this longing and waiting and praying, no words are the right words but Arthur demands. Huddled together as the sun moves across the sky, I sputter out the years apart...abandoning Papa, Miriam and me, school, Mama the Ghost, apprenticeship, Leo, the strike. Shadows from nearby buildings stretch across the lawn, and still Arthur listens, alive in his hunger. I can't stop 'til it's sated. Then it's my turn, but I can only ask it in a whisper.

"After we moved there was no way for you to find us, but it haunted me...Did you...did you write to us? With no answer, did you think we'd abandoned you?"

"Stop Irving, enough guilt. I never wrote."

"But..." My silent 'Why?' hangs between us.

"Little Irving, such a baby." His words are so like Miriam it takes my breath away. Bitter lines drive the sweetness from his face. "Go home to what? To my *schmuck* of a father...to beatings...to hate and contempt?" His voice is acid. "You think that's better than this?"

I shake my head, unable to let this into my mind. He could've tried for us, but he chose not to. "There was still me and Miriam. Mama."

"Oy, you still don't get it." He raises a finger to his left eye. "This is from a fit when I fell on some scissors." His hand goes to his neck. "In the garden from my hoe." Pulling up his pant leg to show the curdled skin of his shin. "I was carrying boiling water for tea. But," he taps his skull, "the worst is here. Things disappear...Mama's face, the street where we lived, even what happened yesterday. If I have a fit tonight, pouf, you are gone. Endless, inevitable, doomed. I am one of God's cursed." Arthur's eyes shoot past me to the darkening trees. "I am where I am supposed to be."

The sun is only a crescent glow over the treetops. The path becomes flooded with bands of muted children, white-aproned nurses, and mud-covered inmates returning from the fields. From the top of the rise, the Mick orderly is tramping our way.

I grab the sleeve of Arthur's shirt. "I will never desert you again. I swear it on my life."

His eyes crinkle with warmth and he squeezes my hand, almost knocking over his half-shucked pot of peas. "Oops. See what happens when I'm overcome. This is all of today's..."

He doesn't finish his thought. Instead, his hand quakes, sending the peas flying in a spray onto the grass. A second twitch, like he's purposely scattering away his day's labor. On the third spasm, the pot clangs to the ground. From two feet away, the orderly breaks into a run, arms extended, but as Artie pitches forward, I'm the one to catch and ease him to the ground while he continues to shudder and bump.

The Mick stands over him, shaking his head. "Like I said, jumping beans."

I'm on my knees, cradling Artie's head and shaking like a leaf myself, but this convulsion is already easing and his eyes flutter open. "Thanks be to Gott," I breathe as a nurse comes trotting over. Cool as a cucumber, she drops onto one knee, her fingers to his wrist as she checks the watch pinned to her bib. She pulls a pad and pencil from her pocket. "Brief, under two minutes, but I'll have to chart it." She glances at the orderly. "Make certain he gets to the dormitory." She stands, taking in the green nubs scattered around us. "No peas for dinner tonight. I warned them about him." I cannot believe my eyes when she makes to leave so I pluck at her skirt.

She tugs away, "I beg your pardon."

The orderly hops in. "He's the brother, ma'am. Day visit."

"Visiting hours are long over," she huffs at him.

"Sorry, ma'am, I was doin'..."

She flicks her hand for him to stop and turns to me. "It's time for you to leave, young man. Your brother is being attended to."

From the ground Arthur's hand claws my shirt. "Irv...Irv...ing." His voice is a nasal hum. His fingers scratch my arm, begging for purchase. I wrap his hand in mine. He pulls himself up to sit against the bench, licking his lips. He is ghost white and his head lolls, but his eyes are riveted on me. "Go." I lean in to hear better. "Go now...so they'll let you come again."

I glance up at the two guardians surrounding me. I wrap Arthur in my arms for a final hug. "I'll be back," I whisper.

Standing, I turn and march to the black iron gate.

TWENTY-THREE

The yoke of years is lifted. My long-lost brother is no longer lost but he's only as found as he wants to be. In the station house, waiting for the return train, thoughts whirl like feathers in the wind. I was ready to squeeze Arthur into our lives...a home, a bed, care, but no dramatic sacrifice is required. He asks only for affection, which I already have in abundance. Everything's changed but not changed. The confusion is dizzying.

I munch my sister's undelivered fruitcake, dense with honey, nuts, raisins, and figs. At least Miriam will be relieved. I reproach myself as ingrate, grousing about my sister as she saves me from starvation. I fold the brown wrapping paper and brush away the crumbs. Using my coat as a pillow, I stretch onto the bench and doze until dawn, when the rumble of wheels shakes the depot and I board the train in a groggy haze.

I debark at Chambers Street to find a city deranged.

Crowds six deep swarm the pier at the water's edge. Men, women, and children gawk out to the harbor, watching an ominous fleet of gunboats cruise up the river's mouth. They flank a veritable armada of boats and barges steaming past Lady Liberty on their way to Ellis Island.

A guy calls, "Three cheers for the U.S. Navy," and, "Hip, hip, hooray," sweeps the crowd. "Give 'em hell, boys." "Those lousy Kraut sailors are in for it now."

I elbow my way to the street in utter confusion, only to find a battalion of khaki soldiers and a horde of blue-coated coppers. And there, pasted to the station wall, in huge black letters, I learn the reason.

WAR DECLARED!
GERMAN SHIPS SEIZED. SPIES PUT UNDER ARREST.

One night. I'm gone one night and the world has somersaulted. Not just my world, everyone's. For weeks Leo's been shouting that the worst is coming, but I was so consumed with my Arthur stuff, I didn't care. Now look. Leo and Miriam must be going crazy. I jump onto a cross-town trolley.

The tram creeps through throbbing crowds. Manhattan has redecorated itself over night. Red, white, and blue buntings hang from windows and American flags wave by the doors. Passengers jostle to catch the show with whoops, backslaps, and handshakes. The teeming streets hold us to such a crawl, I jump off and hoof the rest of the way on foot.

My stoop is devoid of the usual *kibitzers*. It's Shabbos. The stalls are quiet and the synagogues full, probably fuller than ever today. I dash the stairs two at a time to storm our door. Sunlight pours over the *New York World* stretched open on the table. Leo stands behind Miriam, reading over her shoulder. They jerk around as I burst in, but they are not my objective. Striding the room, I drop on my knees to grasp my mother's hands.

"*Mamashe*, I saw Arthur. He sends his love."

Brows knitted, she shakes her head, so I repeat it in Yiddish.

"*Ikh gefunen Arthur. Er sendz zeyn libe*."

Her hard dry fingers squeeze my hands and her lips form a smile for the first time in an eternity. Tears in my eyes, I turn to the others. "Forget the news. I have so much more to tell."

They listen, rapt, holding hands across the table. Leo mumbles curses at the *mamzer* doctor and Miriam's face works with emotion when I tell about the fit. I apologize about the fruitcake, but she waves it away.

"You had to eat. At least Artie is safe, established, and has no wish to leave." Miriam can't keep the relief from her voice. But she chews on a different item. "Irving, this family history he asked for. How could you allow it's okay to pry on us?"

"What choice did I have?"

Miriam's eyes narrow. "They better not be inspecting for money. We don't have any to give away." And with that she deposits an unexpected kiss on the top of my head and disappears to the back to put up her poor swollen feet.

I, too, should be nailed with exhaustion, but too much has happened. I circle the room, not sure where to put myself.

Leo throws me my jacket. "Cepulski's for us."

The saloon is jammed and the crowd is raucous, rattling noisemakers and shouting slogans. A guy at the bar warbles a tuneless "Columbia the Gem of the Ocean."

Caspar, the waiter, uses a slop cloth to wipe the wet off our table. "My father fled to America to escape the Russian army. Now the Russians throw out the Tsar saying no more war and the Americans take their place. It's one crazy world."

He drops us our tub of beer and walks away shaking his head.

I sip, looking at the men crowding the brass railing. Jews, Italians, Poles, Greeks. Even my dog of a father knew to get on a boat. Perhaps protecting this place is not such an unworthy cause.

The Caruso at the bar breaks into a ditty about Marines and honor and the whole room joins in. "*We will fight our country's ba-attles...*" I tap my foot in time to the singing and it comes to me—with Arthur found and Miriam safe with Leo, I'm a free man...No job...No sweetheart... Of course, I've never set eyes on a gun, but I bet learning is easy.

"Fools. Idiots." Leo pounds the table so hard my beer sloshes over. "Dupes of the master class."

I nudge him to shush. Tonight, such talk could get us our heads bashed in. He sniffs but lowers his voice.

"I will never lift my hand against a fellow worker in the service of our enslavers."

"Come on Leo. I may not study Marx, but I know German U-boats are killing innocent Americans."

"Ach, *Schmendrick*, patriotism is such a sly seductress. She puts on face paint and pretty clothes so you won't see the ugliness underneath."

I trace a line along the damp rim of my mug. "Remember what Mendel said? America may not be perfect but it's better than where he came from. He would have fought to protect this country."

Leo sighs in with exaggerated sadness. "Irving, Irving, Irving...all this time and still you don't get it. No matter which side wins the war, we workers lose as long as capitalists rule the world."

"Well Leo, there are fifty or a hundred guys in this room who don't agree."

He downs his beer and plunks down his mug. "Then it is my job to teach them otherwise."

Six weeks later the newspapers announce that all men ages twenty-one to thirty-one must register for military service. At seventeen, I am excused, but Leo crushes the page into a ball and heaves it across the room.

TWENTY-FOUR

I lean on the icebox, noshing a pickle. Myron Dickstein and Leo have taken possession of our kitchen to prepare for a meeting. Dickstein recites from his notes, a cigarette dangling off his bottom lip.

"You are a citizen, not a subject. Will you stand idly by and see the Moloch of Militarism fasten its tentacles upon this continent? Will you be led astray by propaganda masquerading under the guise of patriotism? Do you know that patriotism means a love for your country and not hatred of others?"

He checks for Leo's opinion, letting a column of cigarette ash hit the floor.

Miriam, in the rocking chair, gives a loud, "Ahem."

Leo follows her eyes. He squashes the cigarette mess with his shoe. "Crafty, Myron, very crafty."

"What's so crafty?" I say between crunchy bites.

Leo examines the pad. "Nowhere does he say, 'Don't Register.' Our democracy-loving president has made those words a crime. So much for freedom of speech. It's a joke, no? The politicians howl that socialism is America's enemy, but they're the ones defiling the Constitution."

"There's nothing funny about tyranny, Hirsch. Watch. Tomorrow we'll lose freedom of the press." Dickstein stands and gathers his papers. "I'll bring the statement on Saturday. Let's see if our coalition will adopt it. Not that a bunch of scatter-brained anarchists, sentimental socialists, and lily-livered Unitarians will agree with anything we Marxists propose." Crushing his butt under his heel, he stomps out.

"Go with God." I bite off a crisp snap as he brushes past me.

Leo chuckles. "I know, Dickstein's something of a *schmuck*. But a brilliant strategist."

"He's a *yutz*." Miriam snips the thread on the baby dress she's repairing. She curls her fingers on the counter edge to heave out of the rocker, ignoring Leo's offer of a hand. She unhooks the dustpan from the wall and slaps it into his palm, pointing her toe to the mess under the table. Leo sweeps and offers the results for inspection.

"Thank you for nothing," she sniffs, folding the dress into a chest of baby things she's collected from our neighbors. "Believe it or not, Leo, you're not the only one who reads the newspapers. I read that socialists are not too popular these days. Gangs roam the streets for those 'traitorous rats' in the pay of the Germans."

He dumps the ashes into the trash bin and brushes off his hands. "We're being careful."

"Careful is keeping your mouth shut."

"Impossible. From all over the country thousands are stepping up to oppose conscription. Who knows what could happen? There is no underestimating the power of the masses to—"

Miriam throws up her hands. "*Oy*, spare us, please." She runs her palm over the closed lid of the baby chest then swivels to him. "The nurse at the settlement house says six, maybe seven weeks. You better be here when the time comes."

"Miri." He reaches for her. She tries to back away, but he's too quick, wrapping her in his arms. "Where else would I be?"

Her belly comes between them. She is not smiling.

Over the next few weeks, the stories pour in. All over the country anti-drafters are arrested, beaten, jailed, sentenced years for uttering the words 'Don't register.' In New York, three from Columbia University are convicted for printing an anti-registration pamphlet. Leo seethes. Miriam balks. They circle each other, wary boxers avoiding the next jab. I dance away like the referee.

Shabbos. He's scouring literature he brought from his last meeting. Every couple of minutes he mumbles, "See...See...right."

"What?" Miriam peels vegetables by the sink.

"A famous woman you've probably never heard of. Irving, explain Helen Keller."

Miriam slashes at a carrot. "Irving can keep his mouth shut. I know from Helen Keller."

"Then listen." He reads aloud, "Congress is not preparing to defend the people of the United States. It is planning to protect the capital of American speculators and investors...Every modern war has had its root in exploitation. See, it's so plain, even a blind woman can see it."

"Easy for her to talk. Helen Keller won't get arrested if she doesn't register."

"Miriam, half the Jews in New York came here to escape conscription. What's the difference between Woodrow Wilson and the Tsar?"

Miriam slings the cuttings into the soup, splashing water over the stove. "Shirley Bernstein's brother works for the draft board. He says married men who support their families are...Oh, wait...It's a word you've probably never heard of. Irving, explain exempt."

Leo drips with disdain. "Men with dependents can apply to be excused. This is supposed to make me feel better? Thousands march off to die, but, hey, no problem, I'm exempt?"

"If thousands have to die, at least you would not be one of them. But if you go to jail, where does that leave me?"

His voice softens. "Miri, my father came in the middle of a pogrom to find us safety. I'm doing the same, trying to make a safer world for my son."

She sets her shoulders and raises her chin. "Go peddle your fish somewhere else, Leo. I'll worry about the rest of the world when the rest of the world worries about me."

She turns and will hear no more.

MY NEXT ARTHUR VISIT. THIS TIME I REMEMBER MIRIAM'S fruitcake. He nibbles as I describe the quarrel.

"So, what did you think?" he asks.

"I think who needs conscription? I'm already in a battlefield."

Wispy clouds move across the sun. He looks good today, eyes clear, a titch less skinny. He says he's had only one fit since my last visit.

"One time...let me think...I'd just started with Yaakov the bookbinder. You must have been six, so Miriam would've been eleven. Coming up the stairs from work, I heard Mama wailing. She was in the bedroom, '*Gut in Himmel. Gut in Himmel.*' You were in a ball on the kitchen floor. Miriam stood in front of you holding Mama's iron skillet like a baseball bat, 'In case he comes back,' she said. I offered to take it, but she wouldn't let go. 'You'll just start shaking and drop it.'" Arthur sighs. "This is not a woman who'll trust to the goodness of the world."

We're on the bench outside his dormitory. The clouds pass away from the sun. I shade my eyes the better to see him against the glare.

"By thirteen, fourteen she started asking me about the words men threw at her on the street, so I explained." He snatches up a blade of grass and slowly rips it into long strips. "That's when she whispered, 'Papa looks at me funny, too.' One night, at dinner...Papa's sitting like God on high, his fork in one fist and his knife in the other. 'Any daughter who brings shame on this house will be banished as a whore.' Miriam didn't bat an eye. 'I'm not the shameful one,' she said. I swear, if she weren't a girl, he'd have killed her. But he never mentioned it again."

It seeps back—Miriam's black eyes, Papa's beefy face. "He once called her a choice piece of meat." Who says that of a daughter?

"You should see her these days, Artie. She waddles like a duck. Mrs. Bernstein from upstairs scolded we should be ashamed, letting her work this close to her time." I rub my hand along the splintered bench. "They're building a wooden ship in Union Square. You wouldn't believe it. Two hundred feet long, with fake wooden canon. To recruit for the navy. You want to know the truth? Sometimes I walk by and think, join up, Leo be damned. Sail away. See London, maybe even Paris. But, God forbid something happens to Leo, who's she got but you and me?"

"You mean who's she got but you." He musses my hair like when I was a kid. "My baby brother, savior of the family."

A bell clangs off in the distance. Visiting hours are over. Arthur puts his hand on my shoulder.

"It's early in the war. Wait and see what happens."

TWENTY-FIVE

June 4th. Registration Eve. The Non-Conscription League has called a huge rally. Leo will not be denied. Miriam clutches me by the collar. "Keep him from being stupid." So here I am, Leo's minder, crushed in a mob that circles the meeting hall, three, four, five blocks in all directions.

Leo is jubilant. "See, *Schmendrick*, I told you...the masses will rise up to oppose capitalist enslavement."

Maybe. I hear plenty of "Emma Goldman's gonna speak," or "Lousy, warmongering politicians..." But I also catch whiffs of "Anarchist bums" and "Alien scum."

I tell Leo that I think we got finks, but it gets lost in the surge. Determined to gain entrance, he plows us over, under, around and through 'til we tumble out to the front of the line. The crowd throbs to get in. Only one unit of coppers stands between them and the unopened doors.

I'm wondering how they're going to manage this horde, when the answer comes in a shriek of police whistles. A battalion of blue-coated coppers and khaki National Guardsmen batters open a path wide enough for a motorcar with a jumbo searchlight. Wham, the lamp blazes on. People jump back, arms over their faces, as the light burns into their eyes. With the crowd subdued, a smug captain announces he will admit only those patrons with legitimate credentials. Leo waves his union card. "I'm a registered representative." The cop nearest us lowers his billy club and we race in.

The hall only holds a fraction of the thousands swirling out in the street. Seeing the scramble, Leo races us to the balcony. Down in the orchestra men and women scratch and crash, but we win seats on the railing right above the stage. Leo is ecstatic, hailing friends and comrades as they file by. It's thrilling. The theatre holds only a few hundred, but outside is the biggest assembly of my life, bigger than the union hall, bigger than the strike march. I look sideways at my brother-in-law. The union. Mendel. Nettie. Arthur. All because chance brought me to Niedermeyer's and Leo Hirsch was my teacher.

"Look." He points down.

Two coppers lead a team of women to a roped off table. The ladies adjust their skirts as, one by one, they set pad and pencil on the desktop.

"Stenographers recording for the authorities." Leo cups his mouth and yells "Remember free speech? Who are the real traitors to democracy?"

A voice barks, "Watch your mouth, buster." We bolt around.

Black mustache, black coat, bowler hat, and two jeering allies. With the tight rows and the steep raked floor, the three of them hang over us. Leo pulls my sleeve not to look.

"Stinking kikes," Mustache razzes.

"Hecklers," Leo breathes. "Let them be."

I sigh in relief. Seems Miriam was wrong. Leo's his own minder.

The lights dim. An organizer steps onto the stage. Grey-haired and dignified, he denounces the Prussianizing of America. He says we must demand our freedom of conscience and remember that we are all citizens of the world. The audience applauds in agreement, except for a few scattered catcalls including from our upstairs neighbors. When we clap harder to drown them out, Mustache hisses, "Chicken-livered coward."

A tall, skinny kid only a couple of years older than I am takes the stage. Hands shaking, he pours a glass of water before he starts.

All three behind us stomp their feet, hooting, "Lilly-livered yellow-belly. Cat got your tongue?" Their cohort around the auditorium picks up the taunt, "Yellow-belly. Lilly-liver."

The rest of the audience claps harder to drown out the trouble-makers and the kid steps forward.

"Ladies and gentlemen." He speaks in clarion tones. "I would like to tell you a great many things but," his arm indicates the coppers and guardsmen dotting the gallery, "the police are here. America will not permit me to say them directly."

Someone blows a raspberry from the orchestra, but the kid doesn't miss a beat.

"I *am* allowed to say that I'm a freeborn citizen and I love American democracy. Tomorrow, June fifth, we have an opportunity to crush a law that threatens to destroy that democracy. It is our patriotic duty to do so. As Patrick Henry said, *'Give me liberty or give me death.'*"

Mustache leans over the back of Leo's seat. "Ship 'em back where they came from." From the black depths of the auditorium, another heckler calls, "Gutless cur." A third boos, "Traitor go home." Up and down the aisles men rise to scour for the rowdies, but it's too dark to see them.

Our young patriot waves his arms for quiet. "I will not allow my government to make me murder. I refuse to slaughter my fellow man under the pretense of a democratic war."

The auditorium rings with roars of "Bravo," "Yahoo," "God bless you."

Suddenly an object whooshes past my ear and shards of glass explode onto the stage. The whole room gasps. Before anyone can move, four more missiles whizz down, erupting in spiny splinters. The bastards behind us are flinging light bulbs.

In a flash, Leo jumps up to face Mustache. "Enough, you *schmuck*." His huge frame creates a wall between the heckler and the stage.

Mustache bares his teeth in a dirty grin. He arches his fist for a swing, but Leo's too fast. Using one arm to block, he pushes with the other, somersaulting the troublemaker head over heels. A woman screams. Spectators scramble from their chairs. The two sidekicks lunge at Leo, but a pack of comrades hops to his defense, dragging the thugs from their seats. Guardsmen careen toward the fracas and I'm shoved to the floor as the coppers swarm in.

It's over in a minute. The gladiators are separated. The perpetrators corralled. Mustache, pulled off to one side, whispers with the top cop. He comes back to where they're holding Leo. Flipping over his lapel, he exhibits a U.S. Marshal's badge. With leering satisfaction, he snarls, "The guy's an anarchist fanatic. Take him away." Trapped under my seat, I watch Leo being hustled out of the stadium, his arms bound with handcuffs.

TWENTY-SIX

P anic. I clamber out of the auditorium and race outside, reaching the street in time to see the top sergeant call Leo a "fuckin' Socialist" and give his face the knuckle back of his hand.

I'm stupid enough to call out, "Hey."

Three blue uniforms turn to me. The closest one, a bald bull with a stubbly beard, stomps over and stabs his nightstick into my chest. "This stinking traitor is going downtown. Now move your ass out of here, you little shit." Leo, his lip already swelling to purple, cocks his head for me to scram. It's torture, but I obey, sliding into the shadows as he's shoved into the van that will take him to the city jail rightly called the Tombs. Leo presses his face to the bars as the cage jolts away from the curb, puffing yellow exhaust. Only after it's out of sight do I traipse to the elevated, brushing away tears. Night trains come slow. Trembling and exhausted, I trudge the stairs to my threshold. Miriam, dozing in the rocker, bolts awake at the sound. She scours the hall past my silhouette. When she realizes I'm alone, her color drains.

"It wasn't his fault," I moan. "Finks were there to provoke. It wasn't his fault."

Her livid eyes accuse.

We're awake when the morning papers hit the streets. It seems that as the event broke up, parts of the crowd clashed with the National Guard. Scores were arrested. Later, at the arraignment, the fact that Leo was only defending himself, that he was already in custody when the riot happened, means nothing. He gets charged along with the rest. When the final verdict is delivered, Miriam and I are in the gallery with a flock of Leo's supporters. The judge is unyielding. "All true Americans must despise these foul minions of our enemy. Their traitorous attempt to undermine a just and equitable law must be punished to the utmost."

Conspiracy to commit treason. Three years in federal prison.

My knees go soft. Miriam is white marble. Across the courtroom, Leo's flaming eyes fly first to my sister then sear into me. I bow my head. Command received. It is my turn to provide.

I reach out to his union. Leo's comrades take up a collection. A socialist midwife volunteers for when the time comes. I secure a well-paid apprenticeship back at Niedermeyer's, under Pincas Gutzman of all people. Once it's all arranged, I kneel in front of the rocking chair, taking hold of Miriam's icy hands.

"We have the rent and what to eat. We'll be okay. I promise."

The chair creaks once under her weight. Her lips are a single bitter line.

Miriam is an island unto herself. As the days go by, I hold my breath, waiting for an eruption—shouts, denunciations, shrieks of reproach. What happens is worse. Steely and grim as her girth swells, she is a seething silence, speaking only out of necessity—"Pay the butcher," "We need coal"—or not at all.

Four weeks to the day after Leo's conviction, Samuel David Hirsch enters the world wearing his father's blue eyes and his mother's black hair. Even Mama wakes for this miracle, her calloused fingers warming his chest as he lies in his cradle. Miriam buries her nose in the warmth of his neck, his baby smell sweetening the air. For him and him alone, her face softens to silk. The rest of the time, she is stone.

The first letters arrive in July. In mine, Leo begs and implores, the child must have arrived, is everyone safe? I don't know what he writes to my sister. She won't open the envelope.

"She'll never forgive," I grumble to Pincas Gutzman as we brush scraps from the cutting table. He heaves up a bolt of khaki fabric for the uniforms that we manufacture. Gutzman was never an intimate, but I find solace in his tough common sense.

"I used to think Hirsch was an arrogant dogmatist. I was wrong. He's a good person. Your sister may be angry with him, but she's a smart woman. She won't throw that kind of man away."

My next time at Letchworth, Arthur agrees. "Give her time."

"If only she would berate or scold or yell."

"That's only for small tragedies. This is too deep." He urges she bring the boy for a visit, but when I suggest it, she waves me off.

It's a couple of nights later that her old boss, Harry Hoffman, drops by with a rattle for the baby. One coo-coo under Sammy's chin, then it's down to business. He's surrounded by *shlubs*. Without Miriam, the bookkeeping is a mess. When can she return? Jiggling the child in her arms, she delivers her cold-eyed stare—the salary? Oh, well, she should get a raise. How much? He runs a finger around his white-starched collar. Twenty percent? Miriam is a Sphinx. Okay, thirty percent.

My sister is a fast operator. The next day she asks Mrs. Bernstein upstairs to wet-nurse and, piff-poof, she's back in the store. It's a lot, eight, nine hours then home to the cooking, the cleaning and the baby, but Miriam was never a slouch. Besides, dropping into bed bone-tired makes it easier for her to sleep.

But Leo leaves a hole the size of a bomb crater, not only for Miriam. In that first scorching summer of the war, I walk the world humming the song he taught me—Patriotism is a sly seductress. I watch as we are sold duty, fidelity, and God Bless America and just as Myron Dickstein prophesied, one after the other, the freedoms fall.

Union Square, the site of a thousand socialist soapbox harangues, now houses a full-sized wooden battleship for the Navy to recruit. Vigilantes patrol the street, cornering men to check their draft cards.

When a man in a restaurant fails to stand for the "Star Spangled Banner," the other diners assault him and the judge charges *him* with disturbing the peace. After our esteemed government passes the Espionage Act, the *Forward* ceases all criticism, lest they be shut down.

Little Sammy is my only consolation. He is the cheeriest of souls, returning every coo and cluck with a chirrup of his own. After a long day's work, the gentle rhythm of his cradle soothes me as much as it soothes him. Miriam feels it, too. She falls asleep every night with her hand resting on his head.

August grinds into a sweltering, muggy September. Our flat is a monument to gloom, with Mama her ghostly self and Miriam walled into a fortress of silence. In the oppressive heat, even Sammy gets cranky. Once again, I spend my nights on the streets, this time in the blanketing summer heat. In utter desperation, I again raise Arthur's proposal.

"It's the country. We'd get away from this shithole weather for a day. Artie says that, as the eldest, he should give the boy his blessings. Doesn't Sammy deserve all the help he can get?"

Something stirs behind her eyes. I swallow down a whoop of gratitude when she consents.

This time we take a motorcar from the Thiells depot, sharing the fare with an Italian couple come to see their daughter. When we make a quick swerve around a pothole, Sammy starts to fuss. The Italian woman eyes them with a sad-eyed benevolence.

"*Mangiare?*" She mimes putting food in her mouth.

"Tired, I think." Miriam acts out tipping her head to one side and closing her eyes.

"*Ah, si. Va bene.* So, I make quiet."

Adjusting Sammy's blanket against the road dust, Miriam retreats into her cocoon.

Artie is pacing the gravel walk by the Administration Building when we drive through the black gates. The auto kicks up a cloud of dust as it rolls to a stop. Miriam steps down, cradling the baby to her chest. The two of them face each other.

Artie holds out his hand. "*Mayn lib shvester.*" His brown eyes glow with warmth.

"*Mayn bruder.*" The baby in one arm, Miriam grasps Artie's hand with the other. His fingers go white in her steel grip. "This is your nephew, Samuel."

Arthur's hand hovers over the baby, barely touching the wispy, dark hair then he bends to deposit the airiest of kisses. Sammy's tiny fist brushes his chin. Miriam offers the child for a hug, but Artie pulls away. "No. I'm not safe."

The Mick orderly appears and escorts the Italian couple up the walkway. That bastard Dr. Barnsby strolls by, stroking his beard as he watches our family reunion.

Arthur leads us away from the dark buildings, into the sloping fields. We settle under a shade tree. Nestled on a blanket, Sammy gets his nap as Miriam props herself against the trunk. For the second time Artie insists on hearing every detail of our life after he was taken. I don't care Miriam tells it different from me. I lie on my back with the green leaves swishing in the breeze, wanting nothing more than this— my brother, my sister, and me together in the warm summer air.

Down the hill, the Italian couple has spread a picnic in the grass. Their daughter sits on the father's lap while the mama holds out a baby doll. It appears the girl is one of those who can't make words, but her delighted grunts carry up to us.

Miriam watches them. "They got lots like her here?"

"It gives the officials pleasure to call this a school but it's a garbage dump for the unwanted. They call them feeble-minded, imbecile, idiot, or moron. Not all are such, but once you're labeled, you're a prisoner for life. Speaking of which..." He sucks on a blade of grass. "I've heard about everything except your husband."

I hold my breath. Miriam smooths her skirt. Please God, we're here with Artie. Please God, let her spit it out. She sits up straighter. Her jaw tightens.

"He betrayed me." The bitterness is acid. "I told him. It's dangerous, keep your mouth shut. *But Miriam,*" dripping mockery as she imitates Leo, "*if no one speaks up, we're all lost.*" She slams the earth. "He wouldn't give up his lousy *cause.*"

"But you always knew that about him, that his heart was committed to these things."

"That was before he'd fathered a child...a *child.*" Finally, she's belting out her Miriam rage, loud enough to startle the crows on the branch overhead. "Only a bastard *schmuck* deserts his family."

"I thought your husband was tricked by a government fink?"

"If he'd cared about us, he wouldn't have been there to get tricked."

"So, this Leo is just a cocky *schmuck?*"

"*Yes.*" She drops her head to her hands. "No. But he left us to starve."

Arthur's eyebrows pop up. "You're starving? Irving, you didn't tell me you were all starving."

Miriam makes a face. "Okay...we're not starving. But we could have been."

"Drivel," Arthur hoots. "The earth could catch fire, God could send the plagues of Egypt, but my sister will never let her family starve. Look what you've lived through. Look what you've done. You are a fierce woman, Miriam. Frankly, it sounds to me like you chose a man to match."

Sammy picks that precise moment to let out a wail. Without another word, Miriam grabs him up and moves away to feed him. When she's out of sight, I put my palms together and look to the heavens in prayer. Artie punches my shoulder.

Miriam rides back in silence while I hold the baby, savoring the heft of his firm little body against my knees. We get home after dark. I deposit him in the cradle. Miriam goes to prepare dinner. It's not until the middle of the night, when I rise for the privy, that I find her at the kitchen table, reading Leo's letters.

TWENTY-SEVEN

Exactly one week after our Arthur visit, a bony, sharp-nosed redhead in a white linen dress and straw hat stands at our threshold, a leather portfolio dangling off her shoulder. Miriam, who answered the knock, holds the door half-open.

"How do you do?" The woman extends her lace-gloved hand. "Florence Archer here, from Letchworth Hospital. Come to meet the family of Arthur Friedman. His brother consented to an interview."

"That was six months ago." I stand, pulling up my suspenders. It's noon on Saturday and I've been relaxing with a book.

"Yes, we're sorry about the delay. What with the war...our patriotic staff joining up...and poor Dr. Barnsby is rather scattered. I'm certain you understand." Florence Archer's blue eyes are all apology. "The record indicated that you're a household of Sabbath observers, so I knew you'd not be at work. I decided to throw caution to the wind and hope I'd find you home." I've never seen so many white teeth as Florence Archer shows us. "Might you be brother Irving? Is there any chance you could grant me some time?"

Miriam's chest puffs out like an angry bird. "It's Shabbos. You think you can just come waltzing in?"

I step in front of her. "This is required for Arthur?"

"Anything that contributes to our understanding of his sad condition is in Arthur's best interest."

"Give us a minute?"

I close the door while Miriam brays her outrage. "She's got a lot of nerve. Like she's the Queen of Sheba."

I put a finger on my lips for her to shush. "I told them okay, remember? God knows what they'll do to Artie if we say no."

She scowls, but I face her down, a minute, two minutes. She throws up her hands. "If this is about money, she's out."

I plaster on a smile and open the door. "We can manage something. Yes, I'm Irving. This is my sister, Miriam Hirsch."

The woman dips a curtsey. "Honored, to be sure. So many of our poor inmates are abandoned by their family, I truly appreciate your willingness to contribute to our work."

Miriam narrows her eyes. "What kind of contribution?"

"Well..." Florence looks past Miriam's shoulder. "Perhaps we could sit?"

In a final capitulation, my sister stands aside and Florence Archer steps in, pausing to inspect the worn linoleum and peeling paint. Her eyes crinkle at Sammy, gurgling in his cradle. "How sweet." She stops short at the rocking grey-haired ghost.

"Our mother." Miriam's voice is flat with caution.

Florence Archer dips again. When nothing happens, her head tilts in curiosity. She deposits her portfolio on the table, unpins her hat, and hands us her calling card. "Just to be official."

FLORENCE ARCHER
FIELD REPRESENTATIVE
EUGENICS RECORDS OFFICE

"Fancy." Miriam holds it like it smells. "But it doesn't say what you're after."

Florence Archer places a hand over her heart.

"Please believe me, Mrs. Hirsch, our interest is purely altruistic. Using revolutionary discoveries in the science of eugenics, the ERO is working to eliminate mankind's most heinous maladies. We collect

information on inborn physical, mental, and temperamental properties. Epilepsy, your brother's malady, is known to reside within partic-
ular constellations. The sooner we can identify those constellations,
the sooner we can eradicate this scourge from the family of man."

I clear my throat. "So, ah...you want...what?"

The woman preens cordiality. "I want your family...everything you
know about them, stories, tales, memories, anything, for as far back as
you can remember. We're tracing the segregation and recombination
of your heritable qualities." When Miriam throws a look that's says
get this *draycup* out of here, Florence chirps, "Allow me to demonstrate." Pulling out a pad and pencil, she draws a circle and a square at
the top of the page. "According to our records, your father's name was
Isaac."

"It was Yitzhak," Miriam snaps.

"Beg pardon...Yitzhak" She writes "Yitzhak" in the circle. "Your
mother is Libke." Mama doesn't stir at the sound of her name as
"Libke" goes into the little square. "We draw a line to show that
Yitzhak and Libke are married." A new row, two more circles—
"Arthur," "Irving"— and a square—"Miriam."

"This shows that Yitzhak and Libke have three offspring, two
male, one female. And now that I've been here." Florence plunks a
new circle next to Miriam's square, "For the father," and a second
below it, "For the cute little tyke. Might we fill in the names?"

I'm afraid Miriam will bite her head off, so I jump in. "Miriam's
husband is Leo Hirsch. The baby is Samuel."

Scritch scratch. "Ta-dah." Florence holds up her masterpiece. "This
is your family tree. But, of course, it's just the start. The truth of these
people, the story of their personalities, that's the heart and soul of our
work." She taps Papa's circle. "Let's start here. What can you tell me
about your father? What kind of man was he? Everything and anything
you remember, I'll take it all." Her pencil hovers over the page. Her
eager eyes await.

"He was a big guy," I tell her. "Huge hands, a day laborer in the old
country. Over here he got work as a barrel-maker."

The Letchworth woman holds up her hand. "Wait. Can we go back? Dates, specifics, locations, the nitty-gritty, if you have it."

I dredge up everything I can remember from Papa's rantings and Mama's stories, town names, grandparents' names, distant relatives. Florence Archer is a regular speed demon, recording everything as fast as I say it.

"Good, good, this is golden in terms of genetic tracings. But I still don't have a feel for the man. Was he kind, smart, funny?"

Words catch in my throat—What can describe Papa?

"He was a *chazzer schmuck*," Miriam growls. "You don't understand? It means he was a pig bastard. You want I should give you tales of fists and insults? Living them was enough. I don't need to tell them also."

"Your father was a violent man?" Florence Archer glows with seriousness. The pencil hits the paper. "Was he given to irrational fits of temper? Did he attack without warning or cause?" From Miriam to me. "Could we get at least one example? Just a single incident that would epitomize his mania?"

I scratch around for what will satisfy. "Once, I was nine or ten, after dinner, reciting my lessons for Hebrew school, when, bam, I get his knuckles, 'Shut your trap. I'm tired.'"

"Sudden bouts of rage." Scribble, scribble, scribble. "I'll bet he felt persecuted, didn't he? On and on about how the world abused him... I'm right, aren't I?"

Five mouths to feed. Often no work and no money. A kike and a sheeny. I don't bother to answer and she doesn't wait.

"And the mother?" She turns to Mama, tapping her pencil on the table to get her attention and giving a little wave. Of course, nothing happens. "Quite apathetic, I see. Actually, I'll label her as cataleptic. Hmm, is this her natural disposition?"

I clear my throat. "Mama, well, Mama's always been quiet. She was raised traditional—the wife obeys the husband."

"So, a deeply melancholic personality." She scrawls a note, sits up, satisfied. "There it is. The outcome, exactly as Mendel predicted."

My heart jumps. "Mendel who? What Mendel?"

"Gregor Mendel, the scientist Monk."

"Oy." I run my hands over my face.

"We studied him at Smith. I was a biology major." Pride shines like sunlight. "By cultivating peas, Gregor Mendel discovered how traits migrate between generations. Can you imagine? Let's say there's an abnormality, oh, hypothetically, lunacy. It doesn't appear in everyone, but if the mother has the abnormality in her family background and the father has it in his, Mendel's law says that one in four of the offspring will manifest that abnormality. And here we have it." She taps the family tree. "Father paranoid. Mother melancholic. Three children and, boom, one abnormal, exactly as predicted." Radiating happiness, "It's science at its best." She taps her cheek in thought. "You know, Mrs. Hirsch, I certainly hope your husband doesn't have a similar recessive trait in his genetics because then you'd be likely to produce at least two abnormal offspring."

"That's it." Miriam's hand hits the table. "Enough." She is on her feet. "You learned a bunch of bullshit so you call us dirty names. We're not greenhorns who don't know our ass from our elbow."

Jaw dropped open, the woman stammers, "Please, Mrs. Hirsch, there's nothing offensive. It's not my usual role to discuss outcomes in these interviews, but, honestly, I'm doing you a favor. This is scientific fact. You've already produced one potentially defective child. Do you really want to risk having another?"

"Out." Miriam is at the door, the leather portfolio in her fist. When it hits the banister, the papers fly like dead leaves down the stairwell. "Out. Get out or I'll knock your head off."

"Oh my God. It's the whole tribe of them." The woman trips over the chair as she scrambles to gather the rest of her notes but Miriam gets them first and rips them into shreds. Florence Archer's face changes three shades of red. "Go ahead, have your conniption fit." She points at Sammy's cradle. "If that kid isn't deformed, it'll be the next one. Probably it'll be both. No one escapes science." She manages to grab her straw hat as she makes for the exit. "Crazy foreigners."

Miriam slams the door hard enough to rattle the windows.

The silence between us is deafening. Finally, I croak, "Do you think they'll take this out on Artie?"

Miriam ignores me. She strides to the baby. Sammy mews in surprise as she crushes him into her shoulder. Her breathing ragged, she kisses his head and returns him to the cradle.

"Miriam...what she said..." I rub sweaty palms against my pants.

"*Chaleria* ghoul." Miriam spits on the floor. "Let her burn in hell. You heard Artie—once they label you, you're a prisoner for life. *Not my kinder.*" She retrieves the paper shards at her feet. "She's got nothing. If we don't tell, it never happened."

"But, Leo...Artie..."

Her eyes are knives into my soul. "No one will ever know of this, do you hear me, Irving? Not Leo, not Arthur, not even God." She drops the paper and crushes my collar in her iron fingers. "Breathe one word and I will throw you into the gutter." I try to pull away, but her grip is too powerful. "*Not one word.*"

Like chalk dust on a blackboard, Florence Archer's visit is erased from the world. But it's shadow lives on, hidden behind my sister's eyes. It's there watching Sammy gum his first bagel, or when he falls on his tush tottering across the linoleum. It's hidden there the first time he burbles "Mmaammaa" and when he pulls himself into his silent Bubbie's lap.

It's hidden there a year later, when the Spanish Flu takes Mama and the visiting doctor says the child is in danger.

It's there when, burning with fever, Sammy's little body jerks and twists, jerks and twists. It's there as Miriam stares at me across his crib and her face says, "Just like Artie." It's there hour after hour, until the jerking stops and Sammy is gone.

1928
MIRIAM

TWENTY-EIGHT

"*L* *uftmenschen.*"

"Beg pardon?" My doggy-eyed office boy hovers at my shoulder, looking down with me into Union Square.

"*Luftmenschen.* Dreamers. You never heard the word?"

His nasal voice snivels apology. "Mom and Pop avoid Yiddish at home. They want me to be American. What's all that fuss?"

"It's Union Square, what do you think? *Union* Squ...*Oy*. It's a labor rally." *Yutz*. If he weren't Harry Hoffman's second cousin once removed..."The garment cutters have gone out again. It's like magic. One *shnook* somewhere believes he's been mistreated and the whole industry must come to a halt."

"Huh." His blue eyes go flat with boredom.

"Leave the papers on the desk." He drops his delivery and wiggles out.

From workers like this Leo expects the Great Revolution? I press my cheek into the window for a better angle. Somewhere in that mass my *luftmensch* husband is carrying a banner inviting strikers to come "Join the Communist Party."

I'll find out tonight if he had any takers or if some bystander punched him in the nose.

I spritz myself a glass of seltzer. The whole thing gives me heart-burn. I'm employed by one of Leo's evil Capitalists, and no matter what my zealot husband says, it's been a good deal. Hoffman hired me back right after Sammy was born, promoted me to head bookkeeper and when he opened this 14th Street outlet, he put me in charge. Whenever Leo gets on his high horse about the Evil Bosses, I throw him Harry Hoffman. Of course, Leo never gives an inch.

"Remind me, Miriam, which one of you is getting rich off your fancy, clever bookkeeping, you or Harry Hoffman?"

To which I answered, "I got us a bigger flat with real furniture and a comfortable bed. We got decent clothing and plenty to eat. God willing, one of these days I'll have my own store and be as good an exploiter as Harry Hoffman."

Which is why I ignore the rally and return to my trade papers. Supervising inventory is an important part of the business, but book-keepers don't know from merchandise. Fortunately, the head buyer here is a *mensch*. My first week on the job, she walked me to the stock-room, pulled out two dresses, same style, different price.

"How do you tell quality from *drek*?" When I shrugged like an ignoramus, she turned the garments inside out. "Check how tight are the seams, look at the selvage, recognize the feel of good cotton on your fingers. Some manufacturers always deliver what is promised. Others show you one quality and deliver another." She eyed my bobbed hair, my drop-waist dress, my silk hose and strapped black pumps. "You got a body that can carry the latest trend, but you stock for everyone. A woman like me with a bust and hips would look like a hippopotamus in that knit."

I'm lost in *Women's Wear Daily*, when comes a tap, tap. The door creaks open and there stands my brother, all coy and smiley.

"You know, this place is bigger than our old Norfolk Street apartment."

Irving moved into his own place after Leo got home from prison, but he loves making fun of my office. Today I'm not in the mood for teasing.

"Shouldn't you be down there holding Leo's coat while he rants about the sins of the capitalist class?" I throw up my arms in pretend horror. "Unless you're gonna be a scab."

"Of course, I support the strike. But..." He drops into a chair, studying the toe of his boot. "I got a letter from Artie today."

The kidding's over. Ten years we've danced this dance, because right after I kicked Florence Archer down the stairs, Arthur got shipped to a rat hole called the Craig Colony for Epileptics five hundred miles away. I know full well that part of Irving blames me for that. But as far as I'm concerned, it was my milquetoast, never-make-anyone-mad brother who brought that eugenics witch to my door in the first place. At least he's managed to keep what happened locked in his mouth like I told him.

Lacing my fingers together, I lay my elbows on the desk. "So, tell me...what's he got to say?"

"It's what he doesn't say." Irving offers me the letter and my heart kerthumps. Instead of Artie's tight, tidy script mocking the idiocy of his minders, the scrawling tilts and twists like a toddler's cat scratches.

Irving's face drips with worry. "I got to go, Miri. You know those lousy doctors won't tell us what's really going on. If Artie's...if he's...He won't be able to defend himself, see? From whatever they want to do. If they know someone's paying attention, maybe...I don't know. I've got to go, that's all."

I swivel my chair around to think. Outside, the mob is getting more raucous. Through the open window, we hear "Arise ye prisoners of starvation."

"*Meshugeneh*s." I use the heel of my hand to slam down the window.

Irving grunts. "Must be Leo started that. He loves provoking the leadership."

"Look at you with all the latest gossip. Are you going to join the Communist Party also?"

"I have my own beliefs, Miri. Some things I agree with Leo, some things not."

"But you want to walk off the picket line in the middle of a strike. Isn't that high treason?"

Irving looks me right in the eye. "I've done it before."

We got plenty of past, my brother and me. And he's paid his own price for Florence Archer. One girl after another. Never a steady sweetheart, nothing permanent, never risking a child.

He stands. "Anyway, I wanted you should know. I'm catching the train to Buffalo in the morning."

"Irving, wait." My purse is locked in the bottom drawer of my desk. I pull out ten dollars and put it in his palm. "For you or for him, whoever needs it more."

He looks down at his hand and, surprise of surprises, he plunks a kiss on my cheek.

"I'll see you when I get back."

———

BY THE TIME I LEAVE WORK, THANK GOD UNION SQUARE IS EMPTY and I can catch the streetcar to Essex in peace. Irving was so tied in knots, he forgot—it's time again for the *yahrzeit* candles. Our tenth year. Mama and Sammy, both in January, five days apart. I grab a window seat and rattle down Second Avenue, watching the streets fly by.

Sammy would've been twelve, already studying for his bar mitzvah. Of course, Leo would have thrown a fit. *He should be reading Marx, not that religious propaganda.* We'd have had a big *megillah* battle, but I'd have won—some traditions demand to be observed.

"May God comfort you among the mourners of Jerusalem."

In his long black coat and yarmulke, the clerk at Schoengold's Judaica is solicitous. He ties the two candles up in brown paper. I should properly be buying three. Papa also died in January, but I'll be damned if I'll honor that bastard's memory. The commemoratives burn for twenty-six hours. Some things burn longer.

It's still light outside, balmy for January. My head's too full and walking's good for thinking. I stick the package under my arm and stroll Essex along the edge of Seward Park. A tribe of hooligans bumps me, howling, "Last one there is a rotten egg." Must be they're racing to the municipal playground. In winter, the place crawls with kids. I take a minute to lean on the fence and watch. Two girls shriek on the swings while a little *pitsela* on the slide chirps, "Catch me, Mama. Catch me." For a second, I think she's looking at me, then a blonde rushes to the bottom. "I'm here, sweetheart."

Feh. Enough. I'm done. A quick turn and I scoot off to Hester Street. Who needs this? A smart person doesn't crave what she can't have. No matter what Leo pretends, the world doesn't give us any breaks. Spend your life aching for the impossible, all you get is pain.

Half a block up Hester, I pass the darkened window of an empty store. I stop, conjuring the face of that red-haired Archer woman. "Stick it up your ass. There are things besides making babies." I'm ready to spit out more scorn, but I'm stopped short by the 'For Sale' sign covering the door. I step back, the better to see.

I've been on the lookout for a venue for months, ever since Leo made that crack about Hoffman getting rich off me, but even a shitty tenement that hasn't been renovated since Moses crossed the Red Sea takes a chunk of change.

This place is unusual, only two stories wedged onto a small lot between bigger buildings. But it's solid brick with a decent storefront. I press my nose to the glass and cup my hands around my eyes, the better to see inside. In the dim light, I make out a wooden floor and bare walls. My nose twitches. There's an odor—Brine? Vinegar? Oy—pickles. Even through the closed door, the place reeks of pickles.

"You're admiring the smell?" An old *yenta* steps out onto the stoop next door. "Five years I lived next to that stink pit. When the pickle guy moved out, I went to shul and said a prayer of thanks. The King of the Universe must have been deaf, because it's six months and the stench is just the same. The landlord whined he can't unload it, no matter how cheap." She waves in disgust. "*Schmegegge*, he's too lazy to clean it up himself."

Under the "For Sale" sign, it says "'Contact Feigenbaum Properties, Inc. 326 21st Street."

I comb my purse for a pencil.

TWENTY-NINE

The building is top of my mind the rest of the way home. Since the new job, I've been saving every week to an account. I already got a few hundred dollars, obviously not enough to buy outright, and bankers get cagey about lending to a woman. I'm so busy figuring how to work the angles, I don't notice the jabbering coming from inside my flat until my key has jiggled the lock and I walk in on four of Leo's "comrades" sprawled across my furniture. My *meshugeneh* husband has once again poached my parlor for a meeting hall.

"Leavenworth Prison taught me better than any sweatshop—America's autocrats will annihilate any who suggest they should share their bounty. That is the message we must deliver."

As always, Leo is consumed. However he was before, what happened in prison made it ten times more. I jam my hat on the coat tree and cross the room, only to have that slimy fox Myron Dickstein crane his head around me like I'm a cockroach.

"The strike committee takes the position that the union and the owners share common ground. When shops close the whole industry suffers."

"Owners have been duping workers with that argument since the invention of the wheel," Leo barks back.

Gasbags. As if their every word drips manna from heaven.

I kick the bedroom door shut and toss the Schoengold package to the dresser. It knocks over the framed photograph of Sammy looking up at me, his chubby finger twirling a piece of my hair. When Leo first saw it, he pressed it to his heart. "As God is my witness, I wanted to be here for you and the boy."

I thought that meant we were done with the union business. But soon, out came the Leavenworth stories. Weeks of isolation. Beatings. Starvation. Torture. Villainies, he insisted, that could not be ignored. The next thing I know, he's joined the Communist Worker's Party and we're right back where we started.

But not exactly.

His first night home. After. He was asleep. I tiptoed to the hall privy, propped one leg on the bowl and stuck a finger up my insides until I found the tab. A tug and, thuck, out it popped. The midwife called it a cervical cap. I wrapped it in bathroom paper and carried it to the kitchen sink where I washed away his seed. Leo never knew. Not that time or any time since.

From out in the parlor I hear, "Enough for today," the shuffling of feet, and the exodus. A knock, then Leo leans against the doorframe.

"I'm sorry, Miri. We needed a private place to plan our attack."

I'm on the edge of the bed, rolling down my hose. "Attack? Aren't you supposed to be opposed to war?"

"Oh, I'll do battle when the cause is just." He plunks down next to me. "But I am a confirmed pacificist at home." He bumps my shoulder. When I don't capitulate, he does it again.

I *potch* his arm. "You promised no more meetings in my house."

"This was urgent. The cowards of the National Board are planning to sabotage our caucus at the Chicago convention."

"Do me a favor, Leo, no welfare of the masses tonight. I've got other things on my mind."

"What a coincidence...so do I." He inches closer. "I'm negotiating a mutually acceptable surrender."

He drops an arm over my shoulder, nuzzling my neck and my insides quake. Leo. I bat his chest. Even when I want to pull my hair out, still he is Leo, big as a bear, smelling of sweat and fabric dust. His hand slips under my blouse. Another shudder runs through my middle. From the first time to now, it is always the same. I surrender to the pleasure of his touch. But, as we fall backwards onto the bed, my eyes hit the dresser, the package of *yahrzeits* and little Sammy's picture.

I put a hand up to stay him. "Wait." Surprised, he pulls back, giving me room to stand. "I'll be right back."

As I trot to the privy to prepare myself, my mind wanders back to that small brick building with a big, empty window.

THIRTY

J ake Feigenbaum, the do-nothing landlord, is an oily *zhlub* with a mustache and bad skin who leers goo-goo eyes until I snap, "I'm a missus, and I'm here about Hester Street." He goes crafty, rifling his files as if he has so many buildings, he can't remember what's for sale. When he quotes me a ridiculous price, I stand up to leave.

"Wait, wait," he puffs. "Wrong address." He rifles again, says the real amount.

I keep giving him the evil eye. "So? Are we going to inspect, or what?"

On plops his bowler and lickety split, we're at the building. Soon as the door opens, I cover my nose with a kerchief I brought special for the occasion.

"You gotta be kidding." I make as if to walk away.

"I know there's a little odor, but take a minute." Feigenbaum hems and haws. "I'll drop the price a couple hundred."

"Well..." I enter, but I keep with the kerchief as I size the place up.

The pickle guy has stripped it, lock, stock, and barrel, so empty my steps echo off the walls. Feigenbaum said it's fifty feet by thirty. I'll have to measure that myself. The floor's clean. The tin ceiling's still in one piece. When I give a knock, the walls sound solid. I stand in the middle, my face still covered.

This is just what I'd been looking for.

"There's stairs to the second floor off the back storeroom." Feigenbaum still plays the salesman.

"If it stinks like this up there, I'm out." But up we go.

The apartment's a palace. Two bedrooms, big closets, a kitchen with a gas-type stove, a parlor with windows looking right over Hester Street. I open every cabinet and every drawer, checking for rats and mice. Soon as I'm sure the place is clean, I go into a coughing fit. "I need fresh air."

Feigenbaum trails me to the street, where I lean against the wall like it's hard to breathe. The *yutz* pulls out a hanky, wiping his sweaty hands.

"I could maybe drop the price, say, another two hundred."

"It would cost that much just to fumigate," I manage to spit out, catching my breath. "Still...I got to admit, the size is right, and I like the location..."

Feigenbaum can't take his eyes off me as I glance back through the window, tapping my forefinger on my chin. I give it a full two minutes, before a huge sigh.

"It's a mess, but I'm a sucker for near the park. Drop another four hundred, I'll take the dump off your hands."

"You got a deal." He pumps my hand so hard I get an ache. We arrange to meet at his office to sign the papers and he toddles off, humming. I fold my arms and lean against the wall. Pickle-shmickle. A bottle of bleach, good lye soap and a little elbow grease, the place will smell like a perfume store.

THIRTY-ONE

A week later, Irving is back in my 14th Street office.

"After a fit, Artie woke up dreamy. It took a whole day before he came back to himself. This stinking Craig Colony...it's a work farm, all preachy that labor provides stability to these poor, chaotic souls. Truth is, soon as a 'poor, chaotic soul' is too far gone, they ship him off to an insane asylum. When this time comes, Miri, we'll have to find Artie someplace else." He kicks the edge of my desk. "It'll take money."

"Don't look at me. Every cent I have will go into the new store."

"You sure this is a smart move, Miri? Hester Street's already got a million pushcarts."

"Sure, with clothing piled on the sidewalk like garbage. My store will have inside fashions, like at Hoffman's. I'll have big shelves and long metal racks where the customers can slide things around to see. I'll build them a fitting booth for trying on. Then I'll hang come-and-get-it signs in the window, 'Big Sale' and 'Bargains Galore.' Stuff'll be marked down, but I'll sell it with class. You watch. I'm going to make a bundle. Of course," I make like it's all casual, "I'm gonna need a sales-man, you know, someone who's quick with his words to ooh and ah and make the ladies feel like Greta Garbo."

Irving's face opens into a smug smile. "I maybe know a guy like that."

"Yeah, I thought you might."

We enjoy the moment, understanding each other. He goes serious. "Doesn't all that class take dough?"

It's my turn to look smug. "I got a plan for that too."

HARRY HOFFMAN LOVES WATCHING THE CUSTOMERS GO THROUGH the revolving doors of his Grand Street Store. He's such a slight guy, you wouldn't take him for a *macher* except there's always a sharp crease in his classy suit and a white carnation in his lapel. He says he's setting an example for his employees. The truth is, he dresses to advertise his top-of-the-line menswear.

"Shouldn't you be minding my other store?" he kids when I walk in. "Or is there a problem?"

"The store is minding itself for the moment, and you know that with me in charge, you don't get any problems." Harry enjoys those who don't quake in his presence. I take a seat, smooth my skirt, and cross my legs at the ankles. "I'm here with a business proposition."

Boom, his smile is gone. Pleasantries are one thing, but business is business. It's why we get along. I pass him a sheet of ruled accountant paper with the facts and figures of Feigenbaum's building. He runs his fingers down the column and rocks back in his big leather chair.

"You're suggesting I buy this pittance?"

"No, Harry. I'm suggesting you make me a loan because I'm gonna buy that pittance and sell women's clothing."

His eyes narrow. "I sell women's clothing. Why should I lend you money to be my competition?"

"Oy, gimme a break. You sell everything from baby bonnets to men's underwear. A two-by-four dress shop on Hester Street wouldn't lay a glove on you. But, if you're smart, you can make good bucks from the interest on a loan." I lean forward. "You know me. This will happen. If you don't underwrite me, I'll find someone else, and he'll walk away with a steal."

He drums his fingers on his desk. If there's one thing Harry Hoffman hates, it's being beat out on a deal.

"Okay. Let's talk turkey."

FOUR WEEKS LATER, HAULING BROOMS, MOPS, BUCKETS, AND SCRUB brushes, I march into my new building, my brother Irving at my side.

"If only Artie could see this, Miri. You started with nothing, now look at you."

"It's stays nothing until it doesn't smell." I hand him a bucket. "The apartment. Don't come down 'til it's done."

"My boss two minutes and already a sweatshop." He nudges my shoulder and tromps upstairs as I push open the alley door. It's chilly, but with the front door also ajar, the air flow will help fumigate. I'm in my apron, sweeping and picturing the place crawling with customers, when in traipses my husband, a tool bag hanging off his arm.

"I told them at the union hall I had to go help my wife become a capitalist."

He's so cocky and proud of himself, I can't resist. "And they didn't denounce you as a traitor?"

Out comes his big Leo grin. "I assured them that, if you get more than one employee, I'll organize a union." He drops his tools and rubs his hands together. "So, where do we start?"

Twelve years we're married, I never knew Leo the garment cutter is also Leo the carpenter. He says it's the same idea only wood instead of fabric. Soon, instead of pickles, the place smells of sawdust and fresh wood. He brings volunteers from among his comrades. They do it all—sturdy shelves on all the walls, three rows of square display tables, wood and curtains for a fitting booth, and a gorgeous oak counter in the back where will sit my shiny new brass cash register. A few days later a workman hauls in two mannequins with a note attached. "Use these in your window. I'll get my money back faster. Harry."

Leo, busy shellacking the counter, takes one look and dubs the dummies Karla and Freida. "After Karl Marx and Friedrich Engels. So, when you're a rich tycoon, you'll remember where wealth really comes from."

The night before we open, I make a brisket and tzimmes, our first meal in the new apartment. Irving brings the gift of a bottle of schnapps, which Leo happily cracks open. He raises his glass.

"To my brilliant wife. May she be the first person in the world to get rich without exploiting the poor."

"*L'chaim.*" Irving tosses back his shot and they're off.

They toast pickles and Jake Feigenbaum's stupidity.

They toast the comrade carpenters.

They toast Karla and Freida.

They toast the lucky customers to come.

I don't go in for tippling, but they both insist this is a special occasion. With each of their shots, I take a sip. By the time Irving pours the end of the bottle, I'm feeling silly, so when Leo commands, I make the final toast, standing, glass in hand.

"To the future. At last, we know where we're going."

1933
MIRIAM

THIRTY-TWO

I rock slowly in front of the parlor window trying to catch a breeze. July on Hester Street reeks, even after the sun goes down. Once the shops close and the traffic eases, the women flood to their stoops and fire escapes to fan themselves and complain, an art at which the *yenta* next door is a master.

"For once in my life I had a little *gelt* to put into a bank account. Boom, the Crash comes, the bank's gone, and so is my money."

"*Der mensch tracht, un Gott lacht*," her neighbor intones. Man thinks, and God laughs.

Hah. The old hen got *that* right. I look out on the vacant windows and deserted streets where the Depression took hold a year after we opened. Half the shops on Hester Street went under. I managed to keep us going, but it's hardly the opulent future I had in mind. I glance at my lap. Of course, that wasn't our only surprise.

The infant's lips lock onto me and her sapphire eyes close as she suckles, just twelve hours old and already greedy.

"After seventeen years, not every night is Solomon and Sheba," I croaked to the midwife last night during a lull. "When he came in late and let me know what was wanting, I was too tired to run and get the thing. Besides, I figured who gets with child at thirty-eight?"

The woman stuffed a pillow under my knees and patted my hand. "Late life babies are God's gift." A fresh wave attacked my insides, so I couldn't tell her exactly what I thought about God's gifts.

The chair runners click against the floorboards. The baby curls deeper into my elbow. Her mouth releases, and a drop of milk trickles down her cheek. I catch it with a finger and bring it to my nose, then nuzzle her neck, the better to absorb her scent. Nothing on earth matches the smell of a new baby. My heart twists.

When it hit me, what had happened, I could've kicked myself. I'd sworn one dead child was enough. Soon as I could, I asked a woman who would know for a name, someone clean and safe. I walked with his address in my purse. Canal to Christie, Pike to Division, I strode the streets making myself remember the frightened vigils, the edgy caresses, jumping at every twitch, and, in the end, all alone with that keening grief. Forsyth, Rivington, Stanton, I couldn't stop moving. Against my will the other memories came. The needy push of his tiny fingers on my breast. The two-toothed smile, the arms raised in adoration, *Uppy, Mama*.

I turned to the Eldridge Street synagogue. For the first time in my adult life, I mounted the stairs to the women's gallery. Mama and I spent hours here. It was the only time I saw her relaxed, *kibbitzing* with the other mamas, their toddlers playing at their feet and their babies cooing in their arms.

Down at the bimah, the black-suited men in prayer shawls chanted over the Torah scroll. I never learned Hebrew, so the prayers were meaningless, but I closed my eyes, drifting to the soothing singsong. For some unknown reason, the rabbi switched into Yiddish. In language I could understand, he exalted the Holy One, Blessed be He, who consecrates all of creation with his bountiful perfection.

A sudden shaft of red-gold light flared through the stained-glass window to land at my feet. An ice-hot certainty shot through me. Whatever the evils of the past, this life inside me was unblemished, whole, perfect, unspoiled. The conviction flooded every bone and fiber in my being. I dropped my hands to cover my middle. This time, *this* time, I was safe.

She squirms. A gas smile swims over her face, then a grimace as she burps.

A knock at the bedroom door. "Miri?"

Leo tiptoes in and crouches down to brush a knuckle across his daughter's cheek. "My comrades tease I was proving we're still fruitful proletarians."

"What do you mean 'we'? I did all the work."

He runs his hand over my head. "For once I won't argue the point." I haven't seen his face this soft in years. "Miriam, I've been thinking..."

"Oy, I'm already in trouble."

"...about a name..."

"No lousy Marx or Engels. I forbid it."

"An interesting concept, but not my intention." He gets serious. "I know it's a long time ago, but Mendel Stern died protecting the *kinder*. He had no family to carry on his name. I was thinking it might bring our daughter luck if she honors him."

I recommence my rocking. By tradition, we commemorate our family's dead by using the first letter of their name for a new life. My parents were Yitzhak and Libke. One was a beast, the other was his prey. I will not saddle my daughter with that inheritance.

"You got an 'M' name in mind?"

Leo's eyes dance. "Well, Miriam's the best, but it's already taken."

Back and forth I rock. "A young woman came into the store the other day, very trendy, very modern. Her name was Michelle."

"Michelle...modern, for the future." Leo nods. "I like it." Suddenly his eyes fill. "Thank you, Miri, for granting me this. It has haunted me that I was locked away before I could give my son his name."

My jaw tightens. I clutch my husband's wrist. "Swear that this will be different, Leo. Swear it to me. This time, you'll be here."

His face takes on its Leavenworth look. He puts a hand on the baby's head. "Nothing in the world is more important to me than you and this child. I swear on my life, I will not repeat the mistakes of the past."

The mistakes of the past...I release his arm, realizing I must take a similar oath, but not in front of my husband.

———

A COUPLE OF DAYS LATER, LEO IS OFF AT WORK AND MICHELLE IS asleep in my arms. I call down to my brother to put up the "Closed" sign and come to the apartment. Irving dashes in, swathed in concern.

"You got a problem, Miri? You need something?"

"Have you written to Arthur yet?"

"Oh, that." He relaxes. "I've been busy. I promise, tonight."

"No. Do not write. What he doesn't know won't hurt him."

"What are you talking about?"

"Sit. I want to talk." I wait for him to pull up a chair. "Why aren't you married, Irving? You're thirty-three. I know you have girls. Why aren't you married?" His eyes skitter away. "You want I should say it for you? You hear the eugenics woman's curse and imagine an endless parade of Arthurs."

His head drops, acknowledging without words.

"Look." Michelle's tiny fists twitch inside the swaddling blanket. "Look at her. You're her uncle. Would you bequeath her the life you have? Should she live like you, like me, uncertain and afraid?"

He stares at me, eyes heavy with doubt.

"Papa was an evil bastard," I continue. "I hated his guts. But he understood what you and I refused to see—Arthur is a blight. His presence brings only pain. Well, no more. I will scour that pain out of my daughter's future."

"What are you talking about?"

"I'm erasing Arthur from Shelly's life. You are never to mention his name in her presence. My daughter is never to know he exists."

Irving's eyes go wide. "You want to banish him like Papa did? You would condemn him like that bastard?" He is red with outrage. "You've seen where he's been. I've described where he is. Can you imagine what will happen to him without us?"

"What you do for him is your own business. I'm not stopping you. But nothing of Arthur will enter this house."

"What about Leo?" he spits. "Leo asks after him all the time."

"We will tell Leo that Arthur is dead."

The chair falls over as he leaps up. "Never."

"Then get out." I point. "There's the door. Go ahead, leave."

Irving stares for a long time, taking my measure. His voice drops to a raspy whisper. "It's a sin, Miriam. This lie you are contemplating. It's a sin."

"What Arthur brought into our lives is a sin. Look what it did to Mama. Look what it's done to us. Enough is enough. It ends today." I raise my chin. "I'm doing like my husband. I'm putting away the past. My daughter will not walk through this world in fear."

1936-1938
IRV AND MIRIAM

THIRTY-THREE

IRV

The speaker points to a poster-sized photo—a dark-haired woman surrounded by grey rubble, clutching the corpse of her dead baby. I'm in the front row with Leo, who's the lead organizer for the Trade Union Relief for Spain Committee. The audience listens, rapt.

"Badajoz, August 1936, barely four weeks ago. More than fifteen hundred souls were marched into the bullring, women along with men. The machine guns roared for twelve hours. The next day the arena was four inches thick with dried blood. These reactionary army units were billeted in Morocco until Adolf Hitler provided planes to carry the barbarians back into Spain. General Franco uses those planes to rain murder down from the sky."

The guy is reporting about what he witnessed in Europe, where the Spanish generals use German planes and Italian artillery to massacre their own countrymen. The atrocity is on everyone's lips. How the Spanish people freely elected a Popular Front government with sincere intentions to ease the burdens on peasants and workers. How this so enraged the rich, the monarchists and the elite, they implored their fascist buddies for help. How the German Chancellor and Italian Prime Minister jumped at the chance to flex their muscles. How the arrogant Spanish generals expected a snap victory, but the citizens of Spain wage fierce, ferocious resistance.

The lecture is hideous and inspiring in equal measure. When Leo passes the hat, he rakes in a bundle. Afterward, there's no option but a strong drink, so he and I head to Cepulski's. He tosses back his first shot and immediately holds his arm up for a second.

"Take it easy, Leo."

"That woman in that photo, she could've been Miriam. And that little one in her arms..." He shakes his head. "I tell you, Irving, it's a terrible responsibility raising a daughter in a world that conspires to destroy children."

I reach across the table. "That slaughter is an ocean away. It's heinous, but it doesn't touch us."

"Are you deaf and blind? Adolf Hitler spews venom about Jews. That doesn't touch us? Italian fascists imprison Marxists. That doesn't touch us?" He bangs the table. "Everything touches us."

"You're only saying that because your idols in Moscow are rattling their sabers over Spain."

He glares at me. "The despots of Europe are testing what the world will tolerate. Those Russian 'idols' supply Spanish Loyalists with men and guns while the great democracies fall all over themselves running the other way."

"Of course, that's true." I sip my beer, gathering my courage to say what I've been holding back for months. "It's just that everyone knows the Party here takes marching orders from Moscow. It doesn't sit well." The beer is loosening my tongue. "I don't want to insult you, Leo but you got to admit, your comrades get ungodly self-righteous. Open your mouth with an unsanctioned opinion, you're denounced as a bourgeois capitalist collaborator."

I expect the usual violent justifications, but Leo is subdued.

"Do you remember a lifetime ago, when we were trying to unionize the Margolis shop?" he asks. "Mendel Stern, may he rest in peace, said

'Any association will be as good or as bad as we make it. But whatever we do in this life, we are better off doing it together.'" He sips thought-fully. "The Party might be flawed, but it's thanks to the flawed, imper-fect Party that men and women in every country are sending brigades to sustain the Spanish struggle. They know, as I do, that this may be our only chance to hold back the flood." His sigh is so big it almost sucks up all the air. "I would give my right arm to spare my child the future we witnessed tonight. My right arm, my right leg, and then some."

"Cash is probably more useful than your arms and legs. You brought in a bundle tonight."

"Only a capitalist thinks money is the answer to every issue." He stands, shoving back the chair. "I'd better get home. My wife will have my head for coming in so late."

THIRTY-FOUR

IRV

"Ma. Maamaa."

Lips compressed in concentration, four-year-old Shelly negotiates the steep stairs, one hand gripping the banister, the other clutching the neck of a dingy rubber doll. Once she's safely down, she flings herself forward, wrapping her arms around her mother's legs.

"Come. Come upstairs. I'm hungry."

My sister and I rush to unpack a delivery of rayon blouses so they can flatten straight before we open. Miriam brushes a hand over the child's wispy curls. "I'm working, *mamalleh*. Tell Papa to make you."

"Papa's sitting."

My sister's nostrils flare. Kneeling, she grips her daughter's arms. "You go right back upstairs and you tell your father that he has to feed you." She gives the child a tiny shake. "Tell him *loud*. *Make* him listen."

Shelly blinks. Her sharp little chin comes up. Like a good soldier, she about-faces and marches back up, her bare feet padding the floor with purpose.

Miriam rises. She gives the blouse she's holding a rough flap. "It's this way for months. Like he's in a fog. You talk, he doesn't listen. You ask, he doesn't hear." Left sleeve, right sleeve, she folds a perfect square and stacks it on the counter. "Never home. Disappearing half the night." Snatch, flap, straighten, place. "Now, a bump on a log doing nothing."

There's a tap at the front window. A customer is waving. It's ten o'clock and the door's still locked. I attend to business, but as the day progresses, nothing I do can stem the tide of my sister's irritation. "Irving, you paid for the Kaufman delivery without first checking the barrel. You should know by now all suppliers are thieves. You let Mrs. Cohen return that skirt? It's the Depression, idiot...Drop those receipts. How you do deposits, you'll put us in the poorhouse..."

By closing time, I've swallowed my anger fifty times over and I'll be damned if I feel like staying for Shabbos dinner, so I tell Miriam I'm in need of fresh air and I escape to the streets.

The chill air is bracing, as is the satisfying grind of my heels on the pavement as I pound into the park. The playground is empty but for one ragamuffin shivering cross-legged on the ground, his hat out for alms. I drop him a penny but turn up my collar as I pass the gang of tramps warming their hands over a garbage can fire.

God knows, these are terrible times. That's always in the air. Stores are empty and settlement house breadlines extend for blocks, but even the most destitute woman needs to put a rag over her body and Miriam always finds the cheapest wholesalers so we can undersell everyone else in the district.

Thoughts of the Depression lead me through the park toward the *Daily Forward* building, where Marx and Engels are still enshrined over the doorway. Since our economic collapse, plenty more people have become interested in what those guys have to say, but to me that building will forever be the place that led me to Arthur...Arthur who, thanks to Miriam, is once again an exile.

The day my sister announced her decision, I threw my things into a satchel and grabbed the first train back to Swansea, thinking, *If I tell him face to face, I can soften the foulness of this fresh betrayal.*

What a fool's errand. My brother was vaguely cheerful, never quite sure where he was or what was going on and clearly beyond comprehending my message. I realized with sickening irony that the only person genuinely horrified by Miriam's edict was me, so I turned around and came home.

It was late afternoon. I walked the long blocks from Pennsylvania Station to Hester Street. The store was closed, but the back lights were still on. Miriam was at the long counter, changing Michelle's diaper. Leo came down from the apartment. He wrapped Miriam from behind, resting his chin on her shoulder and reaching a hand to pet the baby's arm. Without taking her eyes from the infant, Miriam's head fell against Leo's chest, a smile on her face.

How often has my sister been allotted such moments? Etched in my soul is the expression on her face as she lifted Sammy's limp, cold, little body from the crib. I considered her lonely nights while Leo was in prison. And, of course, Papa. Through it all, she persevered, my life buoy, pulling me to safety in her wake. It was utterly beyond me to ruin her contentment now. I pushed open the door and went back to work.

Still, you got to wonder...what is it for Miriam, day in and day out, living with such a lie? Does Leo sense it? Is that why his gaze wanders off as if he's listening to words that aren't being said? I glance back to the Seward Park Library where I unburdened my soul to Nettie Bloom. Who does Miriam turn to in need? I shove my hands into my pockets and drop my head. When I agreed to keep my mouth shut, I became her accomplice. I may despise the lie, but I cannot abandon the liar.

By the time I get back, the store's locked so I go in the side entrance. I tilt my head with unease. Something's not right...then I catch it—no aroma. The smell of Shabbos dinner should be filling the building. I climb up, a bad feeling in my gut. Miriam is rigid at the parlor window, arms folded across her chest. At my footfall, she spins around.

"Did you know?" The fury in her voice skewers me to the wall.

"Know what?"

Her eyes narrow, evaluating my honesty. She raises her right arm, pointing down the hall.

"He's going to Spain. He's joining a….a…What does he call it? A brigade." She hollers in the direction of the bedroom. "Isn't that right, Mr. Hero of the People, Mr. Deserter of Children?"

Leo steps into the hall, closing Michelle's door behind him. "Shush, Miriam. You'll frighten the child."

"*I'll* frighten the child?" My sister's mouth twists. "You got a lot of nerve. *I'll* frighten our child."

Tall and grave, Leo walks into the room offering no apology against Miriam's onslaught.

"Leo, what's going on?"

His eyes never leave Miriam's face. "I've been trying to explain to my wife why I must go fight in Spain."

My jaw drops as the breath leaves my body. "What?"

"See." Miriam sneers, "Even your adoring lacky knows this is a disgrace."

"Miriam, do not put words in my mouth." I approach Leo calmly, putting my hand on his shoulder. "Please…I don't…Can you…"

The tension notches down a peg as he steps back to address me.

"Fascism is a plague, a black death. For months we've been saying that if Spain falls, all of Europe will go. We'd be next. Look around—their agents are already here. It's too late for the Jews in Germany. Once they've knocked America's door down, it will be too late for us."

The sudden whine of a police sirens screams down Essex. Miriam waits for the noise to pass.

"Fascism. Marxism. This-ism. That-ism. You always have an -ism, Leo." Her shaking hand points toward the floor. "Right here in this room, you swore to me. *Nothing and no one.* You promised…and I believed you. I let myself believe you."

"I'm going because of that oath. I'm going in fulfillment of that oath."

"Don't blow piss up my ass and call it rain. You're going so you can charge up a hill waving a giant red flag and an adoring legion will erect a statue in your honor. Leo Hirsch, Hero of the Masses."

Leo's face softens into sadness. "No, Miriam. Not for personal glory. I go to protect my family from that which would destroy us."

"The Depression isn't enough for you? You can't stay and protect your family from that?"

"You don't need me for that."

"I need you." She turns away, her voice barely audible. "I've always needed you. But you're never here."

"Miri." There are tears in Leo's eyes. "To the marrow of my being, I know that Spain is our last chance to save ourselves. Your strength is such a gift." He holds out his clenched fists. "This is my gift. I offer it in return."

Miriam straightens her shoulders and lifts her head.

"Look at you, so noble, so brave. We should put your picture in the *Forward*." Her voice is an iron rasp. "The Gallery of Vanished Husbands."

"Mama?"

The three of us jump as Michelle toddles in, rubbing her eyes. Leo leaps to get her, but Miriam blocks his path.

"The first time you did this, Artie persuaded me to forgive. I won't be a fool twice. If you walk out on us again, do not come back."

She scoops the child into her arms and strides out of the room.

THIRTY-FIVE

IRV

They're called the Abraham Lincoln Brigade. Leo writes that they'd arrived in France, crossed the Pyrenees and crept to Madrid. He reminds me, "Don't be concerned if you don't hear from me. Opportunities to write here are infrequent and posting is fitful." He ends begging me to tell Shelly that Papa loves her. I would love to honor his request, but Miriam would consider it treachery and my sister has had betrayal enough.

In February, the papers describe massive casualties as the Loyalists save Madrid from a fascist assault. I hold my breath until a letter arrives. For the first time in his life, Leo writes, he's fired a weapon. "Turns out, I'm a good shot. I close one eye and pretend I'm aiming at a sweatshop foreman." In April, he reassures me that he was in a different province when the German Luftwaffe bombed Guernica out of existence. Nor is he in Bilbao when it falls to Franco. In December, comes Teruel.

It's a dark February morning when the phone jars me awake. Blinking up at the white ceiling, I need a moment to orient myself.

21st Street, home, my apartment. The jingling rankles until I lift the receiver. A brusque voice, "Am I speaking with Irving Friedman?"

"Yes, that's me." I swing my legs to the floor.

It's urgent. Can I come? I say sure, of course. He gives instructions where. I rub the sleep from my eyes. Sitting on the edge of my bed, all I can think is I have to call Miriam that I'll be late into work.

———

LEO EXTENDS HIS LEG TO SHOW THE WHITE, PUCKERED SKIN. "SEE how the flesh grows back." He hobbles back to the hospital bed. In truth, the leg is held together with packing tape and string, but Leo's trying to keep it light.

This is my seventh visit in as many days. The Spanish fascists did a job on him all right, a regular job. Huge Leo, hearty Leo, immovable Leo. Grey streaks his hair and flesh hangs from his bones like a loose garment. They did a job all right. It is hard to look.

"Will she come?" His face is turned to shield how much it matters.

Maybe I should say yes, after the store closes. He'll fall asleep before it's an issue, because that's what he does, early, when the sun goes down. I could let him believe. But he's Leo. I put my hand on his arm. He nods, staring out the window at the pocket of sun he can see through a break in the buildings. A cough comes on, wet and rheumy. He bends over, waiting for the hacking to run its course.

When he can speak again, "She knows there's not a lot of time?"

I bite my lip. "Miriam is Miriam."

I don't leave until he's asleep. His comrades are covering his cost, the doctors who tend him. Not a big sacrifice. Along with the burns, his lungs have been destroyed by the heat and smoke. He doesn't have long.

THIRTY-SIX

MIRIAM

I'm bargaining with that little *chiseler* May Shaughnessy when Irving saunters in like he's doing me a favor by coming to work. She's fingering one of our best confirmation dresses, an organdy number with a fine silk sash.

"We don't sell on time," I tell her for the third time.

"I'm good for the money. Ain't you heard it's the Depression?"

"You bet it's the Depression. No one is good for the money."

She looks over to the corner. "It's for my Ada. See how nice she's playing with your little one."

I put my hand out for the dress. "We don't sell on time."

"What a gyp." She slams five bucks onto the counter and yanks her kid out the door.

"As if I don't know she owes every merchant for a hundred miles and never pays a dime." I tick open the register to start the day's receipts. "Where you been all day? It's closing time already."

He's at my elbow, his voice low. "Leo wants to see his family."

My hand catches on the zipper as I stuff bills into the bank bag. "No."

"Miri, there isn't any more time. He wants to say good-bye."

Teeth clenched, I give a single head shake just as Shelly cries, "Mama, it broke, it broke."

She has somehow managed to decapitate her doll. The three of us watch the round rubber head roll across the floor and disappear under the skirt rack.

I nudge Irving. "Do something useful for once." I bolt to hide in the back. I hear him sooth Shelly as he goes down searching on all fours and I slump against the wall.

Say good-bye, *again*? Once wasn't enough? He rips my heart out, and after a year, he wants to do it *again*? Months of 'When's Papa coming home?' Months of 'We're fine, you and me.' Months of alone, remembering, worrying. The anger rises, vomit-heavy. For himself, always only for himself. As if only *he* made sacrifices. As if only *his* passions mattered. Now he's dying, he wants us. Because he's dying. Leo's dying.

"Miriam?"

I jolt erect as Irving comes looking. His sad eyes plead. "He was your husband for twenty years."

"I was his wife for twenty years. He left me anyway."

"But out of love. As an act of love."

My brother is a gentle man. But he sees the world as a *man*.

"Love like that, I don't need." Wiping my eyes, I collect myself. "Shelly," I call to my daughter. "Come, *mamalleh*, get your toys. We're going upstairs to dinner."

THIRTY-SEVEN

IRV

A steady March drizzle turns 14th Street glassy grey. Men tug down their fedoras and women turn up the collars of their coats. The soft rain is no deterrent. Over the course of a couple of hours, Union Square fills. The horde overflows the fences, blocking traffic from 14th Street to 17th Street, both east and west of the square. A battalion of mounted police trot at the fringes, but the crowd is quiet. No one is here to demonstrate. They're here to mourn. The entire garment industry has assembled for Leo Hirsch's funeral.

A platform has been erected in the center lawn. From my vantage on the dais, I catch sight of people I haven't seen in decades. Amos Niedermeyer, the union employer where Leo and I met. Who knew he was still alive? And there's Rosa Delacosta, wider than she used to be, with her arms around Sophie Bowser's waist. A few feet away, Esther Mandelbaum, tears on her cheeks, holds hands with a guy I don't recognize. And, oh God, even Pincas Gutzman has come, greyed and shrunken, but in my mind's eye, still that gruff, barrel-chested bear of a skeptic. My eyes sweep over the throng, groping for a small, tawny woman with fiery grey eyes, but Nettie Bloom is nowhere to be seen.

I'm sorry. Even in her sadness, she'd have warmed to this, our people. Squint hard enough and they still look like the young, passionate campaigners who, led by Leo, helped transform an industry.

One by one, the union officials take the stage, lauding the bravery, the brilliance, the undying commitment of this great soul, a man who devoted himself to the betterment of workers' lives. I drop my eyes and bite my tongue, remember how Leo brayed about the spineless cowards of this Joint Committee who regularly sold out the workers by pandering to the industry bosses. If I were a braver man I might comment on this fact when I rise to accept their thanks, but it's pointless. Let the blustering orators have their day. Leo's true compatriots are the workers eddying and swirling through the Square, arguing, debating, challenging, and objecting as they wrangle their way toward a better future.

After the preachers and politicians have had their say, the pallbearers make their way to the vestibule of the funeral home. I take my place behind the black-draped coffin, the only member of the family present. A five-piece band appears, three trumpets, a trombone, and a bass drum. As we slow-walk the coffin up 14th Street to the waiting hearse, they forgo a dirge, beating out an anthem instead.

Arise, ye prisoners of starvation....

The crowd picks up the tune. It makes its way down the long column, circling the Square, from man to man, woman to woman.

Arise, ye wretched of the earth...

I brush an arm across my eyes. The world is such a diminished place now that Leo Hirsch has left it.

1947
IRV

THIRTY-EIGHT

IRV

A shaft of too bright sunlight attacks me through my bedroom window. The view to the East River is a gift as long as you close the curtains before going to sleep, which didn't happen. I throw an arm back to still the alarm without taking my face out of Shayna Weiss' ginger-colored hair, savoring the memory of how her neat pin curls became this frizzy mess last night.

She lifts one eyelid. "What time is it?"

"Time to get up."

"Mmmm." She rolls on her back, stretches, swings back to pat my face. "You're making my New York cases so much fun, Irv."

"We aim to please." I brush a finger to move the locks hiding her freckled cheek. "What poor *schnook* are you defending this trip?"

She sits up, pushing that bountiful hair off her face.

"Oh, our ever-vigilant FBI has uncovered a terrible threat. A U.S. postman has balked about signing this new loyalty oath. He might be a spy. Just imagine the damage the Russians could do if they got hold of someone's electric bill."

Shayna's a dish. We met a couple of months ago at an Abraham

Lincoln Brigade memorial. She's a brainy lawyer whose lover died in Spain. I was there to honor Leo. Ten years, a despicable war, more monstrosities than can be born, but some people stay in your heart forever. 'Fascism is a black death...It's too late for the Jews in Germany...' The things he taught me still abide.

Shayna swings to the floor and meanders to the table in search of a smoke then curses, "Damn it to hell."

I prop my head on my hand. "What?"

"It's getting worse." She holds up the headline in last night's paper, "Ten Suspected Communists in Hollywood Cited for Contempt." Balling up an empty cigarette pack, she flings it toward the waste-basket and misses. "You're lucky you never joined the Party, Irv. Me, too, for that matter."

"It never appealed." I toss off my blanket and retrieve the garbage. "But, so what? The FBI wouldn't want anything from me. I sell women's clothing."

"Oh, honey, don't be naïve. Anyone who ever suggested that our glorious nation might be a teensy-weensy bit imperfect has a target on his back, Subversive, Unamerican or an Enemy Agent. It's a brave new world, but they're still out for blood." She cinches her robe with a jerk. "I better get dressed. There's work to do."

We part on the street, but Shayna's words ride the crowded subway with me to work. A brave new world. It's true. Only two years since the war ended and nothing's the same. The faces on the subway, the news on the radio, the boulevards of Manhattan Island—all altered. I circle the park and dawdle at the corner, considering Hester Street. The pushcarts are gone, their noisy haggling and elbowing banished into warehouses by Mayor LaGuardia 'to keep the streets more sani-tary.' The curbside bundles of scraps for victory drives are no more, along with the guys in khaki uniforms out for a wild time before boarding a ship into God-knows-what. All done. All gone. The street is serene. Businessmen in double-breasted suits and wide floral ties stroll past our store, or window-shopping mamas flicking a glance to their prams to make sure their kids stay well-behaved. "Leave me be," their faces insist. "The chaos is over. I'm doing for myself. It's time to get my own."

Even our window display panders to the times. Soon as the war ended Miriam traded Freida's Rosie the Riveter overalls for a floral cotton dress. Three months ago, she swapped out the padded shoulders on Karla's business suit for a darted crepe jacket sloping into a dainty circle skit. So tame. So sweet. So feminine. Blech. I make a face at the window then, through the glass, I notice Miriam is already with a customer. Odd. We're not open yet. I shade my eyes against the reflection for a better view. Seeing who it is, I scoot in to help.

Sophie Bowser, now Sophie Landau, dabs at her eyes with a crumpled tissue. "The Red Cross found someone. My sister Golda's girl...in a camp in Cyprus. It took two years because the child didn't know my married name. Mama, Papa, my sisters, their husbands, the *kinder*." Her swollen eyes well. "She's the only one left."

Miriam grasps Sophie's hand. "It's the wrong season for summer clothes, but I'll see what I have left in back."

I doff my coat. "Come sit while you wait."

Here's more of our brave new world, the mist of death swirling down our streets like the Tenth Plague of Egypt, pausing at an apartment here, a tenement there, this side street, that house. No Biblical prophet warned us this time. No Moses came to say, "Mark your doors to ward off the Angel of Death." This time the He didn't pass us by. This time He took the first born, the last born, and everyone inbetween.

Miriam drags out a carton left over from the summer. Guessing at a size, they fill two bags with cotton frocks, halter tops, bibbed shorts, lightweight knit sweaters—anything good for a mild climate. Sophie reaches for her wallet, but Miriam waves her off.

"You're doing me a favor. I can use the extra space in back."

As Sophie shambles to the sidewalk, I nudge Miriam in the ribs. "That's how you taught me to make a profit?"

She bats my shoulder. "Clean this up so we can open."

My sister's features have thickened and strands of grey lighten her hair, but she's as crusty as ever. Disposing of the empty carton in the stock room, I think back to Shayna and wonder if Miriam ever acknowledges that everything Leo predicted came to pass. The entry bell jingles, jingles again. Good. We're getting busy. It's too early for such deep reflections.

It's been like this since the war ended. People feel free to *want* again and we're raking the money in hand over fist. Around three o'clock, I finally get to step outside for a cigarette. School's let out and gangs of kids spill into the park. Through puffs of smoke, I catch sight of my niece, Michelle, surrounded by her tribe, looking oh so grownup with her proud new pageboy haircut, saddle shoes, and bobby sox. At thirteen, she's already taller than Miriam.

God, she used to be such a little pumpkin, playing with the register keys while I rang up sales. The day she turned ten, she pushed my hand away. "It's my turn."

Miriam scoffed until Shelly showed she could make change faster than I could, so we propped her up on a stool and gave her a go. The customers smiled at this kid taking cash and *schmoozing*, "Oh, what a cute dress. Don't you want a pretty scarf to go with it?" or "Can we offer you a blouse to go with that skirt?"

But it was no joke. Shelly always made the sale.

I watch the gaggle of them circling up at the corner, exchanging words. Suddenly Shelly swivels on her heel and peels off, blonde and rangy, every inch Leo's daughter. But the scowl she's wearing is pure Miriam.

"Where's Ma?"

"Shelly?" I flick away my butt and follow her through the door.

My sister looks up from her desk. "Yes?"

Shelly dumps her books on the counter and stomps to the back desk. "Was my father a Communist?"

Miriam's brows lurch up. "What are you talking about?"

"Everyone was just bragging about their fathers in the war, so I said Leo died in Spain. That catty Ruthie Schneiderman honked 'My Bubby Gussie said only Commies fought in Spain.' I called her a liar and she sneered 'You don't even know your own father was a stinking Red.' All the kids hooted." Shelly's eyes burn. "Is that true? Was Leo really a Commie?"

"Can we please stop with the name-calling?" I snap, my morning with Shayna playing out right before my eyes. "This 'commie' and 'stinking Red' stuff is crap."

"Quiet." Miriam hisses as a customer wanders in. "After work."

I attend to the patron while Shelly takes the counter, still looking sour. We're all strictly business until I turn over the "Closed" sign at six o'clock.

"Upstairs," Miriam commands.

The living room is dim in the late afternoon dusk. I flick on a lamp and lean against the wall. Miriam points to the couch. Shelly's pout is gone but the corner of her mouth twitches. Miriam sits next to her, arrow straight, hands folded in her lap.

"You're old enough to ask, you're old enough to know. Yes, your father was in the Communist Party. But from now on, if anyone asks, you answer a big fat, no."

"Miri," I step forward.

Her hand shoots out to shush me.

Shelly's eyes are two blue saucers. "Did he...did he do bad things?"

"Bad things?" Miriam snorts. "He abandoned you. I would call that a bad thing."

"But he wasn't a spy or an enemy agent..."

"Feh. That's nonsense. He was a garment cutter who organized unions. He dreamed of the day the Workers would rise up in Revolution, overthrow the big, bad capitalists, and live happily ever after."

Shelly's forehead wrinkles. "What's so terrible about that?"

"Nothing," I pipe in, earning an annoyed squint from my niece while she stares into her mama's face.

"What's terrible is he deserted us in the middle of the Depression. What's terrible is his Workers of the World meant more to him than you. You're getting to be a woman so you need to understand this. When a man gets married, he makes a promise. Family first. It's a sacred oath. Leo broke that promise." Miriam sucks a deep breath. "Listen, *shaindeleh*, I'm gonna treat you like a grownup, okay?"

An adamant nod from Shelly.

"These days it's very risky to know a Communist, like how your friends hooted you today. This is the mess your father bestowed on us. But it means we got to be clever. So, here's what you're gonna do." She reaches for Shelly's hand. "Anyone needles you about Leo, you say he was a stupid guy who got duped by those nasty Communists and he's dead because of their rotten tricks." She gives the hand a little shake. "I admit it's not exactly kosher—but it's the smart thing to do. Understand?"

Shelly's blue eyes shimmer with vigilance. "I get it, Ma."

"Good girl." Miriam reaches around Shelly with a hug.

Every muscle in my body is quivering. "Carnage. Extermination. Annihilation." The words explode out of me. "Leo foretold it all."

Miriam is on her feet. "Shelly, go to your room."

"You stay right here, Shelly. Your mother just fed you a mouthful of hooey."

"Do like I tell you, *shaindeleh*," Miriam instructs.

Shelly looks from her mother to me and back again, then trots down the hall to her bedroom.

I'm so nauseous, I must swallow down bile before I can speak. "Who are you, Miriam? What have you turned into? Twenty years... two children... You loved Leo. I know you did." I drop to a whisper. "You don't even light a *yahrzeit* for him. And now this... this wickedness."

Tears flush my sister's eyes, but her jaw is clenched.

"I'm showing Shelly how to protect herself."

"By teaching her to lie?" It comes out a shout.

"Ugh, Irving. Stop being such a *schmoe*. Shelly understands exactly why I'm telling her this."

"You bet she does. And it's ugly." I run a hand through my hair, struggling to gather my wits. "You're betraying Leo like you've betrayed Arthur all these years."

Miriam bares her teeth. "Watch your mouth," she growls, eyes shooting to the hallway.

For a heartbeat I'm sucked into her panic. It only makes me madder. "Do you honestly believe soiling Leo's memory is good for his daughter?"

"It's better than being hectored by her friends. The world has changed, Irving. It's dangerous to have a Party member in the family."

"We have to fight such injustice. It's the same kind of lie that sent Leo to Leavenworth."

"If he'd kept his mouth shut, he wouldn't have gone in Leavenworth."

The room shudders with fresh rage and Miriam's old, old pain.

"You leave my mother alone." Shelly stomps her foot from the hallway, eyes blazing. Occupied with our shouting, we didn't hear her leave her room. She marches to Miriam's side. "Stop yelling at her, Uncle Irving."

One hand goes to my heart, the other reaches out. "Oh, darling, I'm not mad. I just want you to understand what your father stood for."

"Ma just told me everything I need to know." She spears me with the fury of an angry child.

In the face of such icy zeal, my shoulders sag. Further argument is pointless. Clearly, nothing will pry her from her mother's rancor tonight. I traipse to the door but pause with my fingers on the handle.

"If you ever want to hear a different story about your family, I'm here to tell it."

Hester Street is empty. I ignore the red light as I cross Essex and turn toward the subway. The vacant park is black and gloomy and my heels echo on the sidewalk.

1962-1963
IRV AND SHELLY

THIRTY-NINE

Brooklyn Heights, Winter

SHELLY

Howie has a chest like a rug. His beard comes in so thick I make him shave before bed. With his horn-rimmed glasses and business suit, you wouldn't think he's strong, but his body is a rock. When I tell him I can't believe he can sit at a desk all day and keep his body like that, he makes like a circus strong man. "It's the lingering effects of Basic Training."

These days, Howie works until nine, ten o'clock. "Paying my dues," he calls it. I call it an investment. If he makes partner, we'll get it back in spades. I watch TV and wait up for him. Sometimes he comes in hungry, but not for food. Tuesday is a skip dinner night. Afterwards, we're quiet, him sweaty and tasting of salt, me with my head on his chest, running my hands over the coarse black hairs. He shifts under me, the click-swoosh of his match makes my nose curl.

"My mother wants to come for dinner."

My head snaps up. "Again?"

He reaches for his glasses. They give him his lawyer's face. "Come on, Shell, she's all alone."

"My mother didn't clutch this hard when she was dying." Snatching his smoke, I suck deep. "At least, make her quit going at me about grandchildren."

"She just can't fathom why we're waiting."

"Tell her we can't afford it." I stamp out the butt. "Tell her we want to buy a house."

He runs his hand over his face. "You know how she is."

"I'm not starting a family in a one bedroom in Brooklyn because you're scared of your pushy mother, Howie. But, as long you brought it up..." I reach under the bed to where I stash Sunday's real estate section. "I circled some primo properties."

"Shelly." He sighs, turns on the bed lamp and takes a pen from the nightstand, inspecting the newspaper. Scritch, scratch, big Xs. "Greenwich and New Canaan are restricted. No Jews. Fairfield or Stamford... maybe someday." He tosses the paper to the floor. "Tell me again why it has to be Connecticut. Why not New Jersey or the Island?"

"Jersey is for *shlubs* and Long Island is the sticks. Connecticut has class. And with all those rich *shiksehs*, I could open a really upscale dress shop. You know, high-end inventory and designer originals. It just takes having the starting capital."

"Well, don't look at me," he huffs. "*You're* the one who stopped working to take care of *your* mother." His feet hit the floor. "It's late. I need some dinner." And he's out the door.

I swivel onto my back, throwing an arm over my eyes. Ma never missed a trick. She warned me...*He's smart. He's got a future. But you'll have to push.*

A pot hits the floor in the kitchen. My eyes slam open. He's probably trying to figure out how to reheat the chicken soup. All right, fine. I throw back the covers and stick on my slippers. Men. Doctors, lawyers, Indian chiefs. But they can't find their way to the bathroom without a woman to show them the way.

FORTY

IRV

This high up, I can't hear street noise, only the click-click of an adding machine.

"Your profits are down, nothing drastic, but steady." Harry works out of an old rent-controlled apartment, but he owns a fancy condo in Miami. Not for nothing he's an accountant.

"You know, Irving, with your sister gone, maybe you should start thinking retirement. It's a lot to manage alone. You're no spring chicken my friend."

"Thank you for that new and startling information. Now tell me, please, if I'm going to die a pauper."

We review the accounts receivable, quarterly taxes, profit and loss sheet. It's not wonderful. I tell him to cut my salary three percent and pump it back to the store.

"You don't need an accountant, you need a miracle worker." He helps me into my coat and puts his hand on my shoulder. "Want my advice? Go find a rich widow."

Outside, a cold wind blows up Houston Street. It's still early. I button up and stroll across to the East River. Gas fumes off the highway mix with the stench from the water. Cranes haul containers from a merchant ship docked over in the Brooklyn yards. Everything gets imported nowadays, shirts, dresses, coats, all cheap from Japan. Keep this up, they're gonna put me out of business.

I amble back, Delancey to Rivington, right past the tenement where we lived with Papa. You'd think the dump would rot, but brick is brick. Only the garbage in the street changes—and me. A gust of cold air chills my bones. I shiver. Enough with ghosts. I'm alive and I have a business to run.

HESTER STREET'S STILL QUIET WHEN I ROLL UP TO THE GATE. I PUT my hard-boiled eggs in the back fridge and bump up the thermostat, to hell with the cost. Miriam always kept the heating bills down, but I get cold all day alone, especially after closing, when I struggle over the paperwork at which I am still so inept. I remember to move the "Help Wanted" sign from the corner to front and center in the display window. Employment agencies charge an arm and a leg, and I don't feel like paying for a classified. Harry proposed I save a bundle on rent by moving into the upstairs apartment. I shudder. Haven't I got enough ghosts without taking one for a roommate?

I squeeze down the narrow aisles, twisting around the tables of sweaters, blouses, and shirts, past the round skirt racks Miriam was so proud of when we first opened. There's so much stuff. Day by day the place looks a little messier, a little less appealing. I see it. I know it. But all by myself, I can't fix it.

I'm huffing and puffing hauling a carton from the back storeroom, when the bell tinkles and in comes Mrs. Jimenez, dragging her youngest, who must be seven. I brush off my hands. This is the part I'm good at.

"Let me guess." I point at the child. "First communion time, right? Children's dresses are right over here."

Of course, Mrs. Jimenez has to examine every piece with a tsk tsk

tsk. She takes the one I showed her first, a white organdy with puff sleeves and white velvet sash. She holds it up close to her face. "There's a spot."

I was counting how long it would take her this time. Still, I walk the dress to the window as if I'm really checking.

"Just a dark thread."

"Nah, it's damaged." She goes as if to put it back on the rack, and stops. "Drop it ten, I buy it."

"I'll take off one and throw in a pair of party socks."

She gives me the evil eye, but she accepts. The bell tinkles on their way out.

I understand this woman. I understand all the women who amble the neighborhood these days, the Puerto Ricans, the Jamaicans, the Chinese. They know the world can rip them to shreds, so they got big teeth to bite first. Miriam had those teeth. My niece Shelly is equally fortified.

I slit open the carton and shake out Christmas blouses in red or green satin remembering how Shelly always got sulky about the holiday specials. Miriam offered she could have anything she wanted, but Shelly pouted that it would be fake because Jews don't have Christmas.

"We have Hanukah," Miriam soothed.

Shelly snooted up her nose. "Hanukah stinks." It was an omen. These days she thinks the whole neighborhood stinks.

Again, the door jingles. "Hey, Mr. Friedman."

The sun is beaming right through the window, so I shade my eyes to see 'til the silhouette steps out of the glare. Marisol Ramos from up the block. These modern teenagers with their dangly earrings and black eyeliner usually want something my store hasn't got. Still, I put on my best welcome smile.

"Hi there, young lady. What can I do for you?"

She gives back my smile twice over, pointing back at the window.

"I'm here about your sign—the help you wanted."

I'm so surprised that I drop my matte knife. Marisol bends for it.

"I know, I know, you're thinking, like, she's that naughty little *chica* who used to mess up my stuff with her dirty hands, right? But look." She wiggles her fingers in the air. "I wear nail polish now."

I run a hand over my face to cover my smile. I know the girl's people. Valeria, the mama, is a garment worker no less, and the shop steward for her local. She talks union with me whenever she comes in. Marisol's always been a good girl, sharp as a tack. I doubt I can use her, but hey, I started working younger than her.

"Come have a chat."

She follows me to the office alcove and plops into a chair. I fold my arms across my chest.

"Tell me, Miss Ramos, why do you want to work at my store?"

She takes such a deep breath her earrings jangle. "First thing about me, I'm great with fashion. I know all the styles from *Seventeen* and *Ingénue*." She glances around the shop. "Mami's been saying you could use someone like that since Mrs. Hirsch passed."

Hoo hah. Second time I bite my lip not to smile. Seems I'm gonna get an earful of neighborhood gossip.

"Then I thought, you know, the *madres* know me, so they'd buy off me to be nice. I'd be an asset, right? That's the word in school, an asset. Also, you wouldn't have to pay me too much, being I'd kinda be a...whatchamacallit...an apprentice. I type and I'm studying book-keeping—"

"Bookkeeping?"

"Oh, yeah. I got an A. I'm a math dynamite."

The desk in the corner is piled with receipts and invoices that need to be entered, not to mention a couple of letters to suppliers that I've been putting off because my hunting and pecking takes forever. This little charmer is starting to sound interesting.

"Your mama won't start fuming that you're working and not studying?"

Out comes the huge sigh. "Papi just got laid off." The black eyes are suddenly not nearly so young. "I'm the oldest, you know? I gotta take care of us."

A shiver goes down my spine. I'm on the stoop at Rivington, looking at another pair of dark eyes. *I'll take care of us.*

The kid is still going. "I'm done with class by two fifteen. I would race right over..."

You quit school, I'll cut off your schmeckle.

"Mr. Friedman?"

I point a finger at the girl. "No job should interfere with your education."

She lifts her gold cross necklace to her lips. "Swear to God, Mr. Friedman."

"Come after school. You can start tomorrow."

FORTY-ONE

SHELLY

Tradition says if you cut onions in front of an open window your eyes won't sting. It never worked for me. The tears are brimming when Ida stomps into the kitchen, ka-thunk, ka-thunk, ka-thunk, her cane like a pile driver on the linoleum. It's been a year since she broke her ankle and I don't believe for one second that she needs that cane.

"They're too big." She shoves her thick finger into the onions. "You gotta chop smaller for latkes."

Dinner with my mother-in-law...the favorite part of my week.

She stops to pass gas on her way to her prune juice. "God curses me that I can't push it out without help."

"Ida, why don't you go relax in the living room?"

"At the rate you're going, we'll be dead before we eat."

"Howie."

In like a shot, he takes her arm. "Come sit down, Mom. I'll put the TV on."

"Why's so late? It's not like she's got any children to take care of."

She's at full scowl by the time I put the food out, but it doesn't stop her from dropping five latkes next to the roast chicken on her plate. "So, what's the story with Shelly and work?" She slathers on the sour cream. "Is she going back?"

"Hello, Ida. I'm right here."

"Pardon me, your majesty." She gobbles a forkful. "So, what about it?"

"I've told you. I'm taking a little time."

"A week is a little time. Five months is retirement." Ida gives me a cold appraisal. "You're in okay shape but you're twenty-nine. You're making such a tragedy about your mother dying, have a baby to carry on her name."

I kick Howie under the table.

"You know, Mom," he slabs a chunk of white meat onto his plate, "Miriam wasn't as gung-ho about grandkids. She always said there's a lot more to life than children."

"There, that's the problem right there." Ida points her fork at him, "Your wife wasn't well-brought up—a mother more interested in business than babies, a commie father and a bachelor uncle who, frankly, I'm betting is a *fagele* with the boys. No wonder she's messed up."

My fork hits the plate. "Ida."

Her face goes wide with innocence. "What? Relax. I'm only saying what's good for you. This sitting around thing, it's not natural. A marriage is not complete without a baby. My son agrees with me. Go ahead, you tell her, Howard."

"Yes." I turn to my keeping-his-mouth-shut, staying-out-of-the-line-of-fire husband. "You tell me, Howard."

He puts down his knife and fork, dabs his mouth with his napkin and covers his mother's hand with his own. "Shelly and I appreciate your concern, Mom. We will really think about what you said."

Ida pulls her hand away and slaps his wrist. "Okay, fine, make a joke." She makes a boardinghouse reach for the latke platter. "But God won't let you hold your breath forever."

The next morning Howie leaves for work with Ida's nastiness still soiling the air. I sip my coffee and watch his back disappear up the street, my solid family man, my up-and-coming lawyer, my good provider. He doesn't walk like a spineless *putz*.

I light up a Newport and idly thumb *The Brooklyn Eagle*, our local weekly, automatically checking the ads. Pretty sparse, mostly local shops. Now, that's plain stupid. With the holidays coming up soon, the smart move is to hit up the stores with big advertising budgets. I should know. I learned from the best.

Paunchy Sonny DelCecco, E.J. Korvettes' Marketing Director, guzzled a sloppy corned beef sandwich through the whole interview. I was twenty-one, fresh out of college. Didn't matter. He knew talent when he saw it and hired me on the spot. The guy nearly bust a gut when I gave notice last year, but a sentimental Italian with four kids wasn't going to argue about my dying mother. I go back to the window, staring at the empty sidewalk. The cigarette smoke eddies like fog through the yellow sunlight.

It was sunny that day, too. A hot summer Sunday. Ma couldn't make it too far by then, so we took a bench at the nearby church and she amused herself checking out the hoity-toity parishioners.

"Oy, a woman that *zoftig* should not be wearing horizontal stripes. Let me tell you, that little number is a fortune at Saks. My knock-off costs less than half and fits twice as good." Suddenly, out of nowhere, tears welled out of her tough old eyes. "*Gut in Himmel*, how's my brother gonna pick inventory? And, God help us, Irving with money..."

Her face wilted into apology. "You understand, *mamalleh*? Ordinarily the store would go to you, but, after all these years, it just wouldn't be right. You'll inherit the building. It's mortgage free, worth ten times the business. His rent will cover the taxes...unless he drives the store into the ground. Ach, Michelle, promise you'll keep an eye on it, yes?"

I squeezed her hand, "I'll try, Ma. It'll be okay."

"No, it's not okay. But it's all I can do."

A silver-haired docent passed by, leading a gaggle of gawking tourists. "Notice how the setting lends this glorious neighborhood landmark an air of graceful calm."

"You mean graceful money," Ma huffed. She was sick, but she was still salty. Her eyes clouded up again. "Opiate of the masses. That's what Leo always said...Religion is the opiate of the masses. Remember how he wouldn't say Kaddish for Mendel Stern?"

This was new, this drifting. It started with the chemotherapy. Something will ring a bell and she's off, spewing stories I've never heard before. She'd always been so tightlipped, I feel a tad guilty, like sneaking into someone's private diary. But not guilty enough not to take advantage.

"So, I guess Leo wouldn't go to shul. Anti-religion and all."

"Your father was a stubborn man. 'A man must stand by his beliefs.' That's almost the first thing he said to me. My brother told me I'd met my match in him."

"Uncle Irving said that?"

Those dim eyes suddenly popped into focus. She flicked her fingers, "No, no, I meant someone else." She turned acid. "What did that advice get me? Desertion. Betrayal. You know who paid the price for Leo's perfect world? I paid the price. You paid the price." She grabbed my hand, growling, "Men's promises are made of dust. Never wait for a man to do for you," crushing so hard my fingers turned white. "Swear to me...if you want something, you'll go get it yourself. If you don't do it, no one else will."

My chest heaves with a nameless ache. I buried her with that lecture ringing in my ears.

I go back to the table and idly flip through the paper.

LOCAL EVENTS CALENDAR—ADELPHI ALUMNI TO MEET.
DRIVE TO BEAUTIFY BROOKLYN STREETS.
SEASONAL DINNERS FOR THE UNDERPRIVILEGED. BEGINNER
BRIDGE CLASS, 10:00 AM WEDNESDAY, GRACE EPISCOPAL CHURCH.

Grace Church. That was the place. That's where I was with Ma. I drop into my chair, re-read the note. Bridge. That's the ticket—a card table, hors d'oeuvres on a crystal platter, icy cocktails in martini glasses. Could there be anything further from Hester Street? I run my hand over the page. Beginner Bridge. People in Connecticut play bridge. That's how we move up. That's where we want to go.

Forty-Two

IRV

The 7:40 express is mostly empty. Early Saturday morning, most people are coming into Manhattan, not leaving it. I take a seat next to the window, pull out the book of cross-word puzzles and get three words by the time we zip past the poor *schnooks* standing on the local platforms in Queens. It used to be only rich people took the Long Island Railroad. Now, half the Lower East Side lives out there. The puzzle's half done when I get off at Great Neck. I stuff it in my coat pocket for the ride home and walk past the business district. It's cold, especially in the shadows. I tighten my scarf as I head to the residential streets with their picket fences, wide lawns, and their bare winter trees. Not a sound, except once in a while a bird.

"Good mornin', Mr. Friedman." Oria is on duty. She's here three years, working weekends when her husband can stay home with her kids.

"Hello, young lady, how are you this fine morning?"

She pulls her sweater tighter around her yellow uniform. "The sun's okay, but I wouldn't mind a little heat along with it. My oldest wants to go to a university upstate. I tell her she better get used to the cold all right." She glances down at the sheet on her desk. "He's in his room today, Mr. Friedman. The new doctor is with him."

Arthur's chair is under the window and the sun is shining on his placid face, almost unlined, even now. A short fat kid in a white coat stands at the foot of the bed, reading the chart.

"Hi Artie." I put a hand on my brother's arm.

Not a smile. Not a blink. It's okay. I'm not expecting anything. He hasn't spoken a word in years.

"How do you do?" I offer out a hand. "Irving Friedman here."

"Right. The brother." The kid's nod sends his glasses sliding down his nose. "I'm Doctor Abramowitz." I get a split-second smile. "You brought him to us in..." He's leafing through the record like it's maybe the Talmud.

"Nineteen forty-eight."

"Right, right, right." He flips the pages. "I'm here to get familiar with the case...Epilepsy...brain damage...perpetual care..."

I hang my coat over the bed. "Doctor, you want to know about my brother, you can ask me."

All I get is the top of his shiny head. "I'm just looking for the accurate medical data." He's flipping pages and I feel like flipping my middle finger.

"Hey, I'm standing right here, sonny. What do you want to know?"

He jumps like I hit him. "Oh, oh, I just...."

I knock myself as an idiot. Offending this little *pisher* won't help anything. "You'll excuse me, Doctor. I missed my coffee this morning."

He's at the chart again. Apparently, he can't think if he's not reading. "He was in state institutions...Oh, Jesus...the Craig Colony?" His brows go up and he looks me in the eye. Even this *schlemiel* knows the story.

"'Til I had money to get him out."

He clears his throat. "If it's any comfort, Mr. Friedman, if he was this deteriorated, he'd probably stop noticing."

"So I've been told."

"YOU ARE A FOOL." MIRIAM WAS GRATING POTATOES. HER ARM swung so fast I thought she was gonna take off her knuckles. "You're finally making money and you're going to throw it away on a living corpse? Artie would *plotz*. He was a realist."

"You're a realist. Artie was a realist. Between the two of you I have all the reality I can stand."

"I won't contribute. Not one cent. I have a child."

"No one is asking you for anything, Miri. This is on me."

DR. *SCHMEGEGGE* IS BACK AT THE CHART. "FUNNY, I WOULDN'T expect him to have lingered long in this condition." He lifts his lips in what's supposed to be a reassuring smile. "You come from good genes, Mr. Friedman."

"Thank you for your opinion."

Oria hands me a letter on my way out. The management wants to inform us that they are raising the rates. Again. They apologize, but it's necessitated by the increased cost of living. They're holding it to three percent. They hope it doesn't cause any inconvenience. I stuff the thing into my pocket as I walk out the door. How nice of them to be concerned.

It's late afternoon by the time I trudge the grey concrete ramp and cross Penn Station to pick up the #1 train at 34th Street. I make it to the florist at 86th and Broadway a bit before he closes, put together a bouquet with his last dregs, and head down the hill to the fancy apartment building at the corner of Riverside Drive.

"What do you think?" I show my prize to Jose, the doorman.

He winks, "Mrs. Shapiro's a sucker for irises."

Life's such a crapshoot. There's no telling where people are going to end up.

I couldn't believe my eyes last year when Esther Mandelbaum came strolling into the store. I wasn't sure it was her, with her neat bouffant hair and jeweled glass frames, nothing like the spindly girl squinting over a typewriter in our *fakakta* basement. Turns out, after Margolis closed, Esther got a job typing in the union office, married a labor lawyer and moved to the Upper West Side. The lawyer passed away a year ago. She was down in the neighborhood buying a bar mitzvah suit for her grandson. We ended up going to Little Italy for dinner.

"Let's see," she said as she served up the antipasto, "Rosa married a baker from the Bronx. They have a shop on Arthur Avenue that makes the best cannolis in New York. She certainly looks like she eats enough of them." Esther's eyes twinkle. "She's chairwoman of the Democratic Party precinct up there, so God help the Republicans. And Sophie Bowser Landau moved to Detroit in fifty-one. Her husband was with the UAW. And, of course, everyone knows about Nettie Bloom."

"Of course."

"How's your sister? I don't remember her at Leo's funeral." Esther reached for my plate to spoon me the spaghetti. "Now there was a true radical. Not many men his age went to fight in Spain."

"Miriam never forgave him. Her daughter was only four."

Esther's suspended her fork over the food. "Yeah. It's really hard when two people see the world so differently."

I felt a stab of gratitude. There aren't many left who remember what I remember. When we separated on the sidewalk, I made sure to get her phone number. And here I am, such a regular, even the doormen know my name.

Waiting with the door open, Esther offers her cheek for a peck and takes my coat. The living room couch is plush and comfortable. The smell of roasting meat drifts in from the kitchen. I float for a second in the glow of the room, but I pull myself straight when she hands me a glass of schnapps. The liquor makes a satisfying burn in the back of my throat.

"I went to see Artie today."

Esther holds her sherry glass with both hands, takes one tiny sip, studying the hazel liquid.

"Don't you think it's time Shelly knows? This is ridiculous. We're not in the *shtetl* anymore."

I hold out my glass, and she pours me a second. "An oath is an oath. I wouldn't have told you, but after Miriam went, I needed someone else to know. Suppose something happens to me?"

There's a ding from the kitchen. Esther stands. "The roast is done."

I follow her to the table. After dinner, we clear the dishes. She washes. I dry. When the drainer's empty, I lay the damp towel on a hook. I put my hand on her shoulder and follow her into the bedroom, two old friends taking a little pleasure at the end of a long day.

It's way after midnight when I dress quietly so as not to wake her. I'm alone walking the wide, dark blocks to the subway, except for the doormen who survey the street from the safety of their lighted hall-ways. I get lucky when a train rolls into the subway station as I come through the turnstile. The only other passenger is a drunk, curled asleep across the bench. I sit at the opposite end, cross my arms, stretch out my legs and doze 'til my stop.

My apartment is quiet as a tomb. The super must've pumped up the steam, because the air is dense and heavy. I don't bother with the lights. I just toss my coat across the couch and go stand at my window, looking out at the city asleep in the velvet black night.

FORTY-THREE

SHELLY

The brass handle on the church door is frigid. I yank twice, but it's tight as a drum. Damn. The newspaper definitely said Wednesday. I turn a circle but there's not a soul to be seen in the grey, dank morning. Give up and go home? I tighten my coat against the chill. Maybe I'm missing something. I trot back to the corner. Ah, there, a half-open door on the side street, hidden behind a bush. I quick march down the block and into the dark corridor, but when I reach the end of the hall, I startle to a stop.

The painting is maybe seven feet high. A shrouded woman, mouth gaping in a black scream, reaches to receive Jesus' hacked and bloodied carcass as it slides off the cross.

"Gruesome, isn't it?"

I turn to the voice behind me and swing from the hideous to the sublime. The guy is a Greek god. I don't know which god, but it has to be one, because this man is literally breathtaking—cobalt blue eyes, cleft chin, chiseled nose, tanned, with enough sandy-blond hair for a Brylcreem commercial.

"Uh..." I stutter, stumped for any words adequate to the situation.

His voice drops to a stage whisper, "The thing's a bequest from a rich patron, so don't tell anyone I said that." He offers his hand in greeting. "Skip Putnam. You look kind of lost. Can I help?"

I get myself together enough to pull out the *Eagle*. "Would you have any idea where they're hiding this bridge class?"

"Piece of cake." His smile is exactly what that face deserves. "Just follow me. I'm the instructor."

Oh, this is gonna be fun, I think as Skip Putnam leads me around the corner to a large event room guarded by an elderly secretary distributing registration forms. I allow myself one final glance as he glides away, then get down to business, giving my information, pinning on a nametag, and stepping back to suss out the room. It's exactly what I imagined—oak rafters, stained glass windows, a damask tablecloth with a silver tea service. I sneak a peek at the back of a saucer as I pour myself a cup. Royal Albert. Well, of course.

The crowd, all female—it's a workday, after all—chats in polite little circles. I sip my tea, counting Bergdorf dresses, Saks skirts, even a couple of minks. There's something in the way they're standing...I tuck in my tummy and pull up tighter. I could be Donna Reed or Doris Day, all chipper and suburban, except that the "Saperstein" glued to my chest feels like a flashing neon light.

A button-nosed blonde with a shoulder-length flip glances my way, by accident or on purpose, I can't tell. She telegraphs an inviting smile. I stroll in her direction just as Skip Putnam claps his hands for everyone to find a seat. The blonde, tagged "Diane Morrissey," waves for me to join her table.

During Skip's five-minutes-to-greet-each-other, Diane introduces her pals Joan and Linda. The 'Three Musketeers' are celebrating their kids finally starting kindergarten, "Thank you, God."

"How about you, Shelly? Kids in school?" Diane asks.

I go into my song and dance...the draft, waiting so I could put Howie through law school. They deliver so many oohs and ahs you'd think no woman ever held a job before.

Diane is almost offended. "That husband of yours better appreciate you."

"Oh, trust me, I make sure he does." They snicker and I settle back with the Good Housekeeping Seal of Approval.

Skip Putnam strolls to the podium. He's really young, maybe twenty-three or twenty-four. I would've picked it up before, but age is the last thing you think about when you first set eyes on Skip Putnam.

"Forget cards," Joan whispers, not quite softly enough, "I'd come just to ogle."

The flicker across Skip's face is almost imperceptible. He rests his elegant hands on the podium.

"A word of warning before we start. This game is addictive. At Yale, I spent more time at the bridge table than at the library and, look at me now, a pathetic hustler with no future and no ambition." He bows his head in mock sorrow and waits for the room's objections to die away before rallying with, "Just don't say I didn't warn you," and signals the secretary to pass around his mimeographed instruction sheets.

I turn to my table. "Do you know anything about this kid?"

Diane cracks the cellophane on a deck of Tally-Hos. "Rich as bejesus. Daddy's on the church board. That's how we got the class." The cards slurp as she begins to shuffle. "Shall we give this game a try?"

More complicated than hearts, more challenging than canasta—this is not a game for dummies. By the end of the first class, we've barely scratched the surface.

"Let's make this a foursome next week," Diane says as the crew comes to empty ashtrays and fold up chairs.

"Delighted." I give my warmest smile then stroll away with the right light wave. I'm at the exit, pulling on my gloves and swimming in satisfaction, when Skip Putnam ambles down the hall, buttoning a black cashmere coat so creamy Korvettes couldn't stock it even in Better Men's.

"Mrs. Saperstein, I'm so glad you found your way. I think you have a knack for playing the game."

"And you have a knack for teaching the game."

I bask in his twinkle as he pushes the door open, where a gust of frigid air hits us full on before swirling up toward the deep charcoal clouds overhead. We scurry up toward Hicks Street, bending hard against the wind. Another blast catches us at Joralemon and the sky opens in a roaring downpour.

"This is terrible," Skip shouts. "Want to get in somewhere and wait it out?"

I nod and we jump into a Greek diner on the corner. The windows are fogged and the air steamy from the smell of wet wool. Over the clang of the dishes and shuffling of feet, the hostess shouts names off a waiting list. Once we're settled in a booth, Skip leans back, his wet hair dangling over one eye. Our waitress, Shirley according to the stitching on her uniform, gawks as she leaves us coffee and menus. I can feel every woman in the room doing the same, and I can't resist a little preen.

Skip extends a pack of Kents across the table. "I'm glad you enjoyed the class, Mrs. Saperstein." He runs his hand over his hair and, aw, the cute cowlick disappears. "I was pretty nervous."

I snake out a smoke and lean in for him to light me up. "Shelly, please. And you can relax. You charmed our pants off. Tell me, did you really spend all of college playing cards, or was it just a good opening line?"

"It *was* a good line, wasn't it?" His cobalt eyes disappear behind the rim of his coffee mug. "Kind of true, though."

Shirley pops back, pad and pencil in hand. Skip orders a burger, fries, and a coke.

"You want it deluxe for an extra dollar fifty?"

He's studying the menu. "Can I keep it plain?"

"You can get it any way you want, honey." She winks as she sidles away.

"So...no interest in school?" I ask when we're alone again.

"Yale was..." He waves his hand. "Inevitable. Fourth generation. Father to son...that kind of thing."

"Where I came from, nothing about college was inevitable."

"Where might that be?"

"Oh, far, far away...at least six subway stops." I hope he'll let the joke lie, but his head's cocked, waiting. "I grew up on Hester Street."

"That's downtown Manhattan, right? How did you make your way here?"

"I did what a million other people did, worked my way through CCNY, in my mother's store as it happens. I graduated. I got a job. Worked harder. Along the way, I got married." I hold out my arms. "Voila."

"I'm impressed. I'm sitting here with a self-made woman."

Flicking the cigarette ash with my thumb, "You have to be, when nothing is...inevitable. You know. Mother to daughter. Second generation...that kind of thing."

Skip leans back, checking me out for real. Shirley comes over, my tuna sandwich in one hand, his coke in the other, and his burger platter balanced on her forearm. I spread a napkin over my lap and pick up my sandwich.

"So, what did you *not* study when you were *not* studying at Yale?"

Skip is slapping the back of the ketchup bottle. "Bowing to the demands of tradition, I graduated *not* studying economics." A huge red dollop slops onto his burger. "Darn."

"A subject not of your heart's desire?"

"Hardly." He scowls at the mess on his plate, lays on lettuce, tomato and bun, and works on picking the thing up without dripping all over himself.

I munch an inch of my tuna sandwich, musing on that grotesque painting in the church hallway. "Art history. If I'd had the luxury of not supporting myself, I'd have majored in art history."

Skip drops his burger and stares. "Seriously...art history?"

"You think a girl from Hester Street can't enjoy art?"

"No, no...it's just such a coincidence. I wanted to paint. That's what I would have done if I'd had the chance."

Looking at his hundred-dollar coat and million-dollar face, I'm tempted to ask how he couldn't have anything in the world he wanted. "Why did you not have the chance?"

Skip is wiping burger drippings off his fingers. "That's a long, dull story."

I point to the torrents of sleet still battering our window, "I'm not going anywhere."

"Really?"

I prop my chin on my palm. "Really."

He's quiet, swirling a French fry through a hill of ketchup. "Dad's a major collector. I grew up with Pollack, Mondrian, even a small Picasso. When I said I wanted to go to art school instead of college, he was quite cool. He took my little canvasses to Clement Greenberg... yeah, the Clement Greenberg who probably wrote your textbook. Greenberg's no fool. He suggested I demonstrated a 'sweet aptitude,' which Dad deemed damning with faint praise. 'Prepare yourself for the family business or consider your future without my financial support.'" Skip pops the French fry into his mouth. "And that was the end of that."

"Hunh." I look out through the rain-splattered glass. "*Luftmensch*."

"I beg your pardon?"

"*Luftmensch*. It means Dreamer. My mother used it as a curse whenever I threatened to do something...oh, something that seemed impractical, something that was...abstract. Mama would suck herself up to her full five-foot-one and point her finger like a gun. 'No more *luftmenschen* in my family. You want support for college, you study what makes a living.'"

"Didn't your dad have any say in the matter?"

"My father died when I was four."

"Oh, Sorry. The war?"

I tilt my head, evaluating. Does Leo make me unsavory or exotic? Given what the kid just told me, I take a chance.

"He died in the Spanish Civil War."

Skip's jaw drops. "Wow. Was your father a Red?"

I mime looking around dramatically, and lean forward, a finger over my lips. "Shhh. It's my family's great secret. We don't talk about it."

Skip puts a hand over his mouth. "My lips are sealed."

I sit back. "So, what about you. You said your dad wanted you in the family business and here you are, out teaching cards. Are you from a tribe of gamblers?"

"The bridge class is a charity thing for the church. Our business is real estate—Putnam, Burnham and Pike. We're plastered on half the new building sites in Manhattan. You're looking at the junior-est of executives, the rookie who needs to prove his right to the exalted name he bears."

"And how do you do that?"

Skip's laugh is grim. "Haven't the vaguest. Got any ideas?"

It hits me like a punch in the gut. Blood pumps my ears and my vision clouds. The idea's crazy. But it's perfect. I'm afraid he's going to see so I dive into my purse for another cigarette, mumbling, "Excuse me, I'm looking for a light."

BY THE TIME I GET HOME, I'M ON FIRE. I SPEND THE AFTERNOON with a yellow legal pad, jotting notes so I don't lose anything. When Howie calls to say he'll be home early for dinner, I'm flummoxed. Dinner? I scrounge up a jar of Ragu and a box of spaghetti. The minute Howie walks through the door the words tumble faster than I can corral them.

"Whoa, whoa." He hangs his coat in the closet, brushing a piece of lint off the sleeve. "Slow down. I'm not following."

"What's not to follow? I want to sell my building and use the profit to finance our house in Connecticut."

He trails me into the kitchen and I give him the whole day, from bridge—"You went into a church...a *church* for God's sake?"—to the diner, to discovering I'm in the presence of real estate royalty. Howie listens, chin down, arms folded across his chest. When I stop for air, he weighs in.

"It's an arresting premise, Shell, but I'm afraid there are serious obstacles. First—" Up comes his forefinger. "Why would a firm like Putnam, Burnham and Pike, who are, by the way, among the biggest players in luxury real estate in this city...why would PB and P soil their pearly-white hands on the rat infested Lower East Side? That's number one. Number two, even if you could convince this poor *schnook* to buy your little two-by-four building, it would hardly bring in enough cash to buy your way into your fantasy Connecticut. And three, you're ignoring the fact that your only living relative earns his living in that building."

I smack the top of the jar against the countertop to pop the seal. "Is being a wet blanket a law school graduation requirement or just your personal preference?"

He does the single eye-brow lift. "May I remind you that wet blankets are very useful in putting out fires?"

I dump the sauce in a pan, flick on the flame. "Don't treat me like an idiot, Howie. And do me the courtesy of hearing me out."

With a go-ahead wave of his hand, he goes back into listening position. I take a deep breath and start again.

"Just before Ma got sick, she mentioned that the old *gonif* who owns the buildings on either side of the store approached her looking to sell. She was actually considering it until...well..." I brush that out of my way. "As far as I know, those buildings are still on the market. Do you see where this take us? It's not just my itty-bitty little store that's in play. It's three adjacent properties—half a city block. That's what I want to pitch to Putnam Junior."

Howie chews his lip. I have the satisfaction of ten seconds of his absolute silence.

"I'll grant you this—a parcel that big definitely changes the equation, but your store is still only one small third of the package. I don't get how that changes your profit structure."

"That's because you're a scaremongering lawyer, not a visionary marketer." Either he doesn't notice the dig or he lets it pass. "There are actually a couple of ways to play this. We could buy the other two buildings ourselves, and sell them at a profit as part of the package…I know, I know…" I raise a hand. "Too risky and we don't have the capital. I agree. There's another, safer way—the middleman. What Ma in the garment business used called the Jobber. We broker each piece of the sale, getting a big, fat commission every step—finder's fee, broker's fee, your charges for the legal work…we might consider asking for a piece of the final development project, once that's designed. Add that to the cash from selling the store…" I beam, "We have our down payment and then some. Maybe even enough to buy outright."

"Hmm…maybe." He walks into the living room, pulls off his tie and rolls up his sleeves. "But I still don't see Putnam, Burnham and Pike coming to the Lower East Side." He snaps his fingers. "Unless…"

"What…what…unless what?"

He points at me. "Seward Park Co-op."

"The big housing project? What has that got to do with this?"

Howie glances into the kitchen. "Your water's boiling over. Go rescue your spaghetti and I'll explain."

And, as we dive into my pathetic excuse for an evening meal, Howie educates me on new changes in federal housing regulations, construction financing in blighted neighborhoods, and the predatory New York real estate market. After months of bickering annoyance, I'm reminded why I married this shrewd hunk of a guy.

When he's done, I light up a smoke and take a minute, eyes half-closed, seeing a split-level ranch with a bay window, the "Three Musketeers" noshing canapes and jealously admiring the new Danish Modern décor. From out of my fog, I hear Howie cluck, "There's still the matter of your uncle."

My eyes snap open. "What about Uncle Irving?"

"He's your tenant and that store is his bread and butter."

I tap my cigarette at the ashtray. Ten years of marriage has taught me—redirect, refocus, reroute. "I guess I never told you this, but Ma was convinced Irving couldn't handle that business on his own."

"Actually, she wasn't off the mark. I had a meeting with Harry, the accountant, as part of my executor work. He mentioned that Irving was in trouble. Apparently, the store's not doing so well."

"See, Howie? That's exactly what I expected. That's why selling now is such a good idea. My uncle walks away with pride, not as a failure who drove a thriving business into the ground."

"But what's he supposed to do for income?"

"Come on, the guy is in his sixties. I'm sure he's made plans. Ma did." When Howie looks skeptical, I throw in, as if it hadn't just occurred to me, "Besides, I assumed we would send some of the proceeds his way, you know, contribute to his nest egg. After all this time, he deserves a little bonus." I get up and walk around to massage the rigid muscles of his neck. "That's more than fair, don't you think?"

"Maybe...maybe." Howie runs his hands over tired eyes and his head drops back against me.

"We'll be doing Irving a huge favor. Trust me. My uncle's going to thank us in the end."

FORTY-FOUR

IRV

The showroom door's been broken so long it's cut a groove in the concrete floor and the windows are black with centuries of fabric dust, but Manny Zuckerman owns the best knock-off shop in the business. Every year, after the Press Week shows, he goes to Saks and Bergdorf's to get their hottest items for his pattern guy, Abe, who opens them up, stitch by stitch, and figures how to make them 95% cheaper. We came to Zuckerman's three, four times a year so Miriam could pick the inventory.

"Irv, good to see you," Manny calls over the steady click-whirr from the machines behind the factory door. He puts a hand on my shoulder. "My condolences about Miriam."

"With what I know about picking inventory, I figured I'd better get some ideas about the Spring Line. I know it's early, but you got anything to show?"

"Sure. I'll tell the girls to bring it out. But it's good you came by anyway. I was gonna call you." He walks me into his cubicle where the clatter fades to a dull hum. "I wanted you to be the first to know, we're closing up shop after the summer season."

My heart goes kerplop and I feel my stomach drop.

"You're kidding. What happened?"

"You want some coffee, a bagel?" He yells back to the girls to bring out the spring samples, and he pours me a java. "It's a lot of things. The boys don't care about the business. And with these cheap imports, it's getting harder to make a living. Did you know Feinstein's went under? Who needs the *tsorris*? This way at least I'll get a little time with the grandkids."

"Pardon my French, but that's bullshit. You'll be bored to death. And that Japanese stuff is crap."

"Yeah, but it's cheap crap." He wipes a spot of cream cheese off his mouth. "I been forty years in this racket. Enough is enough." Someone knocks on the glass. "Here's the girl. Have you seen this new style from England called mod? They got something called a mini skirt."

Preview over, I stop in the lobby to pull on my gloves. Outside the double glass doors, hand-trucks jump the curb as racks of product roll from factory to showroom and back again. Sales reps stand mid-street, thumbing their order books. Car horns toot the double-parked delivery vans. It's the Garment District running at full tilt. I step into the fray, watching my shoes tick the concrete as I traipse east. Manny's been in business as long as me. Next year, he'll be just another one of my ghosts. The sign will come off the door, the loft will get rented and, pouf, a lifetime gone like you never existed.

"Move it, buddy." A beefy asshole shoves me against the wall as he pushes past. *Schmuck*. I turn to give him hell, then, whoa, something's up. A mob has flooded 37th, surging toward Seventh Avenue. I'm nervous there's a fire or something, so I pull myself up a set of stairs for a look-see.

No, it's not a panic. The guys in the crowd are scrambling to tie signs around their necks as they walk. "ON STRIKE. THE NEW YORK TIMES." "LOCKED OUT BY THE NEW YORK MIRROR." "ON STRIKE. THE WORLD TELEGRAM & SON." I slap my forehead. Of course, the big newspaper strike. The whole city's been spooked about it for days. The printers must be having a rally at the *Times* Building. Hah. Without a newspaper, how would I have known?

I elbow my way through the mob to Seventh Avenue. Jesus. No wonder I got shmooshed. The picket line's enormous. Mounted police strut around, nudging the strikers onto the sidewalk. Well, at least these cops aren't swinging billy clubs. The light goes red and I'm trapped at the corner. Shorty me can't see, so, like a kid, I pull myself up onto the base of a streetlamp.

Mostly men. Well, sure, lead print forms take muscles. For us it was girls, young, beautiful girls, dressed in their best black coats, with yellow sashes pinned across their chests. These guys are wearing knit caps or earmuffs, but those women marched in *hats*. Broad-brimmed hats. Feathered hats. Plumed hats. And underneath, faces of iron. I drop back down to the sidewalk, eyes burning at the memory.

Next to me, a young blonde taps her foot. "Come on, come on. I have to work." Behind her, a guy with a goatee and silk ascot is snarling, "Luddites. Damned fools and Luddites." He shakes his fist. "Morons, idiots, and Luddites." Blondie elbows herself away and the rest us of give this *nudnik* room, but he doesn't stop.

"Three years of writing. Six weeks of rehearsals. Brooks Atkinson came, the *Times* lead critic himself. I'd have had a rave." His face is getting redder and redder. "I wrote a masterpiece and no one is going to read about it." He shoves past me, hollering. "The joke's on you, assholes. Those computers are coming. You are the carrion of history."

The light turns green. Even through the intersection, Ascot shouts, "Cretins, imbeciles, and Luddites."

In my day, a *schmuck* like that would have lost his teeth for cursing a picket line. Sure enough, a bruiser in a wool cap and pea coat, steps forward.

"What'd you call us?" Ascot shuts his trap, but the bruiser keeps coming. "You got a complaint, buster?"

A mounted cop clomps over. "Move it along. Come on, move it."

Brawny throws Ascot a finger before circling back to his buddies. Batting his arms against the cold, he asks, "What the hell's a Luddite?"

How many meetings? How many lectures, speeches, classes? Some things stay with you forever. I can't resist.

"Pardon my two cents, but in olden days, Luddites believed factories were destroying their livelihood, so they set out to wreck all the machines."

Brawny pokes one of his buddies. "Makes sense to me." They snicker.

The light changes again. I have to either duck under the barricade to join or get out of the way of traffic. I offer a handshake.

"Best of luck, gentlemen. Up the Union."

Brawny cups my palm in his bear paw. "Thanks, brother." His calloused hands are like leather, probably from hauling rolls of newsprint to the presses. Not all that different from rolling bolts of cloth down a fifteen-foot cutting table. Nowadays my hands are doughy soft, but once upon a time I was a workingman, too. The picket line moves forward. I walk down the subway stairs, hearing an echo of women's voices raised in protest as I descend into the dark.

FORTY-FIVE

SHELLY

Diane's grumpy. "Holiday shopping's such a mess. I can't find any sales."

"You think that's bad?" Linda keeps arranging and rearranging her cards. "My Uncle Wally's funeral was last week. There was no way to post the death notice so the chapel was practically deserted. Poor Aunt Olive was distraught."

They're up in arms about this printer's strike. I've been too consumed working out the details of my plan to spare it any thought.

Joan's fingers rustle a crystal bowl of mixed nuts. "Edward says the union guy, Bertram Parks, belongs in jail. That's what Edward says."

"Hmm?" I'm tracking Skip out of the corner of my eye. My partner, Diane, took the bid so, once I lay out my cards, I'll be free to leave the table. When I see him amble over to the refreshments, I push my chair back. "Coffee time." I stroll to the cornucopia of sugar-dusted snowballs, holiday toffee, and gingerbread men wearing red and green sprinkles. Skip is examining a perfect, round butterball.

"Look at this masterpiece." He pops it into his mouth. "How's a guy supposed to retain his manly physique?"

I smooth the skirt over my flat tummy. "Hard work and exercise."

"Are we talking push-ups or squats?"

"Jumping through hoops." I retort and earn his wry smile.

Using a pair of tiny silver tongs, I reach for a saccharine tablet. "Seriously, though, I have to say, I've been thinking about you."

"Pleasant thoughts, I hope." His eyes hint more than a joke.

I release the tablet into my cup. "Remember when we had lunch, you mentioned you're in the market for a project? I may have what you're looking for."

"You're ruminating on a tidbit I mentioned weeks ago?"

"What can I say?" My spoon tinkles my porcelain teacup. "You made a big impression. Oh…" I point to Diane who's waving me back. "I'm being summoned. Let's do lunch after class. I'll tell you all about it." I saunter back to the table before he can say no.

Diane is sweeping up the cards. "I think you should have taken the bid. You'd have pulled in more tricks."

I toss a glance back to where Skip is staring after me.

"I'll do better next round."

We're in the same booth by the window only this time it's sunny. From the way he's holding back, it's clear Skip can't decide if he's being seduced or scammed.

I reach across to tap his hand. "I promise, this won't hurt a bit."

He gives me the stink-eye, but loosens up as I spread open a map of lower Manhattan I bought special for the occasion.

"See there?" I point my newly manicured red fingernail to the patch of green at the corner of Essex Street and East Broadway. "That's Seward Park. Very historic. Home to the United States' first municipal playground."

"Is this about those squats and pushups?" Skip is still working to find his footing. I let it pass.

"Just a few weeks ago, this map went out of date. Those streets at the north end of the park, Pitt, Attorney, Ridge, and the rest, have been trimmed away to make room for Seward Park Co-op, four towers —over eight hundred middle-class units, applauded as a blessing that will reinvigorate the whole district. You might have heard something about it."

"I'm in the business, remember, Shelly?" Skip's voice is tinged with annoyance.

"Of course." I remind myself that it rankles Skip to be treated like an ornament. "See where Hester Street goes into Essex? That's where I grew up, two doors in from the corner. My mother bought the building for a song thirty-five years ago. Her store is still there, directly across the park from those gorgeous, beautiful, pristine new high-rises."

"Well, I'm sure that's nice for your store, but..."

"Oh, Skip, honey." I grab his arm. "The store is chicken feed. I came to you because I've stumbled into a real estate development dream." I point him back to the map. "The building to my left corners Essex, a great commercial spot heavy with foot-traffic. The building to my right is a decrepit doublewide tenement. The three lots together take up half the block. The guy who owns the other two, Jake Feigenbaum, is an old lecher who used to pinch my tush while trying to make it with my mother. He's in his eighties and desperate to sell so he can move to Miami Beach and die ogling young girls in bikinis."

Skip is hooked enough to snicker.

"I visited the old wolf and batted my baby-blues. He ended up agreeing that if I could close a sale easy, no fuss or muss, he'd give me a rock-bottom price. Consider this—" I lay my palm over the map. Please God, let me put Howie's lessons to good use. "The Feds and the City are bending over backward to attract private developers into urban renewal. Loans, subsidies, tax breaks. They changed the zoning to make it easier to build mixed-use residential/commercial spaces for middle-income renters. And here I am, with options on a huge swath of property across the park from the most attractive new real estate in the whole district. The possibilities are enormous. Think of it—mixed use residential/commercial space privately owned but subsidized with public money. It's a pot of jam."

In the silence, the sunlight plays over Skip's chiseled face, all trace of playfulness gone. He retrieves a pack of cigarettes from his pocket and lights up, letting the smoke float into the bright glass of the window.

"You know, Shelly, no matter what it looks like, I'm not a fool. Putnam, Burnham and Pike make their millions from luxury residential and high-end commercial properties. Cleaning up the slums for the poor, oppressed masses? They'd laugh me all the way to the unemployment line."

"Only until they go into decline, because, like it or not, urban renewal is where the money is. Look, Skip, you sat right in this booth and told me your future depends on bringing home something exotic, something brand new. I'm taking you at your word. This is a prize, wrapped up in a Christmas ribbon, just waiting to be plucked. And, just for the record, I've never considered you a fool." I wait until I see him believe me. "Don't just take my word for it. Come look it over and you be the judge. I mean, what have you got to lose? I'm okay company, right?"

The blue-eyed twinkle makes a momentary appearance. "You're fabulous company."

It's so genuine, I'm taken off guard and blush.

Skip studies the scene out the window for a minute. "Like you say, what have I got to lose?"

Out on the street, he gives me a last, searching look. "I hope you're not leading me down the garden path, Shelly."

I raise my hand. "Girl Scout's honor."

One side of his mouth goes up. "When were you ever a Girl Scout?"

"Well..." I wink.

He anoints me with a last stunning smile before he disappears up Joralemon.

MY JAW DROPS WHEN MY STARCHY HUSBAND WALKS INTO THE kitchen whipping out a split of champagne. He deposits a congratulatory peck on my cheek, and pops the cork over the sink. I quick hand him a couple of juice glasses.

"Swear to God, Howie, the next time we do this, we'll be drinking out of real champagne flutes."

He clinks me. "As the old saying goes, 'From your lips...'"

"'...to God's ears.'" We share a grin, and down the hatch it goes.

Howie grabs the bottle and trots to the living room. "Come on, tell me the whole story." He takes the couch, stretching his legs across the coffee table. I drop into the easy chair. He listens with closed eyes as, for the second time, I give him my blow by blow of a conversation with Skip Putnam.

Howie lifts his glass. "I have to hand it to you, Shell. I worried this dimwit would be too thick to follow the economic argument, but you nailed it."

"Give the kid a break. He has enough *chutzpah* to come with me even though it's utterly out of left field."

"I suppose." He reaches to pull pad and pen from his attaché case. "Now, to brass tacks. First issue—when will you meet with your uncle?"

I choke as my drink goes down the wrong pipe. "What are you talking about?"

"I'm enumerating next steps. Top of the list is informing affected parties about the impending sale. That's standard procedure."

"No. No, no, no." I'm on my feet, waving my hands. "It's way too soon."

Howie's brows come down. "I beg your pardon. You've just arranged to walk a potential buyer through the property. How do you do that without telling the current occupant? Besides, we have to give Irving reasonable notice so he can get his finances in order. He's at least sixty-two, right? That makes him eligible for Social Security. I assume your mother paid his withholding unless...was he her employee or her partner? I never quite understood that relationship. There are potential annuities he might be invested in, and..."

"I said *no*." My voice comes louder than intended. We stare at each other, equally surprised. "I'm sorry. I didn't mean to shout." I circle the room, rubbing my neck. "Look, Ma trusted me to be a smart business-woman. She knew Irving's not a money guy. I don't want him to mess with this before it's in the bag."

Howie pushes his glasses up from where they've slipped down his nose. "You have every legal right to sell what you own. What do you imagine he can do to you?"

"I don't know. But my gut tells me to keep him out of this until the very last minute. I can't explain it. It's just instinct."

"Well, your instinct is wrong. You have both a legal and moral obligation to tell your tenant that he is under threat of eviction. And, honestly, I'm amazed at your resistance. He's family, for Christ's sake."

A guy who puts his family first. Ma carved it into my brain. And here he is, my family man husband, who also happens to be a nitpicking stickler, his face glowering in its stubborn pout. I calculate the effort it would take to talk him down.

"Okay, you win. But, swear to God, we're asking for trouble."

FORTY-SIX

IRV

I circle the shop, checking the stock and straightening the displays, whistling to the tippity-tap music coming from my old Underwood. All those letters and me not typing any of them, not to mention the ledger up-to-date and the receipts entered. With Marisol Ramos on the job, work feels manageable for the first time in months.

The door jingles. Look at this—another teenage drop-in. I'm guessing Marisol's hawking for me at school. Yesterday I sold two cashmere sweaters and a pair of woolen skirts. From the look of the high-heels and tight capris that just walked in, I'm betting this one's in the market for something else. The girl cranes her neck, looking toward the back.

"*Oyes Marisol.*"

Marisol half stands at her seat. "*Hola, Lydia.*"

They *schmooze* in Spanish for a minute then Marisol says something about *trabajo* and goes on with her typing. The Lydia girl ambles the aisle, brushing the counters with her fingers, picking up a sweater here, a blouse there.

Suddenly, Marisol's on her feet. "Hey, hey, hey."

I turn quick enough to see a pricy leather belt disappearing under Lydia's blouse. I'm at her in a flash, my palm out, making like I'm ten feet tall. "Put it here or I call the cops."

Lydia gives me a scowl that would kill a horse, but she hands over the belt. I point to the exit.

"Peh." Lydia flicks her wrist, but obeys my command. When she gets to the door, she halts, gives us the finger and yells, "Later for you, Ramos." She slams her way out.

"*Bichiyal*," Marisol spits after her.

"Oy." I shake my head. "I hope you don't got trouble now."

"No sweat, Mr. Friedman." Marisol tosses her hair. "I been handling punks like Lydia Barna since I'm three." And she goes right back to work.

Since she's three. I wander to the front and stare out the window. For me at three it was Izzy Schwartz. Jake Rosenzweig and his gang who thugged for the bosses. Strikes, unions, two World Wars and we still can't dethrone the bastards. I catch my breath in a wave of sorrow. Leo. My sister. Arthur. All those struggles. Here I am, still holding down the fort, and what did we accomplish? Nothing's changed.

"Hey, Mr. Friedman, I don't get it."

I shake myself back from the past. "What?"

Marisol comes over with the letter she just finished. "I don't get this."

To the editor,

For weeks now I've been listening to New Yorkers curse Printers Local 6. I too miss my crossword puzzle, my gossip columns, and my daily comics. But, please, ladies and gentlemen, where are your priorities? Sure, strikes are hard on the public. They're hard on the owners too. But we must never forget that strikes are hardest on the strikers, who spend their days in the freezing cold walking on picket lines, not earning a penny to feed their families. The workingmen of Printers Local 6 are front line soldiers in the eternal battle between capital and labor, and we should stand with them the same way we stood with the men who stormed the beaches of Normandy.

Workers of the world unite. You have nothing to lose but your chains!

Irving Friedman

I popped out this gorgeous missive last night after watching Walter Cronkite, where the mayor, the governor, even the Secretary of Labor, bitched and moaned about the selfish union leaders and the gullible printers.

"What's not to get? Good typing, by the way."

"I don't get where this goes? Which editor? There's no newspapers."

I whack myself in the head and laugh so hard I get tears. I was so irritated with all the bellyaching, I didn't think about how to publish it.

"Toss it into the garbage, Marisol. Clearly, I'm an old man with too much time on my hands and not enough company."

She points her painted fingernail at the last sentence. "You have nothing to lose but your chains—neat idea."

"Much appreciated, but I can't claim credit. That's from Mr. Karl Marx."

"Ay." Marisol bites her lip, eyes going wide.

"Marisol?"

"No, nothing Mr. Friedman." She makes to go back to the desk.

"Miss Ramos, you are a prized employee. If there's a problem, please, fill me in."

Her cheeks get pink. "Mami said to keep it secret...but...Old Mrs. Schneiderman in our building, when she heard I worked here, she spat on the floor and called you 'that dirty red.' That's not true, is it, Mr. Friedman? You're not really a Communist, right?"

Gussie Schneiderman, sullying my name yet again. Gussie Schneiderman, who buried children in scrap bins. Gussie Schneiderman who

whacked Tonya Wojcik and caused a riot. Gussie Schneiderman who...
I swallow down the memory of that horrible fight.

"No, Marisol, I am not a Communist. But it's not because communists are bad guys. Many, many, fine, brave people believe Karl Marx
had the right idea."

"But, the priest says all Communists are godless Christ-haters.
They'd turn us into robots like in *Nineteen Eighty-four* that we read in
school."

I rub my head and turn a circle. Some things never change. I ran
into Myron Dickstein the other day. He's a rheumy old fart, still
wailing about the American press, just as annoying as ever and equally
just as right.

"Listen." I take Marisol's arm and walk her to the front window.
"Once upon a time those streets hummed with zealots who devoted
their lives to making a better world. Some were anarchists. Some were
Trade Unionists. Some were Marxists. Many of those 'dirty commies'
sacrificed their lives so your mama could have a good, strong union
and there would never be another Triangle Fire."

"What's that?"

I shudder. "And your own mama a garment worker."

"You mad I said anything, Mr. Friedman?"

"No, no, of course not." I pat her shoulder. "Go back to work,
sweetheart. I just got a lot to think about."

At night, in my living room, a cup of tea in one hand, running the
other over the spines of my shelves, every volume in its proper berth.
What else have I got to do? An old man living alone accumulates
books. I brush past the thin pamphlet of *The Communist Manifesto* that
Leo gave me, so fragile it could fall to dust. But that's not what I'm
looking for as I feel around for what would hit the spot. When I see it,
my heart warms. I put down my cup to use both hands taking it off the
shelf.

A Sweatshop Childhood, by Nettie Bloom. I run my fingers over her
picture on the back flap. The hair is grey, but the face is just as beautiful. "Dr. Nettie Bloom, the former director of The Women's Bureau

was an advisor to Secretary of Labor Francis Perkins and to FDR. She currently holds the Endowed Chair for Social Policy at Barnard College. *A Sweatshop Childhood* gives us a moving portrait of a life spent fighting to improve conditions for America's working women."

I sit down and thumb through the pages. Who can guess where our choices will bring us? Nettie grabbed the brass ring and trotted off to Boston. I look around my silent apartment. This is where my choices led me. It's not great. And yet, Leo, Miriam, Arthur...could I have done one thing different?

I'll bring this in for the girl. You never know. Something might take.

FORTY-SEVEN

SHELLY

The insult comes flying through the chain-linked fence under the thudding of the basketball. It's in Spanish, but the kissy-kissy pucker-pucker is unmistakable. So is the nasty leer. I tap my foot on the sidewalk, willing the light to change and contemplating how I'm going to murder my husband. The second I see green, I charge across East Broadway, but, as I edge around the park, I slow to a crawl. When I stop dead across from Hester Street, an ancient babushka shoulders me aside. I elbow back, and drop to sit on a splintered wooden bench, ignoring the dank winter cold. Every bone in my body cries out that this is a disaster.

Nothing will make Uncle Irving okay with losing the store. If I'd told Howie from the start, he would have balked, and we'd never have gotten off the ground. For a crazy moment, I consider ducking out and lying to him, but that's ridiculous. No, the trick is to manage my uncle. But how? I chew a fingernail, my eyes randomly sweeping the street.

Until ten years ago, I could've named every merchant and half the tenants in these rotten old buildings. Not anymore. Well, Tannenbaum's Hardware is still on the corner. Or at least, the faded yellow sign still has that name over the door, but it must have new owners because the Tannenbaums would never condone the cruddy garbage that's passing itself off as merchandise. No matter. If I get my way, that's one of the buildings we'll demolish. On impulse, I cross over for a closer look.

A window is broken on the third floor and the rickety fire escape is a disaster waiting to happen. I bet the building inspectors dinged Feigenbaum good on that. I stroll, running my hand over the faded brick. On the left edge, the door to the upstairs apartments is a tangle of white graffiti and half-ripped handbills. It's supposed to be securely locked, but it gives way with an easy prod. I step in and immediately cover my nose against the stink. All the ceiling bulbs are out. The pale light filtering through the filthy window highlights the cracked yellowed tiles. I close my eyes. What was I? Six? Seven?

We were playing Hide and Seek. Mikey Blank was *It*. Stuie Applebaum and I ducked behind these stairs, certain no one would find us, but Mikey cheated and kept one eye open. Stuie and I were giggling in the shadows when we heard "Ready or not, here I come." Mikey jumped in and, bang, tagged Stuie, who immediately scooted into the street. When I offered my arm for the tag, Mikey didn't touch it.

"You want out, show me your privates."

Mikey was big, with a mean, grubby face. I wasn't supposed to play with him, but he'd forced his way into our game. I began to whimper.

"Aw, is the little baby crying?" He stepped closer. "Drop your drawers."

Just past him, the sidewalk gleamed with bright sunshine. All I wanted in the whole world was to get out to that street. He came another step closer. I gritted my teeth, ducked my head and butted him right in the gut.

That's all it took. Before he could touch me, I was running to the store, screaming like a banshee. Ma was fast as a freight train, onto the sidewalk with a baseball bat. Mikey tried to scram up the block, but she caught him by his collar.

"See this, you little *putz*?" Ma waved the bat an inch from his nose.

"You come near my daughter again you'll have this in your face. You got that?"

His head went up and down three times before he scrambled away looking scared enough to shit his pants. She walked me back to the store, propped me on the back counter and gave me a sucking candy. When I was settled with no more sobs, she took both my hands.

"Listen, *shaindeleh*. The world is full of bullies. They'll always want to push you around. Today, you pushed back. You pushed and got free. That's what you got to do. You think someone wants to hold you back, you push them out of the way."

I step out, letting the door slam shut. Real live traffic swirls around me, trucking down Essex or turning left onto Hester. The world is full of bullies. Ten-year-old Michael Blank. Finicky Howard Saperstein. Sentimental, inept Uncle Irving. Fair enough. I know what to do.

Ready or not, here I come.

FORTY-EIGHT

IRV

Marisol's breath comes in quick puffs as she spits her disdain into the chilly morning air. She's pulled me out of my nice, warm store to observe the lamentable condition of the two ancient mannequins who adorn my front window.

"Have a heart," I beg. "They were already secondhand when Harry Hoffman gave them as a present in nineteen twenty-eight."

"It's Christmas, Mr. Friedman. They're dressed in sleeveless cotton."

This was the last thing Miriam did before the hospital. She was so shrunken and small, like a kid playing dress up with her dolls. I run my hand over the cold glass to brush away dust.

"The one on the right is Karla, the other is Frieda. It's for Karl Marx and Frederick Engels. You can read about them in the book I gave you."

"I'll read that if you'll read this." Marisol holds up the December issue of *Vogue*. The cover shows red walls, yellow lights, a Christmas tree, and fancy-wrapped packages. The happy-as-a-candy-cane model kicking up her heals sports a green wool suit, pearl button earrings and a black felt hat.

"Why does she need a hat to open Christmas presents?"

"Cuz it's fun." Marisol shoves the thing into my hands. "Pretend you're walking down the street." She holds out her arms, doing a fake mince. "Tra -la-la-la-la. You look over at the window." Her face droops with disgust. "Summer stuff? In winter?" She pretend minces away. "But, if you see *that*," pointing to the magazine cover, "*Ay, tan bonita.*" She flounces up to the door. "You come right in." She twirls, giving me a giant, satisfied smile. "See?"

"Forget the clothing business, you should get an Academy Award."

But, of course, the kid's right. This window should not be a permanent monument to my sister. But it hurts my heart. I flick a finger at the magazine.

"If my customers saw that model in my window they'd call Welfare because it's clear she's starving to death."

"Ha, ha, ha," Marisol mocks. "Come on. Mrs. Hirsch knew everyone wants to look good. That's why she went out of her way to make the window special."

Out of nowhere a husky voice pipes, "Always listen when a smart woman gives you good advice."

Sweet as you please, my niece Shelly comes sauntering down the street, as if she walked here every day, instead of exactly never since her mama died.

"Hi, Uncle Irving." Arms open, she come close for a hug.

What am I supposed to do, scold her like a naughty child? I swallow my pride and give a bustle. Her cheek's soft and she smells of good perfume.

"Marisol," I step back, "meet my niece, Mrs. Michelle Saperstein. Michelle, this is my new assistant, Marisol Ramos. Marisol has your old job."

"My steppingstone to bigger things." Shelly offers a handshake. "Pleased to meet you, Marisol."

Marisol takes in Shelly's belted woolen cloak, the soft leather gloves and black pumps then flings a glance to her magazine. I can guess what she's thinking. Meanwhile Shelly narrows in on my window.

"I gather you two are having a marketing debate. That's right up my alley. Want a hand?"

"Please," I wave an arm. "Be my guest."

Shelly pulls off her gloves, one finger at a time. "Come on, Marisol, show me what you have in mind."

Marisol's face lights up. Eager as a puppy, she follows Shelly inside and the two of them hit the racks, rifling the merchandise like a couple of old hens. I swallow hard, thinking what a kick Miriam would have gotten seeing Shelly back in the store. An hour later Karla imitates Jackie Kennedy in a white wool dress and a pillbox hat. Frieda's the party girl in black crepe with a rhinestone necklace from the costume jewelry.

"Just like *Breakfast at Tiffany's*." Marisol claps.

Shelly rubs her chin, nodding. "I think Ma would approve."

I'm swallowed up in an ocean of memory. Once upon a time, Shelly was also a delighted child, sinking her face into the sweetness of fresh fabric, learning to count at the cash register, learning to read from the labels. It washes over me in a wave, until she pulls on her expensive calfskin gloves, cinches her belt and says, "Can I catch a word, Uncle Irving? Marisol can hold down the fort, right?"

"*Si, si,* absolutely." Marisol glows. She hasn't taken her eyes off Shelly since she walked up to the store.

Outside the sky is cold grey. We cross Essex and find an empty bench. Behind us, a gang of little hooligans bounces around the playground, making bang-bang-you're-dead games with their toy guns. I wait until they chase up the block before I pat my niece's hand.

"Thank you, Michelle. That was a difficult task for me, but it needed to be done. Miriam would've had a fit if she knew we were displaying summer clothes in December."

"That's why I came, Uncle Irving. Ma was worried about you in the store on your own. It really weighed on her. She begged me to keep an eye out in case you needed help."

I give a sad smile. "I was twelve and your mama was eighteen when she took charge of my life. I grew up but, God bless her, she always believed I would fall apart without her."

"Please don't take this the wrong way, but I understand her concern. Honestly, I've never seen the shop look so shabby." She sees my face and up come her hands, "The racks are disheveled. The stock is all rumpled and messy. I noticed a big red 'Past Due' on an invoice by the work desk."

I clasp my hands in my lap. "Big adjustments take time. I'm one person doing the work of two. Actually, if we're talking about Miriam, she always worked like five people, so it's that much more. But it's improving. I got myself some good help."

"It'll take more than a sixteen-year-old counter girl to fix your problem, Uncle Irving." She plays with the fingers of her fancy glove. "You know, Howie is Ma's executor. When he was with the accountant, Harry mentioned that your profits are way down."

Patience is one thing, but this is getting on my nerves.

"Such snooping is uncalled for, Michelle. My business is not your concern."

"I wasn't snooping and frankly, Ma made it my concern. That's why I'm here. I've gotten wind of something...something Ma would have grabbed up with both hands. Soon as I heard it, I knew. This is fate telling me how I can help my uncle and honor my mother's dying wish."

Something in her tone puts me on edge. "What are you talking about?"

"I've been contacted by a prominent real estate firm. It's still very early on, hypothetical really. They're considering some huge development project on Hester and Essex...I don't know...something to do with the new co-op. Anyway, they're interested in buying my building. Like I said, nothing's definite. But, from our initial conversation, they're willing to pay top dollar. I mean, big money. If this thing goes, we'd make a mint. See? It's the perfect solution. Exactly what we're looking for."

"You're planning to sell the store out from under me?"

"Just listen before you panic, please. Yes, I might sell the building. Yes, that means the store would go, but, I promise, you'd be fine. Just like us, you'd walk away with a bundle of cash."

I'm on my feet, my whole body flashing hot and cold. "You honor your mother's memory by pulling the rug out from under me without a word of my consent? Miriam's life's work, my livelihood, gone like they're *drek*?"

"Uncle Irving..." Shelley reaches out for my hand. "Please...I know this is out of left field. That's why I came to talk today, to give you time to get used to the idea. And it still might not happen. But the truth is, the store can't last the way it's going. If you wait too long, you'll end up with nothing. With this deal, we'd give you a percentage of the take. You can walk into retirement with a nest egg, cash in hand. Believe me, this is in your best interest."

Don't blow piss up my ass and call it rain. I count the beats thumping in my chest. I am in the presence of Miriam and Leo's daughter and I can't trust a word coming out of her mouth.

"Michelle, there is no way to describe what your mama and papa have meant to me in my life and no way I can repay what I owe them, so it breaks my heart to tell you that you're peddling a load of horse-shit and your mother must be turning over in her grave."

Her cheeks go beet red. In the silence, the air vibrates between us. Then, she stands. "You're the one who's full of shit. My mother would have cheered to see me parley that pathetic little building into a small fortune. She'd have puffed out her chest and walked the streets brag-ging her daughter was a genuine *macher*."

"God help you, Michelle, you don't even know who your mama was. Severe, tough, a shell of steel, sure. But inside was a heart the size of Manhattan. How could you not know that...most of her heart was given to you?"

If looks could kill, I'd be dead in the gutter. Shelly turns a full circle, her gloved fists raised to heaven. "Jesus Christ, how did I get stuck with this *schmuck*?" Back in my face, "You leeched off my mother your whole life. Why is it you never went out on your own, Uncle Irving? I never knew."

"You're right. You know nothing."

"I know I come from a hard-headed businesswoman who always fought to win."

"That's the tiniest part of where you come from, Shelly."

"Well, it's the part that I care about."

She cinches her coat and settles her purse on her arm. "Get this—you have no say in the matter. If this deal goes through, that building's coming down. Prepare yourself."

She turns on her heel and stalks away.

FORTY-NINE

SHELLY

The floor shimmies, the wheels screech. I hang on the subway strap, seething.

Your mother would turn over in her grave. Like hell, you stupid, self-righteous old fart. I'm breathing so hard, the person next to me steps away. Standing still is impossible, so I stride down the aisle and, ignoring the rules, throw open the forward door and hop the gap to the next car. I keep going, one, two, three, all the way to the front, where I can stand at the window and watch the blazing headlights bore holes into the black tunnels.

Losing my temper was not part of the plan but, God damn it, no one gets under my skin like that sanctimonious old bastard. The train swings around a sharp curve and I'm bumped against the wall. He's done this to me all my life. All my life, as if everything I do is wrong, watching, checking up on me, keeping count. Ma excused him. "It's not mean. He's trying to look out for you." I told her if he wanted to look out for someone, let him get some kids of his own.

Another shimmy. This time I brace a hand against the window. In a jolt of sudden brightness, we shoot into the milky winter of the

Manhattan Bridge, the wheels clattering over the East River, brown and ugly beneath us.

God, I hope I didn't blow it. Who knows what he might do now that he's mad. I bang my fist on the glass window. If only my smug lawyer of a husband hadn't bullied me. I suck deep breaths, willing myself calm. Panic won't help anything. What's done is done. If this turns into a battle...well, whatever Howie's failings, he's good in the trenches. At least I can count on him for that.

The train rattles into Jay Street and the doors swish open. I scurry home to Rector Street and throw open the apartment door. "Howie?"

He's standing in the living room, his face veiled in caution. "Hi Hon, we forgot. It's Mom's birthday."

From the couch, a grey-haired head slowly turns in my direction, my mother-in-law Ida, her livid face a sinkhole of reproach.

It's too late to cook, so Howie orders in Chinese. We choke down the wonton soup and egg rolls under Ida's litany of rebuke. "I sacrificed my life for you and this how you treat me? An afterthought, a nothing, a piece of garbage."

Howie is a broken record. "I'm sorry Mom, really sorry."

It's so relentless, one could almost feel sorry for him. Almost, because at least she's not going after me. I keep my mouth shut and my head down until, from out of my fog I hear her carp "I bet Michelle wouldn't treat *her* family this way."

Something flits across Howie's beleaguered face. "Frankly, Shelly's got her own family issues. She's selling her mother's building."

From deep into the moo goo gai pan, Ida's head shoots up. "Doesn't her *fagele* uncle own a store there?"

Lights flash. Sirens scream. Bombs explode. I signal him to shut up, but Howie is too busy placating.

"That's why we lost track of your birthday. She was preoccupied about dealing with him."

Ida's face goes full sneer. "I should have known it was her fault." Her beady bird eyes scour over me. "Some nice girl you married. She treats me like dirt and chisels her own family."

I glower across the table, but his eyes skitter away.

He coughs, wiping the sweat off his upper lip. "Ready for your fortune cookie, Mom?"

Bam, my fork slams onto the table. Seizing the empty plates, I storm into the kitchen, turning the faucet on full to drown out the sound of their voices. I stay there the rest of the night, until Ida's nastiness runs out of steam and Howie takes her down to find a cab. I stomp to the bedroom, throw on a nightgown and scuttle under the covers—on my side, face to the wall.

We were in a lousy motel in North Carolina his first furlough out of Basic, the knotty pine walls, the stinkbugs slamming against the window screen of that Southern sweat box. Lying in bed, his fingers tracing the sweat dripping between my breasts, my professional man, my lawyer with a future, he made promises. *You and me, Shell. Watch. Together, we'll conquer the world.*

I don't move a muscle as he comes into the room. The closet door slides open. I hear the slush of his pants against the floor, the rasp of a hanger on the metal rack. The mattress bends under his weight. I tug the blanket tighter and move away.

———

MORNING. HE'S WORKING A WINDSOR KNOT INTO HIS TIE WHEN I stumble into the bathroom. Our reflections regard each other in the mirror. He puts up his hands, gesturing surrender.

"I grant you, it wasn't my finest hour." But Perry Mason is never far away. "In my own defense—we *did* forget her birthday. And you know as well as I do that arguing with her only makes things worse. I admit that I may have been overly conciliatory, but what else could I do? She's my mother, Shell." He straightens his shoulders and sucks in his gut, "Anyway, I acknowledge that I could've done better by you."

Good lawyer words, but I know the truth. It'll be the same next time...and the time after that.

"What do you say, Shell? Can we move on?" He gives me the

Groucho Marx eyebrows. "You could fill me in on your visit with Irving. I know it got lost in the shuffle."

Click, click, click. I tap a fingernail on the edge of the sink. A distant strain floats up from memory, the Hester Street *yentas* out on their stoops. *So, he has a few faults. What man doesn't? But such a good provider. A man like that, you never have to worry where your next meal is coming from.*

Who knows? Maybe that's the price you pay.

"It's late, Howie. You better get to work. I'll tell you the whole story tonight."

"That's a deal." He pecks my cheek and prances out, mistaking my answer for forgiveness.

FIFTY

IRV

In quiet moments, I circle the store, touching the wall where Miriam nailed up our first dollar, testing the strength of Leo's sturdy shelves, adjusting hangers on the racks. It is a deathwatch. No matter how big my "percentage of the take," without this income, I can't afford Artie's care. One or two months with no rent, the place will kick him out. Maybe I should buy a rocking chair, just like Mama. My hands tremble, picturing him in my small apartment. It's what Miriam warned. I am again to be the poverty-stricken caretaker to the living dead. Nettie flew up to the stars. Leo rode to glory. Miriam forged and built. But my life is an empty circle, ending where it began. The darkness would bury me but for the rays of light arriving every afternoon with my sunny apprentice.

Thanks to her, under sentence of death, business has suddenly boomed. Yeah, sure, we're in a holiday season with no newspaper ads to attract my customers uptown, but I'm convinced the new window display is responsible. Marisol claims all the credit, ringing up each sale as if she personally sewed the garment, humming ditties like, "Come on, baby, do the locomotion..." to every ding of the register.

"You better do right by that *muchacha*," Mrs. Jimenez scolds, buying three scarves and a wool cardigan on her way out.

I'm trying.

We're at the register, totaling receipts. It's been a crazy week, open 'til eight-thirty, nine o'clock every night. Even though it's school, Marisol insists on staying after I've shut the front lights and turned over the "Closed" sign.

"Shouldn't you be studying for finals or something? It's the end of the term, no?"

"No sweat, Mr. F. I'm Honor Roll and Arista, all As," she snaps her fingers, "like that. My teachers are pushing college, college, college."

"And?"

"Nah." She's rubber-banding a pile of twenties. "I got three little brothers. Papi says '*Los hombres son para la escuela. Las mujeres son para bebés.*' Men are for school. Women are for babies." She hands me the packet and starts on the tens.

"Have you read that book I gave you? Nettie Bloom's papa proclaimed, 'Women don't read Torah.' It didn't stop *her*."

"But she was a Wonder Woman. You know she got her books from Seward Park Library right where I do my homework. Her boyfriend took her."

"Of course." I allow myself a sagacious nod. "He had a crafty way of courting a smart woman. But Nettie was the real cunning one. She went for the boy, but she stayed for the books." I tap Marisol's skull. "I know another cunning young lady who should stay with the books."

"Aw, Mr. F." She waves me off. "You know, Mami said no one at the union hall remembers anything about the strike Dr. Bloom described, but the basement where they all worked...it's right on my block. It's a record store."

A haberdashery, a Judaica, a dry cleaner, a stationary store, a luncheonette, a luggage store, and now with the records, I've tracked it for forty-five years, but for me, forever, it is our messy, hopeful, noisy, joyous strike office. I have only to close my eyes and memory pierces my heart...Leo's posturing...Esther at the typewriter....the whack of Nettie's hammer...Mendel's laugh...so clear, so vivid. I was once surrounded by heroes, and in one moment, a single instant, I made a choice. Where would I be if I had made a different choice that day?

"You okay, Mr. F?"

"What? Oh..." I notice I'm holding a stack of greenbacks. "Look, we're done."

I stuff the cash into the bank bag along with the deposit slip then go to the storeroom for our coats while Marisol gets the light. When I come back out, she's pressed to the front window, peering into the dark street.

"Wait up, Mr. F." She twists her head, pressing her face into the glass. "It's Lydia Barna and her stinking boyfriend." She stamps her foot. "*Puneta*. She said she'd get me back."

The coats hit the floor as I join her at the window. My night vision isn't so good anymore, but I catch some movement under the streetlamp close to the corner. Heat flushes my body. Is this also part of The Great Jester's grand design? First the store, then the girl?

I jerk her away from the glass. "Go call the cops. Now."

She rushes to the phone while I grab the just-in-case baseball bat we keep under the counter. Thirty-five years I've never had to use it, but the time has come. I fling open the door.

"Hey you," I call. "Hey, *schmegegges*."

I storm down the street, bat raised, a regular Mickey Mantle, swinging once, twice, like I'm practicing for a homer. The shadows under the streetlamp dance and weave.

"You wanna take something from me?" Swish, swish, the heavy wood singes the air. "Come and get it."

The hulking black shadow steps into the street. "Come on, old man, let's see what you got."

A distant siren whines from up the block. The shadow twists to wispy threads. Shoes pound the long street and echo into the park. I'm rooted to the spot, standing sentinel 'til I feel Marisol at my shoulder.

"That was crazy, Mr. Friedman. Hector's a gang guy. He could'a done anything." She's gripping the matte knife I use to open cartons.

"And you were going to help me with that?"

I put an arm around her shoulder just as we're showered in rotating beams of blue and red. My heart is racing and I have to gasp for air. Something has cracked in my chest. I lean over, propping myself up on the bat, but all I can think is *Enough. Enough you gutless, chicken shit. Enough.*

It's your turn to fight.

FIFTY-ONE

SHELLY

I'm hopping from foot to foot, pumped as a prizefighter, when Skip's little green Triumph tootles up to the curb. The top is down.

His cobalt eyes challenge. "It's a balmy day. Are you game?"

I whip out a scarf to tie around my head. "I'm game for anything."

He hops out and, with a grand sweep of his arm, ushers me into the leather bucket seat. I position myself so as to flaunt my long legs and pert, neat, delicate ankles and watch him sneak a peek before he guns the engine, toots the horn, and off we go. Whatever else happens on this make-it-or-break-it trip, being with Skip Putnam is a mammoth breath of fresh air after the suffocating, oppressive courtesy that has reigned in my household since Ida Saperstein's foul visit.

Zipping across the Williamsburg Bridge, the wind's too turbulent for conversation. I relish the crisp tingle of the air against my face and the illicit pleasure of Skip's knee pressed close to mine. But as we come down onto Delancey, I gather myself back to business.

"Remember, this is not Sutton Place," I call out, reverting to my script. There's no hiding a hundred and fifty years of rot. If I admit it before hand, I don't come across as a shyster.

"I stand warned," Skip shouts back.

Once we turn onto Norfolk it's quiet enough to talk, but I let this part of the neighborhood speak for itself. The grey, narrow streets, laundry-strung allies, piles of steaming rubble. I let him circle double-parked cars, stop short for a feisty jaywalker, get caught behind a delivery truck. At one traffic light, a cigarette-smoking teenager bangs the hood, braying, "Hey, buddy, I'll park this baby for ya."

"Not Sutton Place," Skip mutters.

It's the sort of comment I was waiting for. "That's why we're here. PB and P already owns Sutton Place."

Skip chews on that as we turn onto Hester. I point to the far end of the block. "That's it, over there."

He navigates a parking spot the size of a postage-stamp and kills the engine. We step out and lean against the car, taking in what Ma called her midget between giants. It's Saturday. A graffitied accordion gate covers the store's windows and door. I wasn't about to bring him around Irving.

"So that's your store?" Skip glances up and down the block. "Did you live on this street?"

There's something unexpectedly naked about showing him this. The dingy buildings, the squalid streets...I can't keep self-consciousness from creeping in.

"Up there, on the second-floor."

Skip sticks out his hands, an artist framing a picture. "Ought to put up a plaque—childhood home of real estate genius Michelle Saperstein."

I bat his shoulder. I should know Skip Putnam is not a heel. I shake myself back to action. "Let's get down to business."

With their lousy security doors, it's easy to gain access to both of Feigenbaum's derelicts. We climb the rickety stairs, walk through the decrepit halls, tiptoe around the garbage and rot. One tour and Skip agrees they're unsalvageable. Back outside, we stand side by side, pacing off the full area we'd create by demolishing all three structures. It's more than half the block.

"Now comes the real kicker." I grab Skip's hand and pull him to Essex, where we can see four clean modern high-rises shooting up over the trees.

"My mother and I watched them go up, floor after floor like one of those time-lapse things in the movies. Twenty stories each. Housing for fifteen hundred middle-income people. People with disposable income who want good schools and a safe neighborhood. Shall we take a look?"

Skip tucks my hand under his arm. "Lead on, McDuff."

We enter the grounds from Grand Street. In the unseasonable warmth, the courtyard is busy with dog walkers, baby carriages, and strollers. A tribe of roller-skating boys commandeers the path from three jump-roping girls who holler, "No fair," and chase the rowdies to the playground where they all end up in a game of Tag.

"He pursued her until she caught him," Skip cracks.

We've come to the first tower. The young woman in front of us doesn't blink when we trail her through the security door. She disappears into the elevator, but Skip and I stop and gawk. The murals. I'd completely forgotten about the murals.

The figures cover the whole length of the wall. On one side a sturdy, overalled workman, maybe twenty feet long, lies prone, two ears of corn growing from the crook in his elbow. Facing him across the elevator shaft, equally as massive, a woman lies beneath a set of broken shackles, her strong body protecting a sleeping infant. Set between them over the elevator door, Albert Einstein's benevolent face beams down, with the quote, "A new type of thinking is essential if mankind is to survive and move toward higher levels."

The press was all over these murals when the buildings opened. They were commissioned by the unions, a celebration of the working class. I open my mouth to explain, but Skip's already gone in for a closer look, walking up and back the length of the lobby.

"The Detroit Industry murals? You know...Diego Rivera. Did you ever see them?"

I shake my head. "Never been to Detroit."

"I was seventeen, on a class art trip. God, what an experience. I couldn't wait to get home and rave to my art collector father. Mistake. Big mistake. Huge. Old Shro, that's his nickname, Old Shro loathed..." Skip's voice fills with sarcasm, "The destructive Communistic rhetoric of Rivera's art." He touches his hand to the wall. "Mind you, this guy is no Rivera, but..." He squints, searching for a signature. "I wish we knew his name."

"Hugo Gellert." A middle-aged blonde with a grocery bag halts in the entranceway. She puts down the bag and folds her hands over her chest, sighing with pleasure. "There's a different one in each building, but this is the one I bring my students to see."

Skip cocks his head in a silent question.

The woman smiles. "I teach art at the local high school. Often thankless, but it has its perks, bringing the kids to see this being one of them." She gathers up her groceries and heads to the elevator.

My mind snaps into gear.

"Beg pardon." I step forward. "We're, ah, exploring the co-op. If you don't mind my asking, how do you like it here?"

"Oh, it's a joy. We were living out in Queens but jumped at the chance to move back." She watches the numbers count down on the electric elevator display. "You know, the garment unions underwrote this whole thing." The doors open and she steps in.

"My father worked for the garment union," I say, desperate to keep her selling for me.

"Really?" Her arm pops out to hold the door. "Ask him if he remembers Tonya Wojcik. That was my maiden name."

"Oh, he passed away a long time ago."

Her blue eyes go warm with sympathy. "I'm so sorry. I owe those people a lot. When my mother died working in a sweat shop, half the industry went out on strike."

"You were living in the suburbs and you chose to come back?" Skip's voice is sharp. "Did I get that right?"

"These are our people. We have a common history, a shared background. You can't find this kind of community scattered out in the suburbs. We have reading groups, theater parties, weekly card games. We manage not to murder each other talking politics."

The doors start buzzing with venom. The woman smiles an apology. "Best of luck to you," she says as she steps inside. The yellow elevator numbers rise, 10, 15, 17. When the down arrow lights up, Skip and I head for the exit door.

It's a slow ride back to Brooklyn, the gold of the setting sun gleaming off the rearview mirror. When we pull up to my apartment building, the words burst out of him.

"It's not just the stable rent and decent housing, Shelly. She's talking about community and, oh, I don't know, comradeship. This thing you and I are planning, it can't compete with that."

A wave of heat flushes my body. It's now or never.

"Don't you get it, Skip? We're not there to compete with Seward Park Co-op. We're there to *leverage* it. Those tenants pay a price to live there, along with rules, regulations, and requirements. Not us. Our renters will get the gravy that Seward Park brings without having to pony up for it. It's something for nothing. You can make a fortune selling something for nothing."

"I don't know." He scours the darkening sky, his hand tapping the leather steering wheel. "It's utterly out of left field for PB and P. We'd have to sell like crazy."

I clutch his knee. "Haven't you noticed? That's my specialty."

"Lady, there's nothing about you I haven't noticed." His head falls back against the cart seat. "Okay, partner. You've dealt the cards. Let's play them out."

I seize both his hands. "You won't be sorry, I promise."

A fading sunbeam highlights his flawless face. "I'm already not sorry." He leans in and his warm lips brush mine with the lightness of a cloud.

Floored, I snap the door handle and leap away. Without taking his eyes off me, Skip guns the motor. The car jerks and the Triumph fishtails the corner.

FIFTY-TWO

IRV

I am a man in need of advice. Esther is the only one who has enough of the story to grasp my situation. Her reaction is immediate and firm. Get a lawyer.

"I'm having some people in on Friday for a holiday get together. You're coming. One of Harvey's old partners, a retired estate attorney, will be there. Besides," she places a soft hand on my chest, "you could use a little amusement now and then."

It's quite a notion. I can't remember the last time I contemplated anything as simple as amusement.

Friday night I send Marisol home early and close the store at a normal hour. I dust off my blue sports jacket and my best silk tie and trek to the Upper West Side. Esther answers the door, looking classy in black wool and pearls and I ponder again her change from the squinting, spindly scarecrow I first knew. That's what a successful, comfortable life can do for you. I toss my coat on the pile in the bedroom and wander back to the living room to hide in a corner while Ella Fitzgerald purrs under the clink of glasses and titter of chat.

These people started from nothing like me, but look what they have accomplished. Lawyers, doctors, professionals. From the way they're leaning in so close, the two couples crunched on the couch must be old friends. Same with the three guys so politely gathered by an open window to smoke their cigars, where one waves his arm, obviously telling a joke.

Catching me skulking, Esther drags me to a kitchen counter covered with half-empty liquor bottles, pours me a jumbo glass of schnapps, and introduces me to a guy who grew up around the corner from me. We compare notes. Turns out his mother-in-law is one of my customers. Pretty soon we're bemoaning the Great Baseball Betrayals of five years ago, when the Giants and the Dodgers moved to that ridiculous California. Who would want to live in constant sunshine anyway?

It's been so long since I've conversed such pleasantries, I almost forget I'm here on a mission, but Esther doesn't. Toward the end of the night, she walks over with a tall, stoop-shoulder guy in a bowtie, Alan Shapiro, the retired estate attorney. He and I move to a quiet nook behind the refrigerator.

"I'm told you're a good guy with a problem." He offers me a cigarette, which I refuse. "Want to fill me in?"

"Now?" I look around at the pockets of people getting tipsier as the night wears on.

The guy bends in so I'm the only one to hear. "Frankly, parties bore me to tears. You'd be doing me a favor if you'd give me something worthy of my time."

I know hooey when I hear it. This man is offering me a kindness. Who am I to scoff it off? So, squirreled next to Esther's Frigidaire, the room thinning out around us, I lay out my predicament. When the party rolls down to Shapiro, Esther, and me, he and I get more comfortable on the couch as Esther quietly gathers glasses and empties ashtrays.

Shapiro has the eyes of a hawk. "If I understand you correctly, you and your sister had a clear discussion that the real estate would go to her daughter. What about the rest of her estate? How was that to be disposed?"

I shrug. "I assume it all went to Shelly."

"You mean you haven't personally seen or been at a reading of the will?"

"After my sister died, I had other things on my mind. Shelly's husband Howie took care of all that."

Shapiro looks appalled. "Well." He sits back, folding his arms. "At least we know where to start."

Coats on, phone numbers exchanged, Shapiro and I shake hands and he walks to the elevator. I wait in the doorway to say good night. Esther, an apron over her fancy dress, has the room all tidied and the dishwasher chugging away. I take her hand between both of mine.

"There are not words enough to thank you."

Her brown eyes crinkle behind her glasses. "You're very comfortable looking out for others, Irving. It's okay once in a while to let others look out for you." She plunks a kiss on my cheek and closes the door.

FIFTY-THREE

SHELLY

The walls are ivory. The plush carpet muffles sound to a hush. A Jackson Pollack presides from the mantel. Add a Picasso pencil sketch, a Mondrian on one wall, and Rothko on the other. The family brownstone where I'm about to meet Mr. Schrödinger Putnam, Senior. Swallowed up in the lavish white couch, one leg stiffly crossed over the other, I'm finding it hard to breathe, much less be ready for the Big Sell.

"You should have warned me," I hiss to Skip. "How does anyone think, surrounded by this...this...?"

"I didn't expect to be here." His face is thick with consternation. "Dad doesn't usually conduct business under the Great Art."

I compress my lips and stifle my violent urge for a smoke. Okay. I can handle this. I force steadying breaths. Pretend it's not real. It's out of a movie set, so put on a show. You've studied the script. You know the pitch cold. Do what you've rehearsed. You've got it licked, Shelly. Breathe. You've got this licked.

The door swings open. The man who strolls in is tall and lean and he glows like polished silver—silver hair, silver tie and silver blue eyes.

The eyes inspect the room, owning it just by looking. This is his room. All the rooms of the world are his.

"Skipper." Schrödinger Putnam's voice holds echoes of his son's, but deep with authority.

"Hi Dad. Thanks for meeting with us."

Schrödinger's eyes crease with something that imitates warmth. "Well, when my son and heir comes to me with an utterly bizarre business notion, I have to be Johnny on the Spot." He tilts his head in my direction. "May I surmise that this lovely lady is the source of your sudden ardor?"

Skip steps forward as I stand up. "Dad, I'd like to introduce Mrs. Michelle Saperstein. Shelly, my father."

Putnam's palm is silk. "A pleasure, Mrs. Saperstein. Skippy told me you met in his bridge class. May I venture that you're not a regular member of our congregation?"

"I was a drop in. But everyone was so welcoming, I felt right at home."

"Well, good for them." He waves his arm for us to sit then occupies his wingback chair with the elegance of a king taking the throne. "Now, as I understand it, you've beguiled Skipper with a scheme to purchase three festering tenements on the Lower East Side." He extracts a cigarette from an ornate silver box at his elbow, taking his time with the matching lighter. "I'm curious, Mrs. Saperstein, as to how you connived to suggest that Putnam Burnham and Pike would ever consider that an appropriate venture."

His hooded eyes stare me down through the screen of his cigarette smoke and I feel like a gnarled, double-dealing witch clawing to defraud his stupid, gullible son. I cross and uncross my legs, chafing under the look.

That's when I catch on. I know this game. I drank it with my mother's milk. It may be dressed up in this hoity-toity art and the fancy-shmancy cigarette case, but Putnam's *shtick* is as old as the hills —before you negotiate, dominate. My jitters drain away like water through a sieve. I sit back, relax, and drape my arm across the back of his overstuffed couch.

"I'm delighted to walk you through the proposal, but, please, my friends call me Shelly."

A blink and a quick nod of his noble head. "Shelly."

Folding my hands under my chin as if pondering deeply, I look him right in the eye. "Let's be real, Mr. Putnam. Like it or not, new waves of immigrants are flooding into this town from Puerto Rico, South America, and China. The Lower East Side is the City's traditional first stop for any immigrant population. It's a slum. It's always been a slum. But here's the thing—it's also a seller's market for decent, low-cost housing."

I stand, the expert delivering a lecture.

"For the last ten years our country has depended on public funds, tax dollars, and government bonds to finance gargantuan public projects as a way to deal with low-cost housing. But times are changing. There's backlash about all that government spending. So, the politicians have come up with a new tactic. They're throwing around subsidies, tax breaks, and government grants like Christmas candy, all to attract private developers into the urban renewal market."

I lean across the back of the couch.

"And that's where we come in. This is the golden moment. The smart players are going to snap up those subsidies so fast it'll make your head spin. PB and B is an established, respected old firm but if you don't step up to the plate, you will be left in the dust, an archaic relic of a by-gone age."

I go back to the couch to add a dollop of flattery. "You must know this, sir. You're too canny a businessman not to have thought it through."

Putnam stubs his cigarette out in his crystal ashtray, lightly brushing his fingers.

"Well, Mrs.—Shelly, your analysis of current market conditions is certainly cogent."

I acknowledge the compliment. No need to tell him my brainy lawyer husband spent days coaching me on every last detail.

Putnam turns to his son. "Anything to add, Skipper?"

Skip, who has been leaning against the mantel, stands to attention.

"Yes, Dad, I do." He faces his father head on. "You've been grooming me to run the family business all my life. Occasionally I've balked, as you well know, but I also paid attention. I've studied current trends in real estate, tracked where the real profit centers are. Shelly is right. Our approach to the market is antiquated. If I'm the future of the firm, give me a shot. Let me show you what I believe that future is."

"Well, well, well..." Putnam looks from Skip to me, back to Skip. He rises, strolling to the bay window at the front of the room. Hands behind his back, he rocks on his heels, the shadow of raindrops dappling the fabric of his elegant suit. When he swivels around, he looks at me.

"The board has to approve acquisitions of this size. They'll require a prospectus with financials detailed to the penny."

I move to stand with Skip. "We can do that."

A tiny smile twitches Schrödinger's lips. "Oh, I'm sure you can." He comes to take my hand. "Welcome to the PB and B family, Shelly. This should be an interesting experiment."

FIFTY-FOUR

IRV

Agust of cold wind takes my fedora. When I grab for it, I elbow a passing co-ed, earning a look that says, *Who are you, old man, befouling my concentration?* Barnard College is so dense with learning you can inhale it. I move closer into the wall so as not to hinder this flock of women swirling up the stone stairs, heads bent, hair bobbing under woolen caps, their boots pounding the concrete in their rush to knowledge. Once upon a time, Nettie Bloom was one such woman. Her skirt was longer and her hair, too, but I can see her clear as day, a street flower blossoming when it finds the sunlight at last.

Another cold blast. I angle my body to catch less of the wind. I need a minute, here on the steps, to gather my courage. Forty-six years is a long time and I'm an old man whose life got stuck a few blocks from where it started. Nettie Bloom lives in my heart fresh as the day we stood on the library roof, but it's monumental *chutzpah* to think that this advisor to presidents remembers me at all. I was not worth a name in her memoir, just "a fellow worker" who wooed her with books. But life's given me a new task in my old age, and I've sworn to forego cowardice.

I turn and push through the revolving doors.

The guard yawns, "History Department? Third floor." before slumping back to his half-doze as I lug myself up another long staircase. I guess even passing visitors to paradise have to earn their admission.

An empty corridor. My heels click like castanets on the marble floor as I read the names on the doors. Hers is second from the last, the nameplate embossed in gold. I take a moment to run my hand over the letters then close my eyes and knock.

"Come in."

She's at her desk, holding a fountain pen, looking up over the rim of her glasses. Her iron-grey hair brushes the collar of a rich, navy-blue suit. Fuller, rounder, lines on the forehead, grooves to the lips, but the piercing grey eyes are the eyes of my memory. Even seated, this is a person of substance. Dr. Nettie Bloom.

"Can I help you?" The voice holds a tinge of the old neighborhood.

"Um." I doff my hat. "Um, pardon my interruption. Uh, maybe you might remember...My name is Irving Friedman? If you recall..."

Her eyebrows fly up in surprise. She tilts her chair back, scanning me so hard it stops my jabbering.

"Irving? Irving from Norfolk Street?"

"Well, I made it as far as Hester Street."

Her face opens into a lush smile. "My goodness, Irving Friedman." She scurries around the desk to grip my hands in both of hers. She's thicker around the middle but she still comes only to my chin. "Yes, I see it now. You still have that look that says you're not quite sure of your welcome."

"Well, out of the blue, it's a reasonable concern, no?"

"No. Not one little bit. Come, come and sit." Waving me to a chair, she pulls a second from the corner so we can face each other. Hand over her mouth, she inspects me again, more slowly this time.

"I can't believe it. Irving Friedman...It's been what, forty, fifty years?"

"As I remember, you were sixteen, off to Boston for a little schooling." I glance around the room. "I guess it was a good trip."

A corner of her mouth turns up. "Seems to have turned out okay." Her hands slap her knees. "But I'm still flabbergasted that you're here. I mean...where, what, how? Fill me in. Your life...everything."

"Oy, everything is a lot. Let's see, well, I'm still in the old neighborhood. My sister Miriam bought a building and made a store selling high quality women's goods..."

"So, still in the rag trade?"

"I stayed a cutter for a while until the store, and since then, a salesman."

"I bet you're a doozey—a way with people and a gift for words." I blush and she giggles. "And still modest. How about family? Children...grandchildren?"

"I have a niece. Miriam's daughter from Leo."

"Ah, Leo." Nettie shakes her head. "I heard about Leo." She sighs. "What a tragedy. A great loss."

"Miriam passed last August. I manage the store now."

"Oh, I'm so sorry. I know you two were close."

"After all these years you remember these things?"

"What do you take me for, a *schlemiel?*" She looks past my shoulder, her grey eyes focused like she could see into the past. "That strike never left me—the Pinkerton goons, Klara Wojcik, Mendel Stern. That was my beginning." Despite the age lines and the grey hair, that flinty resolution still abounds.

"Excuse me, but if I remember correctly, the young zealot I knew was around before the strike, after her mama died passing the banner into her hands."

She's so startled, her hand goes to her throat. "I guess that's true." She looks at me with awe. "I can't think of another living soul who would know that."

"Old friends. They remember you before you were *you*."

Her eyes crinkle. "And you, old friend, I remember you, too." She reaches for my hand. "Tell me, did you ever find your brother, Arthur?"

My throat tightens. She remembers his name. I look down, turning my hat in my hand.

"We had the blessing of a little time together before...before life conspired to interfere." My voice comes out thick. "I would never have gone looking if not for you."

She pats my hand. "For two dumb teenagers, we did pretty good by each other."

"Well..." I clear my throat, "well..." I must do something to prevent myself sniveling. "Well...so...with all that goodness, I didn't earn a nice mention in your book. I was just a 'fellow worker?'"

She knows it's a joke, but her answer is not. "I knew about Leo...connections to the Party. After McCarthy's House Un-American Activities Committee, a lot of people needed to stay anonymous. I was being careful."

"Oy, Nettie, what we lived through, all of us...the Marxists, the anarchists, the union organizers—so much faith that with enough pushing the world would twist toward goodness. Look what happened, just look."

"I still believe that. Don't you?" When I don't answer, she points outside. "Keep an eye on the young people. You've heard what they're doing down South—the sit-ins, the Freedom Riders, that James Meredith installed at the University of Mississippi." She pulls my sleeve, tugging me over to the window. "Keep your eyes open. Maybe it won't be the workers' paradise we imagined in nineteen seventeen, but it seems like that was a flawed idea anyway. I don't care. We had an idea. It wasn't perfect. Now we try a different idea. One generation passes the torch to the next. The important thing is not to get it perfect, but to keep struggling."

Outside, the diamond hard sunlight bounces off the women walking through the snow. "All these years and you still believe."

"Absolutely. It's why I teach."

"Um, speaking of which —"

"A-ha." She bumps my shoulder, just like the old days. "I figure you if you showed up here after fifty years, you got to be on the make. *Nu,* so, tell me."

"Well, I know this smart, beautiful sixteen-year-old girl. Her mother's a garment worker and a union organizer, but her father insists that education is wasted on women."

Dr. Nettie Bloom's grin still lights up the world. She holds up her hand for me to wait, returns to the thick leather chair behind her desk, pulls out a pad and picks up her pen.

"Now, give it to me."

When I'm done, she shoves her notes into a file folder and scribbles "Marisol Ramos" on the lip.

"There are scholarships, grants, endowments. We can do this." She pulls a business card from the drawer. "Just tell her to call me."

I stuff it in my coat pocket, pick up my hat, and stand. Nettie threads her arm through mine and walks me to the door.

"You know, Irving, you changed my life that day on the roof of Seward Park Library."

This time I can't hide the tears. "And you changed mine."

She reaches up to kiss on my cheek. "*Zolt zein mit mazel*, Irving."

"*Zolt zein mit mazel.*"

The door clicks gently behind me.

FIFTY-FIVE

SHELLY

We're a week out. I'm at the kitchen table organizing fact sheets, financials, and charts, everything in triplicate—me, Skip, Schrödinger—when the doorbell buzzes. A blue-suited messenger hands me a letter from Alan Shapiro, Esq., Attorney of Record for Irving Friedman. Unless Mr. Friedman receives a copy of his sister's will *immediately*, Mr. Shapiro will request an injunction be placed on the sale of 42 Hester Street.

The floor drops out from under me. I fall against the wall. So much for Howie's, "There's nothing he can do." I've put up with a barrel of shit from my husband, but at least I thought I could count on his smarts. Now look. If PB&P gets wind of a potential lawsuit, it could scotch the whole deal, which is, I'm sure, exactly what Irving and his shyster lawyer have in mind. Hands shaking, I dial Howie's number. I don't know who I hate more, my uncle or my husband.

I've worn a hole in the carpet by the time he walks through the door.

"Shelly, calm down." He seizes my shoulders to stop my pacing. "I mean it. Look at me. Relax." He waits 'til I breathe myself off the ledge of my fury. "This is malarkey. No judge in the world would issue this injunction. Shapiro's trying to intimidate you, that's all. It's standard practice. They want the will, so we'll give them the will. We have nothing to hide."

He's so certain, so unruffled, my panic actually dims enough for him to let me go. He drops his coat over the couch and loosens his tie.

"What irks me is that I'd have sworn Irv wouldn't fight us like this." He rifles his pockets for a smoke. "I mean, sure, he's not pleased. He's losing the store, which I grant you, feels shitty, but he's not walking away empty-handed. We're offering him a sweetheart deal."

My fury resurfaces. "I told you. I told you he'd never get it."

"I'm sorry. You were right all along."

Amazement actually overpowers my anger. I can't remember the last time Howard Saperstein apologized without some defensive, picky point of order.

His jaw tightens. "It's unfortunate, really. Now we play hardball." And, like Lazarus rising from the dead, there he is, the guy I thought I was marrying. In spite of everything, my body stirs.

"So, what's the strategy? What do we do?"

"First, we let them have the will." He lights up and flicks the match into an ashtray. "After that, well, give me a couple of days to think."

It only takes one.

Noon. I'm busy adding a final filigree to the prospectus, when the phone rings. Howie's breathless, fired up.

"Drop what you're doing and meet me at work."

"What? What are you talking about?"

"Just come." Click.

His office is tucked away off a back hallway. I barely nod to the receptionist and trot past the typing pool. When I walk in, he's leaning back in his chair, staring out his window. He swivels to face me, his color high.

"I found something."

THREE DAYS LATER WE APPEAR AT THE APPOINTED HOUR. ALAN Shapiro's offices reek of legal dignity, mahogany paneling, brocade chairs, and brass table lamps. But there is nothing dignified about this meeting. It's a face-off. Howie and me on one side, Irving and his lawyer on the other.

Howie oozes disdain. "That injunction threat was blatantly absurd." He snaps open the two clips of his attaché case and shoves over a packet wrapped in blue legal binding. "You'll find that we've followed her mother's instructions to the letter."

Shapiro's face is impassive. "That's for us to determine after we've examined the document."

Irving doesn't take his eyes off me during their whole back and forth. Suddenly he leans forward.

"I beg you, Michelle, stop this. It's a disgrace. We're all that's left. We should not be at each other's throats."

My jaw drops open. "God, Uncle Irving, you're the one with the lawyer and the threats."

"Because you act as a *gonif* who steals what she wants."

"I've bent over backwards to make sure you're covered."

"Throwing a bone to salve your conscience. You know your mother intended the store should stay."

"I know Ma said you were a lousy businessman and I'd better look out for myself."

Irv flinches. Shapiro puts a hand on his shoulder. "Squabbling won't solve anything. We're good. They've given us what we asked for." He starts to rise from his chair.

Howie doesn't move. "Not so fast. There's a matter my wife and I wish to bring up."

It's satisfying to watch Shapiro get wary. He drops back down.

"As you may know," Howie returns to his attaché case, "Miriam's accountant Harry Rothman and I have been running a fine-tooth comb through the estate. It's been quite a revelation. Seems Miriam tucked away assets not referenced in the will. Three days ago, we stumbled onto these in an unopened file box." Using two fingers, he pushes across a manila file folder. He drops his hand under the table to squeeze mine. I squeeze back. Here we go.

Face cautious, Shapiro flips the folder open. I watch him find the red bankbook and the sealed envelope with "For Irving" in my mother's loopy script. When Shapiro opens the bankbook, his eyes go wide. Without a word, he slides it to my uncle. Irving takes his glasses out of his breast pocket and reads. His head shoots up.

"What is this? Howie, is this a joke?"

"Not in the least. It's a valid account. We've been to the bank."

"There's ten thousand dollars here." Irving looks to Shapiro, back to us. "Where did my sister get ten thousand dollars?"

Howie's casual. "Not such a surprise. Miriam was a canny business-woman." He pauses. "The issue is...where does it go?"

I can see the wheels turning in Shapiro's brain. It doesn't take but a minute. "It's in that letter. You found them in the same folder."

"They were rubber-banded together," Howie concedes.

"So, the possibility exists that the letter contains information relevant to the disposition of the asset." Another long pause. Shapiro's mouth goes up in a half-smile. "Well, Saperstein, I give you credit. It must have been tempting."

Tempting doesn't touch it. It was agonizing. Ten thousand dollars just sitting there, begging to be taken. Add it to the potential profit from the sale and Howie's commission, we'd have a house, capital for a new store, and then some. That day in Howie's office, holding the bankbook in my hand, I didn't have to say it out loud. Howie counted off on his fingers.

"One, Harry Rothman witnessed the discovery. Two, the lawyer's likely to interview Rothman as part of his investigation. Three, well...it's a moral issue. After all, Shell," he waved the damned envelope, "it's about your mother's wishes, right?"

I took it, held it up to the light. Ma could've written anything to Irving, a good-bye, a thank you, maybe instructions on how to run the store, which would be totally like her.

"Steam it open?"

Howie ruminated only a second. "This isn't a Hollywood movie. We have to meet with them."

"What the hell is everyone talking about?" Uncle Irving's so flustered his voice is raised.

Shapiro pats his hand. "It's possible that money is yours, Irving."

"And possibly not." Howie's voice is silky smooth. "For all we know, those two items were in that folder by accident. I can make a good case for the money going to Michelle, as with the rest of Miriam's assets. It hinges on the contents of the envelope."

Irv is struggling to absorb what's being said. He runs a hand over his forehead, through his hair.

"Miriam left me ten thousand dollars?"

Shapiro taps the envelope. "Only if she made her intention unequivocally clear."

This dicking around is killing me. "Jesus Christ, Uncle Irving, read the damn thing already."

I've had three sleepless nights. Swear to God, if that file hadn't been locked in Howie's office, by the third night, I would have ripped it open, risk or no risk.

Irving weighs the letter in his hand. Something guarded flits across his face. "She meant it to be private."

Shapiro pulls a letter opener from a wooden tray of office supplies. "Read it, then decide."

Irving compresses his lips. With a deep breath, he slips the metal tip under the edge of the flap. There's a soft slush as it runs the length of the fold. He pulls out the note. I can make out inky script through the translucent white. A red blush starts at his collar and rises to his forehead. He closes his eyes. When he opens them, they're filled with tears.

"Yes, the money is for me to use." He starts to slip the letter into his coat pocket

Howie is martial. "Not until you prove it."

My uncle crushes the paper to his chest. "Alan, they can do that...shanghai a private letter?"

"It's a reasonable request, Irving."

A muscle ticks in his jaw. He turns to me, his voice coarse with feeling.

"Michelle, you have known me your entire life. Would I cheat you? As God is my witness, your mama wants me to use this money. I beg you to trust me and let it be."

The lawyers are dumbstruck. Me too, riveted on my uncle's pleading face. What's the game here? After all the scolding and name-calling and reproach, he hits me with *this*? I blink, groping for clarity. Howie puts his hand over mine, signaling no go. Irving's expression doesn't change. The red bankbook rests on the table. Ten thousand dollars. A small fortune. Irving is a salesman, after all. Besides, that note is from my mother.

I stick out my hand.

Irving's chin drops to his chest. He lays the paper across my palm.

Mein lieb Irving,

Long ago I called you a fool for wasting your money on a living corpse. I was wrong. Family is family. All your life you've been a good brother to Arthur and a good brother to me. It's my turn to be a good sister. There's enough here to cover him 'til the end.

Please forgive me.

- Miriam

The words cut like shards of glass.

"Who is Arthur?"

WE WALK OUT OF SHAPIRO'S OFFICE INTO A FEBRUARY DOWNPOUR. Howie grunts and dashes out to hail a cab. A cab all the way to Brooklyn—I'm so numb, I don't consider the expense. Massive rain-drops attack the Checker, turning the window into a kaleidoscope of distortion. I can't catch my bearings. A family curse. An epileptic hidden in an asylum. A guilt-ridden deathbed bequest. That's a potboiler novel, not real life.

We arrive home in pitch darkness, too exhausted to talk. Howie stakes out the bedroom while I troll the apartment. Paperwork for the sale is still spread across the kitchen table. I randomly finger the pages. We gave them the will. I assume that makes us good now. One thing doesn't have anything to do with the other. I guess. I assume. It's such a muddle. Who can sort it out? In my distraction, when the door-bell sounds, I open without thinking.

Uncle Irving stands at my threshold, hat in hand. "Angry words in a lawyer's office are not a fitting end. We should talk like family."

"Okay then." I step aside to let him in. Irving deposits his sodden coat on a chair and trails me to the living room.

Hearing conversation, Howie pops from the bedroom. "I can't allow a discussion of..."

Irving cuts him off. "I'm not here for that."

I wave Howie off. Reluctantly, he retreats. Positioning myself on the couch, I point Irving to the opposite chair. He leans forward, elbows on knees, gathering himself.

"First, understand, your mama loved you. You were the center of her life. We grew up with so much badness." He makes a fist. "She was fierce that you should never endure such things."

"Please spare me the rigmarole." A simmering resentment burns in my mouth. "At least try for the truth."

"That is as true as anything I've ever said."

"She picked a lousy way to show it. What was she so afraid of? Is this Arthur a raving lunatic or something?"

"My brother, Arthur, was the heart and soul of our family. I have always believed it was a terrible loss that you were not permitted to know him before...before he disappeared."

"God." I get up, turn to the wall then back to face him, "If he was so wonderful, why the mad man in the attic routine?"

Irving waves at the room. "Look how you live, Michelle. Snug.

Protected. You don't know from danger. We watched our brother get ripped away, imprisoned where children were discarded like garbage. When Florence Archer condemned your brother to that fate, your mother kicked her out. Then Sammy died with the same twisting, writhing fits that plagued Arthur. Miriam couldn't forget. Me neither." He sighs. "Imagine believing yourself to be soiled, polluted, unclean. Your mother vowed to spare you from that."

"Because some *shikseh* bitch said you had...what...tainted blood?"

"Once the seed is planted, it worms into your mind."

A realization drops from the sky. "That's why you never got married."

His sad smile confirms it. "You can't escape science. Florence Archer damned us for life."

"Wait...wait a second." I sit, ticking the numbers in my head. "Sammy died in, what, nineteen seventeen? I was born in thirty-three. She waited sixteen years?" My gut twists. "I was an accident, wasn't I, Uncle Irving? A mistake."

"An accident, yes. A mistake? Never."

"But all my life you've both been watching me, monitoring me, waiting for..." My skin crawls.

"No. No. Not ever. Miriam knew you were perfect before you were born."

I press my hands to my eyes. The world is twisting into new, bizarre shapes. Or untwisting out of them, I'm not sure which. I'm barely listening, but Irving drones on.

"Over the years I begged and pleaded. Miriam wouldn't budge. My sister had a great capacity for bitterness. Look what she did about your father. God knows Leo wasn't perfect, but he had heart for the whole world. Miriam kept that from you. And Arthur was an angel, holding on to patience and kindness in a life that would strip you of both. Leo and Arthur, they are the cloth from which you are woven. She sheared them away and left you to flounder." He shakes his head. "I watched it happen. It's my deep sorrow that I couldn't prevent it."

Irving's regrets are his own business. I walk to the window, peer out into the darkness, reimagining the story of my life if I'd known about the family curse. Maybe I'd have brushed it off as ignorant, old-world superstition. Maybe not. How did he put it? *Once the seed is planted?* Would I have been waiting for the ax to fall, scared of every random tic or shiver? Would I have been so cavalier planning a marriage, a family? Maybe Ma wasn't so wrong.

"You two brushed me off, but this thing impacts me as much as you." Howie looms in the bedroom doorway, stern-faced and grim. Flushed with righteous indignation, he marches straight to my uncle.

"I've been sitting in there, listening to your whinging justifications. What a load of crap. All this time you've been wailing and moaning about sneaky, greedy Shelly but it turns out that you're the real crooks, you and her sainted mother. It's basic human decency, Elementary Contracts. You provide full disclosure. Shelly was entitled to know the truth. So was I. Your lies defrauded us both."

Irving bows his head. "I suppose that's one way to look at it."

I shudder, jarred by Howie's hot anger, although the cynical part of me wonders why he didn't support me like this when it was *his* mother going for my jugular. Standing against the window, watching them face off, something else catches my eye, something past them, at the other end of the room—the sale papers and documents scattered on the kitchen table.

The world telescopes. It's like in a Loony Toons cartoon. Irv and Howie shrink into pygmies and the papers swell to the size of bill-boards. It only lasts a second, the room going in and out of focus, but when it stops, my mind is crystal clear. Icy tendrils surround my heart. I've worked so hard. I'm so close. Nothing is gonna stop me. Besides, the bastard owes me.

Head high, back straight, I walk over to where Irving is slumped in his chair.

"You've done enough harm. You've hurt me enough. If you have any decency at all, get out of the way of this sale so I can move on with my life. It's the least you can do."

There's a long pause. Finally, flopping his arms to his sides, Irving rises.

"*Gai gezunt*. I'm done fighting. Take what you want. It's all yours." He walks over to retrieve his hat and coat. "Michelle, do you...have you...would you like to meet your Uncle Arthur? He doesn't have much more time."

"There's really no point."

Hand on the door handle, he takes a final look back.

"*Zolt zayn mit mazl*, Michelle."

"I don't know what that means."

His head bobs in silent acknowledgment and he walks out the door.

Fifty-Six

IRV

The rain has stopped. Reflections from the streetlamp shimmer in the puddles. My feet take me where they will on the dark Brooklyn streets. The issue is to move, to keep walking, to not be still. If I walk far enough, I can leave that ugly scene behind. But the world is too small. All too quickly my road ends on the stones of the promenade that edges this island.

Manhattan taunts from across the river. Its flickering lights bounce off the dark water that flows past the city, past the harbor, out to the deep black ocean. That's how my people got here, in the hold of a rancid steamer...young Arthur, tiny Miriam, wretched Mama, and my prick bastard of a father. If I was a seed in my mother's belly, malice was a seed in his. They were planted in this new world side-by-side. Now Papa is gone. Mama is gone. Miriam is gone. Soon it will be Arthur's turn, then mine. Michelle is the last of us.

I lean over, studying the swirling waters. A million quivering butterflies flutter in my chest, love, pain, loss, guilt—all the warring passions of the day. But, as the dark water pirouettes below me, one sensation dominates. Release. The words have been uttered. The secret is out. No more dark corners. No more hidden lies. Michelle can take possession of our past. It is hers to own.

The East River is that thing, what do they call it? An estuary. The current changes direction with the ocean tide. Perhaps tonight it flows back out to sea. Perhaps it's taking the poison that my father made and washing it far into the ocean, where it can sink to oblivion.

I raise my head. The weight of generations melts into the night air. I have fulfilled my obligations to both the living and the dead. My niece is responsible for her own future and I am free to find mine.

Fifty-Seven

SHELLY

The pop of the champagne cork ignites a chorus of Hoorays. I smooth my dress and suck in my tummy as Schrödinger Putnam waits for the room's attention.

"Let's all raise our glasses to our own native son, my first born, Schrödinger Putnam the Third, and his collaborator, the dynamic young woman whose shrewd business acumen is responsible for this auspicious new venture—Mrs. Michelle Saperstein."

Dipping a light curtsy, I acknowledge the applause. I stand next to Skip, shaking hands with a parade of partners, executives, and staff. Jack Burnham, a bull of a man whose red neck bulges over his white collar, barks, "Isn't there also a lawyer husband somewhere in this fracas?"

I force a smile. "Unfortunately, my husband had another case today."

"Humph. Disrespectful, if you ask me." He pops a canape into his mouth and stamps back to the bar.

My sentiments exactly. "It's all the partners. We need to make a good impression," I insisted, but he refused with a tart, "You're not my only client, you know." It's been like that for weeks—distant, remote, even in his lovemaking. Frankly, with everything swirling around, it hasn't bothered me much. I look around the lavish boardroom. At least he didn't distract me from this.

It's been a mad three-month dash to the finish line, but it's finally signed, sealed, and delivered. I'm queasy with relief. As soon as the line of well-wishers eases up, I wander over to the window. Thirty-three stories down a huge brass statue of Atlas supports the world on his shoulders. *Here's to you buddy.* I sip my champagne. I know how you feel.

"Pleased?" Skip's husky voice purrs in my ear.

I swivel around to his perfect smile. "So happy I'm nauseous. You?"

"Swimming in honey. Dad is crowing to anyone who'll listen that Schrödinger the Third is a chip off the old block. A paean to good blood and breeding. He believes the gods saw fit to end the newspaper strike so he could shout our success to the world."

Skip points to *The Times* Business Section on display next to the bonbons.

Putnam, Burnham, and Pike, one of New York's premier real estate firms, is branching out into the urban renewal market with the purchase of three buildings adjacent to the innovative Seward Park Cooperative. Does this herald a bold new direction for this prestigious old establishment?

He puts a warm hand on my shoulder. "I owe you, Shelly."

"Ah, t'weren't nothin'."

His cobalt eyes gleam. "It was everything."

"May I join this conversation?" Coming from behind, Schrödinger Senior throws a perfectly tailored, eight-hundred-dollar business-suited arm around my waist. "Shelly, I want to offer a personal note of appreciation. I've waited a long time to see my son assume the mantle of leadership at PB and P. I believe you're responsible for that."

I raise my hands in protest. "Oh, no. Skip's been the visionary on this from day one."

"Visionary." He jabs Skip in the arm. "How's that for a reference, boy? Well, Shelly, Skipper's been equally laudatory about your skills and capacities. Which brings me to a question." Father and son exchange a glance, "How would you feel about continuing this relationship?"

"Beg pardon?"

"Join us." He swings his arm to encompass the room. "Become a permanent member of the PB and P family as Skip's project manager. This shindig is just getting started. It's obvious you have impressive management skills. Skip insists it would be a marriage made in heaven." Schrödinger's voice drops. "I guarantee you'd be happy with the compensation."

A surge of heat flashes up my spine. "I...I...I'm utterly at a loss for words."

"Oh, I'm sure you'll find them soon. Direct any questions to Skippy. He has some relevant thoughts on how this matter might proceed." Schrödinger winks. Catching sight of someone across the room, his face twists into its foxy smile as he ambles away.

Skip clears his throat. "I hope that didn't sound too... compromising."

"Is it compromising?"

"This is an absolutely genuine offer, Shelly. I want you. I can't imagine doing the rest of this without you." In a distant echo of his father, Skip's earnest voice drops an octave. "The exact terms are up for negotiation."

On the subway back to Brooklyn, the euphoria is over.

Skip Putnam? In the dark, at night, all titillating and spicy, especially after one of Howie's spells as a jellyfish. You'd have to be a corpse not to think about it. My fingertips caress the folds of my dress and the subway fades to a filmy haze until, in a sudden glare of daylight, the train shoots onto the Manhattan Bridge and Brooklyn looms across the river.

It's a slow walk to Remsen Street. There was that Lana Turner movie, *The Postman* something. Ma came out huffing, "*Goyim.* Only a cheap floozie cheats on her husband." And you'd be trading Ida for Schrödinger. Still...a corner office...my name on the door...Skip wouldn't push. I could make it work—do the job and avoid the pitfalls. It would take a bit of *finagling,* but, hey, am I not one hot little *finagler?*

I mount the stairs, glad that Howie didn't come. I doff my coat. All this thinking has put me in a sweat. My head is throbbing, probably from the champagne. Early as it is, I slip into a nightgown. I'm at the mirror brushing my teeth, still dreamy, when, reflected from the shelf at my back, I notice the unopened package of tampons. I wheel around, staring at the grey and pink box still wrapped its cellophane. With all the work, I wasn't paying attention. Sodden with dread, I start counting. How many weeks? I tap my forehead. For sure before the rush of work. For sure before the revelation.

I'm swallowed by a new wave of nausea. Head lowered, I grasp the sides of the sink and watch all my phantom dreams go slipping down the drain.

FIFTY-EIGHT

IRV

The black and yellow GOING OUT OF BUSINESS signs are already peeling from the windows. No matter. Their job is done. Whatever inventory didn't sell in the FINAL SALE was peddled in bulk to Ornstein's on Canal Street for a pittance, along with any serviceable display tables, the cash register, the desk, and the typewriter. Karla and Frieda sit in the middle of the floor, covered in drop cloths. No one wanted fifty-year-old mannequins but I couldn't stand to leave them here stark naked. I'm waiting for the junkman who'll take them away along with Leo's shelves and the decrepit chrome racks.

One more thing that has come to an end.

Three days ago, I attended Artie's funeral. I made it to Great Neck in time to hold his hand as he breathed his last. Esther was kind enough to be with me at the cemetery as I stood over his grave. Although I haven't set foot in a synagogue in fifty years, I will attend shul every day for the next month to say Kaddish. I have to laugh. How Leo would have mocked me, drinking the opiate of the masses after all this time.

Shades cover the windows. Shadows chill the room. I walk in circles, my footsteps echoing off the empty walls. It's a relief when the front door rattles and I open for the junkman. Only it's not the junkman. Marisol and her mama, Valeria, papa, Rueben and the three brothers, are there instead.

Marisol smiles. "Mrs. Narvaez called when she saw you going in. We thought you'd like some company."

Valeria extends a plate wrapped in tin foil. "They're *tostones,* fried plantains," she says, brushing past. "You need to eat."

Ever since Marisol's Barnard scholarship, Valeria insists on providing me with enough food to feed a horse. Marisol nudges my shoulder. "Mami wanted to bring *Pasteles*, but I said maybe better not 'cause of the pork."

The boys munch cross-legged on the floor, while we grown-ups nosh leaning against the wall. Valeria reports that a ruckus is brewing about the fancy uptown company elbowing into the district, with rumors of possible protests. I chew the information along with my *tostones*.

The junkman arrives. It doesn't take long. The six of us stand on the sidewalk, watching the truck chug around the corner. I go in to flip over the "Closed" sign. Out on the street, I run my hand over the gold-plated "Hirsch and Co. Women's Clothing," still painted on the window.

"She gave me the gift of my life."

Marisol sticks her hand under my arm. "Like you're doing for me."

Side-by-side, we leave Hester Street behind.

1965
SHELLY AND IRV

FIFTY-NINE

SHELLY

The baby kicks, I have to pee and that does it for sleep. I pad barefoot into the living room. Under the charcoal sky, islands of snow dot the lawn outside our picture window. Quaint, charming, just like in the movies. My hand goes to my back, massaging against the six-month bump in my middle. Some happy ending. Mikey's not out of diapers, now this.

I drop my head against the glass, waiting for the paperboy to ride by and the reassuring thud of the newspaper hitting the door to remind me there's a real world out there. I cock my head, listening, but it's still too early. I toddle to the bedroom to get dressed. At nineteen months, Mikey doesn't sleep much past six. The day is deep shit if I'm not ready to do battle when he wakes up. Mikey's a handful.

When we asked, the pediatrician was casual about my epileptic uncle.

"The science of eugenics has been thoroughly discredited."

Howie wore his Perry Mason face and his courtroom voice. "Nevertheless, it is conceivable that her relative's condition is genuinely hereditary."

"Oh, there's a statistically small possibility, perhaps," he chirped. "But I wouldn't worry about it."

Of course, you wouldn't worry. It's not your kid.

Howie stumbles out of the bedroom, rubbing his stubble. "These five o'clock mornings kill me," he mutters on his way to the bathroom.

It's probably our only contact for the day. With the two-hour commute, his long, lawyer hours, and my current state of permanent exhaustion, I'm usually passed out when he meanders in at ten or eleven. I don't think he minds all that much. My honorable husband acts the paragon of fatherly virtue when he deigns to be home. He can't help I overheard Ida wheeze, "You married damaged goods." As usual, he didn't contradict his mother.

The morning piddles away with dusting, vacuuming, polishing. Mikey stays absorbed in his big wooden blocks, a gift from Skip Putnam who was so stunned when I turned down his job, he couldn't muster a word of congratulations. A week later I got the box from FAO Schwartz with a note. "Apologies. I'd like to contribute a little something to your next 'project.' I'm sure he'll be a winner."

I lean over the couch, watching the rise and fall of Mikey's constructions.

Skip telephoned about eight months after my refusal, after I'd given birth. He said the residents of Hester Street were rallying to protest the uptown developers invading their neighborhood. I told Skip it was crap and would blow over, but the spineless bluebloods of PB and P turned tail and ran. The project was suspended, going into their books as a financial loss. I have to assume PB and P had enough capital to cover it. I can't be sure. Skip never called again.

Mikey lets loose with a piercing screech and flings a block across the room. Desperate for a diversion, I stuff him into his snowsuit, cram his stroller into the car, and scramble into Norwalk. It's early enough to catch parking on North Main Street and sometimes a walk in the cold air sedates him. He mewls as I unfold the stroller, but I stick a binky in his mouth and he gets busy thuk-thuk-thuking away.

The downtown shops are opening. I trot lickety-split past Kaplan's

Pharmacy so as not to get captured. Ruth, the pharmacist's wife, is a certified *yenta*. She once wasted three-quarters of an hour quizzing out my life story while I waited for my vitamin prescription. I casually mentioned looking for a bridge club and she snorted, "Forget it, honey. The *goyim* are perfectly happy to get their prescriptions filled at Kaplan's and buy school clothes from Goodman's but admit us into one of their precious clubs? Not likely. The Jewish Community Center does mahjongg Thursday nights. That's the place for you."

I didn't bother to tell her I'm not a mahjongg kind of girl.

We meander a few more blocks, the hardware store, the five and dime. Babette's Better Dresses has the corner, catering to local matrons who prove their pedigree by dressing like their grandmothers.

The December air bites. I tug Mikey's hat over his ears and pull the blanket up to his chin, but I only make it half a block before my back aches and my ankles give out. I drop onto a bench at the bus stop, squinting into the sharp winter sun. There's no shade in this burg. New York has skyscrapers that swaddle you in shadow, but these faded old two-story buildings don't leave you any cover. I lean back and close my eyes.

It wasn't supposed to be like this.

It was supposed to be garden parties and bridge clubs, white pearls and canapés, not spit up and diaper pails and lousy housecleaning. Mikey's head lolls. A thin line of drool slips out his half-open mouth. After we visited the doctor, Howie took it upon himself to contact Irving for a full family history. Apparently, Arthur's seizures didn't start until his teens. We won't know anything for years. Not about this one or the one that's growing inside me.

Regret sits on my chest like stone. I was stupid. I hate being stupid. Ma never made a bad deal, but I got greedy. I glance back at Babette's dowdy window. Every time I walk by, I want to kick myself. Jesus, what I could do here. Every night, in bed alone, the shadows playing across my lily-white ceiling—*Michelle's of Norwalk, Fashions for the Modern Woman*. If I had help. If I had someone to pick up the slack. If I had what Ma had.

I flinch as the baby shifts position. A chill flutters down my spine. My body can't take this cold. Clutching the back of the bench, I heave myself up. Who knows? Maybe I can *finagle* a phone call. Maybe I can sell Irving on forgiveness. After all, am I not a great little *finagler*?

Leaning against the stroller, I totter down the street, conjuring the pitch.

Sixty

IRV

My feet know well the wide, long blocks between Broadway and Riverside at 86th Street. I would prefer to make fewer perambulations, but Esther and I agree that it would be unseemly for me to move in, so I make a point to always leave before morning. The arrangement is tedious, but change is in the offing. Come next month, at the age of sixty-five, I'll be a first-time bridegroom. Meanwhile, I travel up from my 21st Street apartment several times a week, and always for dinner.

Tonight, Marisol is coming. Given the sorry quality of Barnard's dormitory food, she often eats with us, especially on Friday, when Esther's whole clan gathers for Shabbos dinner. Marisol is contemplating law school so she spends a fair amount of time huddling with Esther's son, Paul, an ACLU attorney.

It's the hour before dusk. Paul and his wife, Sharon, sip sherry by the big front window, having doused the lights and opened the drapes. The room shimmers with reflected color as the setting sun turns the Hudson River to flame. Cross-legged on the floor, teenaged Stevie has condescended to play *Clue* with his eleven-year-old sister, Judy. His vehement accusations that she's cheating only elicit her contemptuous sneers.

Esther is finishing up in the dining room. I offer her the bouquet I've brought as a contribution. She pats my cheek and nudges me to pull a vase from the glass cabinet. I have spent my life surrounded by accomplished women and my bride-to-be is no exception—for Shabbos only her best china, the good crystal, and the centerpiece just so.

"A good day?" she asks, as I follow her into to the kitchen to check the food.

"Productive. Have you heard of the Cooper Square Committee?"

"The ones who stopped Robert Moses from destroying Delancey Street?" Her voice is muffled as she leans over the soup pot to give a sniff test.

"You got it." I pat her tush while stealing a gherkin from the pickle dish. "I offered my services as a hale and hearty old fart with time on his hands. After all, I'm retired, not dead."

She swivels to put her arms around my shoulders. "I can certify that, should you need corroboration."

I kiss her for real, long, slow, and delicious.

"Yeow," Judy squeals from the doorway behind us. "Bubbie's kissing Irving,"

Untangling myself, I turn to my soon-to-be step-granddaughter.

"Get used to it. When I'm your new *zayde* you'll see it a lot more."

"Can you at least stop for dinner? I'm hungry."

Marisol picks that moment to saunter in, her boyfriend, Raphael, in tow, happily distracting Judy from those disgusting old people. The girl trills that, "Marisol's bell-bottoms are so hip," and Raphael's ponytailed hair is "super cool." Apparently hip and super cool are great accomplishments.

As the sun sets, Esther corrals us into dinner. I move to sit along the side, but gracious Paul waves me to the head. Esther lights the Shabbos candles and recites the ancient prayer, but the peace is fleeting. Before I have downed three sips of my chicken soup young Stevie asks Raphael if he's a radical in SDS. "My friend Ernie's dad says radicals are dumb punk trouble-makers who should keep their mouths shut and listen to their elders."

Raphael gags and Marisol's face turns red.

"Jack Simon's an idiot," Lawyer Paul jumps in. "These college kids are doing great things. Their only real problem is impatience. It's the incremental steps enshrined into our legal system that lead to enduring change."

"How can you say that?" Marisol's fork becomes a pointer. "Look at the power of the military-industrial complex. The whole system is corrupt."

"Exactly. We should ditch the whole thing and start from scratch." Raphael bangs the table. "Right is right."

The debate rages back and forth, through the soup course and well into the brisket. I sip my wine and wink to Esther across the table. The struggle belongs to the young. I leave the world to them, offering a silent prayer for teachers like Nettie Bloom to guide them into the future.

I'm content to sit here, not with the family of my birth, but where I have found a home.

AUTHOR'S NOTE

One of the great adventures of writing this book has been the deep dive into history. I grew up in New York City hearing family stories about life on the Lower East Side. Those stories whetted my imagination, but you can't write historical fiction on anecdotes alone. You need to do research.

Having moved to Portland, Oregon, I started this journey on the internet, not sure what to expect. I was floored. The wealth of information is staggering: Archival footage of Manhattan in 1911; garment union gazettes going back to 1910; strike anthems on the *Yiddish Penny Songs* YouTube site; turn-of-the-century medical texts about epilepsy; a project that photographed every building in NYC; a complete course on the history of 20th Century fashion; and on and on and on.[*]

On trips home, I discovered the thrill of doing primary research. It started with visits to New York's irreplaceable Tenement Museum and its loving recreation of immigrant homes and habits. On a museum walking tour, I encountered the landmark *Forward* Building which plays a recurring role in this book. Later, in the Tenement Museum's bookshop, I found a compilation of the *Forward's* advice columns, *A Bintel Brief* —another important plot device.

Next came the libraries. At NYU's Tamiment Labor Library, I

asked for anything they had on the International Ladies Garment Worker Union (the I.L.G.W.U.) and watched wide-eyed as a young man wheeled out a carton of papers going back a hundred years. Some were routine, minutes of meetings, business notes and such. But how about *That Reminds Me... Jokes & Stories for Use by Union Organizers*? Or—my absolute favorite—the course catalog from the union's Education Series No. 1, "An Outline of Social and Political History of the United States," to be offered in English, Yiddish and Italian. This is the pamphlet that so delights Nettie on her visit to the union office.

On a stroll through Union Square, I plotted out the location of Miriam's office window and the speaker's platform for Leo's funeral. Then I walked to my appointment at the YIVO Institute for Jewish Research, where I cried over an 85-year-old letter from a young man to his mother, explaining why he had run away to join the Abraham Lincoln Brigade in Spain. You hear echoes of that letter in the final scene between Leo and Miriam.

Back in Portland. One afternoon I had an hour to kill between appointments, so I popped into the Central Library, expecting to find nothing of much use. Instead, I discovered an aging collection of relevant texts, like *Making Both Ends Meet: The Income and Outlay of New York Working Girls* from 1911, itemizing living expenses to the penny. Another author wrote a feisty, opinionated "history" of the I.L.G.W.U. overflowing with diatribes against his ideological opponents.

Now, here's a riddle: How did a Portland, Oregon library come by such an idiosyncratic collection of old books about New York City's garment industry? I asked a librarian, who speculated that the collection might have been donated. I've considered writing my next book about a hunt to discover who collected these books and how they came to survive in an Oregon county library. There's no telling where research will take you.

One final note: All this research, the books, the web searches, the investigations, provided a rich historical framework, but *Across Seward Park* is a work of fiction. There were two great entities working to organize New York's garment industry in the first half of the 20th century: The Amalgamated Clothing Workers of America and the I.L.G.W.U. Neither are mentioned by name in this book. I wanted to follow my characters' emotional journey without the restriction of holding true to real names, dates, and events. Except for a couple of walk-ons (Monroe Goldstein of the National Desertion Bureau, Dr. Charles Little of the Eugenics Records Office), every character and event in this book is a product of my imagination.

[*] I've referenced a trifling sample of these treasures on my website, gaillerhmanauthor.com.

ACKNOWLEDGEMENTS

From the beginning of this journey, I have been sustained and supported by a warm, generous, gifted community of writers.

Kim Taylor Blakemore. Just think, this whole thing began with one of your two-paragraph writing exercises. You are the midwife who brought this baby into the world. Your huge heart, unwavering encouragement, and editorial prowess are the reasons *Across Seward Park* exists. There are no words...

Sue Ann Higgens and Shirley West. My writing companions, who critiqued this book scene by scene. Thank you for your keen feedback, your patience through every iteration, and your consistent fellowship.

Betsy Porter, buddy, walking companion, fellow writer, and generous beta reader. Thanks for your time and support.

Kerry Cathers, editor *extraodinaire*. Thanks for your eagle eye, impeccable grammar, and flexibility with the vagaries of dialect. And of course, your morning sentences.

Alida Thacher and PDX Writers: Thank you for creating such a kind, welcoming space for writers to explore their worlds.

Katie Nelson. When I was flummoxed on how to find the price per square foot of Lower East Side real estate in 1928, you guided the way. Thank you.

My companions on the Morning Write. It's been a gift to watch the sun come up in your company.

The Novelitics community. You are, each and every one, an inspiration.

Laurie Davis. I'm so glad you're incapable of reading without editing as you go.

Rollee Jones and The Knott Street Writers: We outlived the standard life expectancy of writing groups. Thanks for the company along the way.

My patient husband Ken and supportive son Alex. You are my world.

Book Club Questions

1. *Across Seward Park* raises issues about priorities and the choices people make. What do you think about the choices made by Irving, Miriam, and Shelly?
2. Describe Irving. What kind of person is he? What are his strengths? His weaknesses?
3. Miriam puts her obligation to her family above everything else. Leo feels an obligation to the larger world. Do you think it's fair for Leo to ask his family to share his sacrifices? On the other hand, is Miriam's view too narrow?
4. Given the social stigma of epilepsy at the time, what do you think about Miriam's decision to hide Arthur from Shelly?
5. What do you think about Leo's decision to go to Spain? Is it, as Miriam believes, a betrayal of his promise to her, or is Leo being heroic?
6. Is Irving too passive in his relationship with Miriam? Should he have told Shelly about Arthur, whether Miriam approved or not? Should he have put up more of a fight when Miriam told Shelly to lie about Leo?

7. What do you think about Shelly's relationship with Howie? How is it different from her relationship with Skip? How is it the same?

8. Shelly believes that her mother would have approved of her plan to sell the building. Irving insists that Miriam would have seen it as a betrayal. Who do you think is right?

9. How do you picture Shelly's life in Connecticut after the close of the book? What might her life look like ten years later?

10. *Across Seward Park* is a story about people struggling to find their way during a specific historical moment. Does their story have relevance in the current historical moment?

About the Author

Gail Lehrman is an expatriate New Yorker relocated to the Pacific Northwest. Though she has traded the canyons of Manhattan for the mountains of Oregon, Gail has never lost her fascination with her native city and its melting pot history. New York's voices still sing in her ear. Those voices are the force behind her debut novel, *Across Seward Park*.

She holds a B.A. and M.A in English Literature and an M.F.A. in Creative Writing from Columbia University. After a ten-year teaching career, she pivoted into computer programming but continued to feed her creative spirit by studying acting and singing (a skill she sadly never mastered). Life swerved again when she moved to the West Coast with her husband and son. Now a frequent hiker in Oregon's lovely Columbia River Gorge, Gail is also an enthusiastic participant in the rich literary community of Portland, Oregon.

To contact Gail or to learn more about the real history behind *Across Seward Park*, visit Gail's website:

Gaillehrmanauthor.com

Made in the USA
Middletown, DE
14 October 2023

40770349R00172